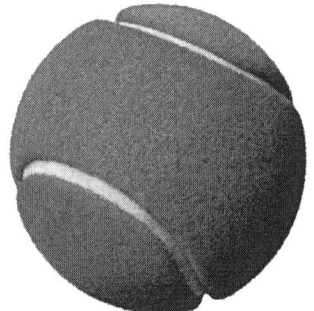

THE MOONBALLERS

A Novel about The Invasion of a LGBTQ2+ Tennis League ... by Straight People **(GAY GASP!)**

JEFFREY SOTTO

The Author of **CLOUD COVER**

Copyright 2022 by Jeffrey Sotto

All rights reserved. No part of this book may be reproduced in any form without permission in writing from the author.

Characters, places and events in this book are fictitious. Any similarity to real persons, living or dead, real places, and true events are coincidental.

Sotto, Jeffrey

The Moonballers: A Novel about The Invasion of a LGBTQ2+Tennis League … by Straight People (GAY GASP!)

ISBN
978-1-9992418-2-7 (paperback)
978-1-9992418-3-4 (eBook)

Story edit by Ali Dean, Bobby Nijjar, Melissa Paladines, and Nathan Tarrant

Copy edit by Liz Parker

Poetry by Jeffrey Sotto

Refractions Books ◆

THE MOONBALLERS

A Novel about The Invasion of a LGBTQ2+ Tennis League ... by Straight People

(GAY GASP!)

JEFFREY SOTTO

For all the Tennis Queens.

"You only tease the ones you love."

— Tom Boehner

DISCLAIMER

This is book is meant to be a Spoof!

This work is a satirical commentary. Any jokes, obscenities and/or graphic details are not endorsed or intended to offend anyone.

I only want to make you laugh.

Also, for those unfamiliar with the world of tennis, there is a guide about the game along with definitions of tennis lingo at the back of the book for your reference.

Finally, from the bottom of my heart, thank you for your interest and support.

PROLOGUE

The Tale of the Racquet Stuck in the Tree
Bonn, Germany
Summer 1987

In the forested area of the nationales Tenniszentrum von Bonn, or the National Tennis Centre in Bonn, Germany, was the biggest tree in the city: a great oak standing at 150 feet tall, and sprawling 15 feet wide. If one looked closely, they'd see a junior tennis racquet—a grey Dunlop graphite with a baby blue grip—firmly stuck in its branches. Deeply wedged and partly hidden by leaves within the dense crown, nobody—including centre officials, local arbourists, and even the odd curious native red squirrel—could remove it from its location.

The tale of how the racquet got there was the stuff of folklore, well known among German tennis circles, and all of children's organized sports leagues.

Once upon a time, there was a little boy named Stefan Porsche. He loved tennis. In 1987, when he was seven years old, Stefan advanced to the state final of the North Rhine-Westphalia "Junior Under 8" tennis championships, held at the Bonn National Tennis Centre. His opponent: six-year-old Peggy Bock. Due to the lack of girls entered, the competition was co-ed for the first time in its illustrious 40-year history. In addition, tournament officials believed mixing boys and girls was a dynamic and inclusive step forward in the development of junior tennis in the country. Every tennis parent wanted their kid to be the next superstar like Boris Becker or Steffi Graf.

A prodigy, Stefan excelled in his tennis lessons, having scored wins over all other children in his class with ease, and even exhausted some coaches in practice. Also taller than most of the kids at a towering four- feet and five inches, he was the state tournament's number one seed. His father, Otto Porsche—whose biggest claim to fame was winning a set off of the professional Manolo Santana in 1969 at a small tournament in Munich—was determined to capitalize on the potential his son possessed. Father Porsche pushed Stefan to train for hours early in the morning before school and late into the night after. It was also important that he look the part; Stefan was dressed to resemble a mini Bjorn Borg, complete with a white Fila headband over his flowing blonde hair, parted in the middle, and inappropriately super short shots.

In contrast, Peggy stood at three-feet and six inches, with a racquet that appeared heavier than her. Her tennis skirt was fluffy and pink—tutu-like—and there were pom-poms sticking out of the backs of her socks. Her blonde pigtails bounced up and down, and when she often smiled or giggled, one would notice her two top middle teeth were missing, giving her a noticeable lisp. Everything about her suggested sweetness—an inability to hurt a fly, let alone beat an older boy on the tennis court. Before the match, she cheerfully greeted her opponent: "Good luck, Thtefan!", chipper as can be.

To say she was the underdog was an understatement.

Heading into the final, Stefan had not dropped any sets and only lost six games total. His serve had never been broken. As for Peggy, Father Porsche—furious that girls now competed with the boys—commented, "she should just be happy to be in the final … good for the little thing."

However, something happened that scorching summer afternoon on the red clay courts in Bonn. Perhaps it was his father constantly pointing to the trophy and yelling at Stefan from the stands, or Peggy swinging freely and having fun, having no expectations on her.

Whatever the reason, 90 minutes later, Stefan stood in front of his father in the locker room, holding the runner-up trophy. The score was 6-3, 6-1 for Peggy.

"I'm sorry, Vater," Stefan said, his eyes welling up. "Vater" is German for Father.

Otto, arms crossed, spewed out a tirade in German so fast that it was indecipherable to others within earshot. One could assume it wasn't encouraging. He concluded his rant in English, shaking his head: "You lost, Stefan. You lost ... *to a girl.*"

A collage of images flooded Stefan's head: the red clay of the court, shots sailing out (all of which were his), the fluffiness of Peggy's tutu-ish skirt, the gap in her teeth when she smiled with the winner's trophy, and the amusement of the crowd when she dropped it because it was too heavy for her to carry. The montage concluded with the most dramatic scene of the day: little Peggy Bock jumping up and down in victory after the last point, then suddenly crying in embarrassment because of an unfortunate incident. From the stands, Father Porsche had thrown a banana at her, hitting her in the face. He was quickly ejected from the stadium while her parents cursed at him and cleaned the banana goo smooshed on her cheeks with a towel.

When asked what spurred this heinous act, Father Porsche responded, "I was ashamed of my son."

Stefan's sadness turned into hysteria, and he ran into the hallway and then outside the players' facility, crying. Racing into the forest near the stadium, he got lost in a maze of trees, his vision blurred by the tears flowing from his eyes. He stopped to wipe the perspiration, tears, and snot from his face. Looking around and up only to see the great oaks and spruces surrounding and then ostensibly closing in on him, he let out one last piercing scream, scaring the cuckoo birds to simultaneously flee the area in one large flock and creating an ominous sound of wings flapping in unison. He then reached into his backpack and pulled out his racquet—a grey Dunlop graphite one with a baby blue grip—and threw it up high with all his remaining strength. He never saw it come back down.

***

Fifteen minutes later, Stefan's mother found him lying on the ground in the same spot, his face soggy in tears and spittle, having fainted. She picked him up and carried him back to the car to go home, rubbing his shoulders along the way.

What little Stefan didn't know was that within the forest he had fled was the biggest tree in the city, in which now his racquet had become stuck. Consequently, the racquet's origins became famous. Visitors from far and wide across the land would flock to see it; the tale had turned into a warning, a legend, and a point of ridicule for all junior tennis players in the country for years thereafter.

PART ONE

The Torpedo Valley Lesbian Gay Bisexual Transgender Queer Two Spirited+Tennis Association (TVLGBTQ2+TA)

THE EXECUTIVE
(Tennis Skill Rating listed in brackets – Out of 7.0)

PRESIDENT
Stefan "Steffi"/"Stef" Porsche (5.0)

VICE PRESIDENT
Butterball "Bibi"/"B" Deveraux (4.75)

MEMBERSHIP COORDINATOR
Ernest Law (3.75)

EVENT COORDINATOR
Scooter Mann (4.75)

TREASURER/WEBMASTER
Dakota Pearl (3.5)

Chapter 1: Inauguration Day
Torpedo Valley, Ontario, Canada
April 2020

Death by a thousand moonballs is the worst kind of loss in tennis. Moonballs, also referred to as "lobs," are shots hit high toward the sky and are much slower than groundstrokes, or regular shots. As they are beginner level, soft, and of a defensive nature meant to throw off the rhythm and balance of one's opponent and elicit errors to win points, they are considered—pardon the non-politically correct term—a "pussy" way to win matches. It is more humiliating to be on the losing end of that strategy; a devastating shot to one's ego.

Of course, moonballing as the most shameful method of victory and defeat is not an official rule written in stone. Rather, it is an anecdote; a common belief among professional tennis competitors, coaches, recreational players, and most notably, the obsessively driven fathers of child tennis prodigies.

This notion, drilled into his head growing up—heard in his father's voice, thick with a German accent—still ran through Stefan Porsche's mind as an adult as he drove to the tennis courts in the park of the suburb Torpedo Valley, 30 minutes west of Toronto.

"Don't fall for the fucking moonballers. That's not real tennis!," Father Porsche would always say. Stefan put on his Ray-Bans and blasted music to drown out the memory, so loud that neighbouring cars glared at him at the intersection. Ignoring them, he adjusted his rearview mirror, from which a pearl beaded rosary hung, only to admire his dirty blonde hair catching the sunlight, and kept driving while bopping his head to the music. *This is my jam!*, he thought.

Nicknamed "Queen Steffi," or simply "Steffi" in honour of his tennis idol, the famous German professional player of the 1980s and 90s, Steffi Graf, Stefan was the president of the newly formed TVLGBTQ2+-

TA: The Torpedo Valley Lesbian, Gay, Bisexual, Transgender, Queer, Two-spirited, plus Tennis Association. Today was the inauguration of the league and first tennis practice of the 2020 season. Its preceding gay tennis organization, the Toronto Torches, had disbanded in late 2016, for reasons unknown to its members. Adding to the intrigue, the league's president at the time, Francesco Zappone, moved to Italy immediately thereafter; his involvement with the league's crash surrounded by mystery.

***

Waiting at the Torpedo Valley Park tennis courts was Ernest Law, a skinny, short, caramel skinned African-American boy with circular gold-rimmed glasses. Occasionally, people commented that he looked like a young Will Smith, but with hipster-ish style and a coincidentally earnest demeanour. Having spent a short time in 2016 as an occasional member of the old gay league, Ernest was the first membership coordinator of the new one in Torpedo Valley, to which he held much pride. He had been dropped off at the courts by his mother, Joy, who said she may be late picking him up after practice because she had to get waxed—a Brazilian. He was, as many gay men are, close to his mother, but at times he felt horrified by how much she overshared. Her response when he came out to her when he was 18: "Oh thank God, now I don't have to pay a hairdresser, 'cause I have you, Ernest darling!" to which he responded, indignantly: "I'm not that kind of gay, mother!"

At 25, Ernest had failed the G2 driving test twice, both examiners remarking he was "overly cautious to the point of being too slow, compromising safety, and potentially causing road rage in other drivers." Although he felt juvenile having to take transit or bother his mother to drive him everywhere, he did feel a moral superiority for it; *it is better to be safe and slow than be sorry. Above all, not driving reduces my* carbon footprint; a small yet important contribution in mitigating the eventual destruction of Mother Earth at the hands of humankind, he believed.

To prepare for the opening day's festivities, Ernest set up tables, blew up balloons and arranged them like a rainbow, bought gluten-free muffins, organic watermelon, and strawberries; he wrote and memorized a welcome spiel for each player, trying to sound fun and animated as he rehearsed it. There was no manual for the role of membership coordinator. When he got the position via email, he only received the instructions to download the league member list from the website and show up at the Torpedo Valley Park tennis courts on such and such a date to greet them and check them off the list. Hand them the balls and explain the rules. The only other content in the instructions: *This role is 100 % voluntary. No pay. You do this because you love tennis and this is fun for you.* There was no smiley face emoji at the end of that sentence.

Members began arriving. Usually not one to pay attention to such things, Ernest immediately noted what differentiated gay tennis players from straight ones: their impeccable sense of tennis fashion. There were the traditional gays who wore crispy white polo shirts like Roger Federer, with navy blue wristbands which matched their headbands and shoes. Then there were the more showy gays, taking inspiration from Rafael Nadal, sporting muscle tops to display the biceps they had laboriously sculpted at the gym, and shorts so tight to showcase the perky yet firm bubble butt and not so subtle bulge front and centre, or at times, curving to the left. Clothing was just the tip of the iceberg on what divided the league members.

"My shots may be rusty, but damn I look good, bruh," Scooter Mann, the league's events coordinator, said after noticing Ernest staring at his crotch, which seemed to jump out from across the registration table screaming, "do you see me? I'm totally big, right? Hello?!"

"Sorry," Ernest immediately apologized after Scooter saw him staring at his shorts. "I couldn't help but see that you lost some weight from the last time I saw you a few years ago. You got so … buff."

"And everything looks so much bigger, right?"

Ernest didn't know what to say.

"My boyfriend broke up with me over the winter … well, uh, actually it was more of a mutual decision to split," Scooter said.

"Sorry to hear."

"It's all good. I joined Grindr and went on Keto. Started CrossFit. I can lift a tire with my dick, bruh!"

"Lovely."

"Revenge body, just like, what's-her-face-Kardashian said … look at what he's missing now, right?" Scooter smirked, faking a gunshot with his right hand while winking.

"Well, good for you!"

"Thanks. So Torpedo Valley, eh? Not bad for a suburb, I guess?"

"It's the best one outside Toronto." Ernest then looked down at his papers. "You're on court two. And you know, every thirty minutes you move up or down the courts depending if you win or lose. Go left to the higher court if you win, right to the lower if you lose."

"Got it, swipe left, swipe right, swipe away! Ha!"

Practices were always run that way in the old league. Players were assigned a court number according to their skill level, and the objective was move up to the higher level courts by beating your opponent after 30 minutes of play. Court one—the show court in Torpedo Valley Park, similar to the Prestige Clubs in Toronto previously used for the Torches' league—was the only one that had benches to sit on and watch matches. It was the goal to play on it, and winning one's way to earn that right was an accomplishment, even if it was just a practice and nobody was watching except for the players on the lower courts, enviously.

Ernest grabbed a can of new tennis balls and handed them to Scooter, who turned and headed toward the courts. "Thanks, bruh."

"Well, hello there, honey!" Cutting the line and charging toward Ernest was a golden skinned man with a bright smile and open arms.

"I'm Butterball Deveraux, the league's Vice President! But you can call me Bibi! Charmed, I'm sure!"

"Hi. I'm Ernest. I remember meeting you a few years ago."

"Ernest, haa! I ... I *think* I remember you too."

"Haa" was "Hi"; Bibi had a strong southern twang. Ernest couldn't get a word out before Bibi aggressively hugged him.

"Oh no," Bibi said, "is that what you call a hug? Come on, give me a real one. I wanna feel your chest against mine. Don't be shy just cause we're in a suburb. Torpedo is quite progressive. Why, we've got a copy of *Mary has Two Moms* at the Torpedo Valley Library!"

Ernest, wondering how someone could be so friendly after only having met once years ago, grabbed on to Bibi as best he could.

"I was just tickled pink when I saw you submitted your name for membership coordinator. I was like 'Oh ma gawd, that little Ernest Law, bless his heart.' This is going to be a fabulous year!" Bibi looked around the park. "Don't you find it so peaceful out here in the burbs? Whereas Toronto is all crazy neon, Torpedo is kinda pastel ... I just love it."

Bibi, a six-feet one-inch tall, stocky—some might say slightly overweight—man with bleach blonde hair, was half Filipino, half Caucasian, but often mistaken for Mexican. He moved to Canada from Nashville, Tennessee in late 2016. Within a couple of months of joining the Toronto Torches, he had unofficially become the Miss Congeniality among them. He preferred to be called Bibi, but didn't mind if people used "Butterball". The reason? "Cause I gotta sweet ass," he'd say with a cackle. Self-confidence was not a quality he lacked, despite *not* spending hours in the gym, working out, or taking selfies.

Bibi's muse and idol was Dolly Parton. This made sense to every league member; watching his interactions with people made one feel like they were watching the film *Steel Magnolias* with Truvy, Dolly Parton's character, firing one one-liner after another.

Bibi's reputation for being kind and welcoming also contributed to rumours that he was somewhat overly hospitable. Before the crash of the Toronto league, Bibi would show the newbies or visitors to the tournaments the sites of the city, with the welcome tour ending in a view of Bibi's bedroom ceiling or white satin headboard. "People think I'm a hussy?" he would always say, shocked. "I'm Filipino *and* from the south, it's in my nature! And I want to use my talents for something *other* than nursing or nannying!"

"How have you been, Bibi?" Ernest asked.

"Now, we'll have to have some proper bonding time, you hear me?" Bibi said. "I'll have you over sometime for some Southern Comfort and peach pie. We'll do each other's hair and nails, watch some Pornhub, I just love me some good ol' fashioned BDSM … and you know, girl-talk. Oh, you must come over, I will not take no for an answer, Ernest!"

"Um … Okay sure. That sounds like fun."

Bibi giggled in exuberance: "Yay!"

Suddenly, everyone looked toward the parking lot, from which the song *Call Me Maybe* blared from a big black truck.

"Is that …?" Ernest questioned.

"Yup. That's our president, Stefan. Queen Steffi. She loves her some Carly Rae Jepsen. I decided to accept it and then move on." Bibi quipped. "You ever meet Stef?"

"I saw him play a couple of times. He's amazing. But no, we've never met formally."

"What's your rating, hun?"

"Rating?"

"Your tennis skill rating?"

"Oh. 3.75. I took lessons over the winter and just moved up from a 3.5."

"That's probably why. Just between us girls," Bibi lowered his mouth to Ernest's ear, "and I hope you don't take offence to this."

"Not at all."

"Now I love her, but Stefan doesn't really talk much to players below a 4.5 rating."

It was sad, but true. During the time of the old league, players were divided into different divisions according to skill level. The best players played in the "Open" and "A" divisions, followed by "B" and "C" for the mid-level players, and finally "D" for beginners; the latter often thought of as the "boyfriend division." Non-tennis playing partners of players addicted to tennis would hastily join the D level and force themselves to learn how to play in a desperate attempt to get in some couple time.

The different divisions were played at separate tournament sites, and as a result, an A level player wouldn't get to know a C player, an Open player wouldn't get to know a D player, etcetera.

Ernest had heard of this before, but also recalled that one league member, Angelica Berry, said the real reason for the division was, "pure ego ... the Opens and even the A players think they're too good to talk to anyone. Totally stuck up! They have their noses in the air and a dildo up their ass!" Hence, Stefan, though admired for his talent, didn't exactly endear himself to many other players.

The new Torpedo Valley league abolished the divisions, and put all players into one open category to encourage the socialization between all players. No separations. All inclusive. A dynamic step forward.

Call Me Maybe stopped playing. Stefan got out of this vehicle, an immaculately shiny black Ram 1500 pickup truck, black rims, leather interior.

"He's got a nice truck," Ernest remarked. "But that thing must guzzle tons of pollution into the air."

Stefan grabbed his tennis bag and walked purposefully toward them.

Stefan was conventionally attractive; six-feet tall with his chiseled cheekbones and jawline, broad shoulders, toned biceps, and legs for days. His straight locks effortlessly blew in the wind. Dressed in all white, in a polo and shorts that were folded up one cuff, Ernest guessed Stefan to be in his late 30s; apparently, he was quite the sought after twink when he first joined the Toronto league in 1997.

"Hopefully she won't be on her rag today," Bibi uttered.

"What do you mean?" Ernest asked.

"I beat Steffi in our last practice match. Whenever I win, she won't talk to me after. But when she wins—which is most of the time—she loves me, and we're BFFs. We're close, but she moody as fuck."

Stefan stopped in front of them, took off his sunglasses like a movie star—a hair toss and eyes squinting—revealing a hint of his sparkling blue eyes, which made contact with Ernest's. "Who are you?" Stefan had a slight German accent.

Intimidated, Ernest looked back down at the registration list.

"Howdy Miz Prez," Bibi greeted as he went in for a hug. Stefan barely moved in and patted Bibi on the back as they air-kissed.

"Miz B."

"Girl, you look orange. Did you get a spray tan again?"

"I don't know what you're talking about," Stefan mumbled. "Did you like my last Facebook post?"

"Which one?"

"From this morning. The selfie I took after I worked out."

"How is that different from all your other posts?"

"That's my brand. Can you just like it please? It only has 80 likes so far. Actually no, don't like it, *love* it—I'm having an existential crisis. And like it on the 'gram too."

"Yes, yes."

"At least Darren liked it."

"Who's Darren again?"

"You know, my ex from five years ago I told you about?"

"I can't remember."

"Whatever. But you know what it means when an ex clicks like on one of your posts? It's basically an admission that they're inferior to you."

Stefan looked back at Ernest. "Sorry, who are you again?"

"Stef, this is Ernest Law. Not sure if you remember him from a few years ago; he's our new registration coordinator," Bibi said.

"I don't," Stefan blurted.

"Hi," Ernest said shyly, sticking out his hand.

"Ernest. Welcome to the club." Ernest barely felt any squeeze from Stefan's limp but much larger hand.

"I like your truck, Stefan. You in construction or something?" Ernest asked.

"No, I'm a finance executive."

Bibi interjected: "Steffi here is compensating. Big truck makes people think he has a big—"

"Hey, quiet you!" Stefan snapped. He then scanned Torpedo Valley Park. "Not bad for a suburb, eh? This is where we shall rebuild this league, my friends."

Stefan turned back to Ernest. "Let me see the members list."

Ernest handed the clipboard to Stefan. Shuffling through the papers and then limply handing them back, he said, "I don't recognize a lot of those names. A lot of new members."

Soon, a line-up of returning players from the old league formed. Ernest, unable to get his welcome spiel out due to Stefan and Bibi taking over greeting duties, resorted to simply checking off attendees. First was Angelica Berry, the lesbian with a mean one-handed topspin backhand. Then, Daniel Brown, the rare serve-and-volleyer of the league.

"We must do brunch sometime, and out of this godforsaken suburb," Daniel said to Stefan, "Edward just redid our veranda; we got some custom flooring shipped in from Florence—or was it Venice? Oh God, I don't remember. We have a great view of the Distillery. Well, whatever, we must brunch soon, Stef."

"I'd love that," Stefan said.

Stefan rolled his eyes, looking back at Ernest, "God, it's so exhausting when everyone wants a piece of you."

Ernest smiled politely.

Stefan and Bibi began to sound like drones with more members arriving: "Welcome back, you look great!"; "So great to see you!"; "I love your outfit!"; "How's the kale garden coming along?"

Then a couple of unfamiliar faces.

"Hello, gorgeous," Bibi said. "You must be new."

"Yes, the name's Abigail Elle," the blonde—stunningly beautiful—said shyly. "But you can call me Abby."

Ernest found her on his list. "Abigail. There you are."

"Well, I'm always happy to welcome some pretty faces to the league! The lesbians will love you! And damn, you tall too, girl!"

"Thank you," Abby said.

"And what do you identify as?"

"Um, sorry?"

"Top or bottom?"

Abby arched her eyebrows.

"I'm just kidding with ya, doll!" Bibi laughed. "I always like to ask our new members that just to loosen them up." He then leaned into her and whispered, "but really, we need to figure that shit out. I don't know if you're aware of this, but there's a shortage of tops in Ontario! It's dire, honey!"

Stefan interrupted. "There's no shortage of tops, they're just not interested in you."

They laughed. Abby giggled politely and smiled at Ernest.

"Well anyway," Bibi said, "the joke works better with dudes."

Stefan stared at Abby. "We met right, at the Queen's Country Club, or was it the Rosebowl?"

"No, you must be mistaken."

"Oh sorry. Well, welcome."

"Thank you."

Stefan turned around and watched her walk toward the courts.

"Striking, she is."

"What is that smell?" Bibi said, scrunching his nose. The scent of Axe body spray wafted into the vicinity.

"Oh, hello! Who dat?" Bibi said, as he, Stefan, and Ernest saw a muscular young brown man approaching. "Whoa, he looks like Britney Spears' fiancé, Sam Ash-something, you seen him on Instagram?"

Ernest found himself overwhelmed as the guy walked forward, bow-legged. He was very attractive indeed, if one was into tall, brooding, built, "masc" men with square jaws. Ernest suddenly felt a shortness of breath and something odd in his chest. A little flutter.

"But, what's he wearing?" Bibi whispered, "oh my heavens, is that cotton? Like regular cotton?"

The brown man, about six-feet three-inches tall, dressed in oversized grey cotton sweats and white tube socks halfway between his ankles and his knees, introduced himself. "Hi, I'm Khalid. Khalid Adam."

Bibi perked up immediately, extending the back of his hand: "Khalid Adam, charmed I'm sure."

Khalid reached underneath, putting the palm of his hand into Bibi's, and turning it into a handshake.

"I'm Butterball Deveraux. But you can call me Bibi. This here's Stefan, our president, and Ernest, our membership coordinator. Welcome to our humble league."

"Thanks."

"Can we call ya Cal?" Bibi smiled.

"Uh, Cal? Wouldn't that be anglicizing his name? We don't wanna do that," Ernest blurted out, always the one to be culturally sensitive.

Awkward pause. Stefan raised an eyebrow at Bibi.

"I'm not too fussed about it," Khalid replied.

"So, anyway ... how did you hear about us?" Stefan asked, sizing him up.

"I'm a member at the Forester Club. Angelica told me about you guys, and I thought, yeah, sign me up!"

"Great," Stefan said, "you play on their doubles league this past winter?"

"Yeah."

"What level?"

"A-1."

"A-1?" Stefan asked again, surprised.

"Yeah. A-1."

A-1 was the top level in doubles. *This guy must be good. Really good*, Stefan thought, his head backing away slightly.

"And you identify as?" Bibi smirked, batting his eyelashes.

"I'm sorry, what?"

"Top or bottom?"

"Never mind," Ernest interrupted, thinking the question was inappropriate. "You're on court one, Khalid."

"Great, boss."

"Ernest, what court did you put me on?" Stefan asked.

"Three."

"What?" Stefan snapped, sounding insulted. He cleared his voice and changed to a warmer tone. "Sorry, excuse us."

Stefan put his arm around Ernest's shoulders and turned away from the group. "Ernest, court three? Really?" His eye contact intensified: "Do you know who I am?"

"What?" Ernest replied, puzzled.

"You know I'm the president, right? Have you not seen me play before?"

"Yes. But I just thought, you know, give everyone a chance on the show court?"

"That's not how it works, my friend. Switch me to court one, now." Stefan turned around with a big smile and looked at Khalid. "As a new member welcome, I'll play with you on the show court."

"Right on, boss," Khalid said.

Stefan snatched a can of balls from Ernest, and they walked toward the court gate.

Bibi, pasting a smile, stood beside Ernest; their heads moving slowly left to right, following Stefan and Khalid to the gate door. "Good luck gals! Be a swan, be a swan!"

Bibi turned to Ernest, his smile turning into a look of concern: "He cute, but sweet Jesus, that outfit. Cotton is just rotten, honey!"

Putting their bags on the court one benches, Stefan was curious to learn about the newest member of the league.

"Where are you from?" Stefan asked.

"I live about a ten-minute drive from here. I'm so glad your league decided to open up in the suburbs."

"Right ..." Stefan said, "no, not where you live ... I mean your background?"

"Canadian."

"But where are your parents from?"

"Oh ... my parents came from Syria. But that was before I was born."

Stefan nodded. "Neat."

Khalid removed his hoodie to Stefan's dismay: his forearms, with a sprinkling of thick black hair and muscles bulging, made Stefan a bit self-conscious.

Stefan immediately pulled back his shoulders and pushed his chest out. With his trim and very toned body, he was not usually around people who had a more impressive physique.

"Wanna just rally for a bit before we start scoring?" Stefan asked.

"Sounds good, boss," Khalid said cheerfully.

"Start at the baseline?"

"Yeah."

Stefan snapped open the can of new balls, hearing the pressure release like a pop can. He always loved that sound and the smell of the fluorescent yellow balls inside.

The players on the adjacent courts stopped and looked over; it was always exciting to see a new player hit for the first time: to see their level and where they measured up within the skill levels of other players; if they were a threat to the already established stars of the league.

Above all, more important than skill, existing members always gawked at new ones in the case they were attractive; eagerly trying to find if said newbie was single, and if his game deemed him a top or a bottom. Unlike Bibi's more direct method of finding out, it was assumed that an aggressive powerful game marked one a top; a defensive or counterpunching one a bottom. It was a belief that members swore by.

Khalid sensed all eyes were on him. Feeling nervous, his hands began to quiver, and his breaths suddenly felt shorter. He knew this was a prime opportunity for the emergence of the condition that plagued him throughout his competitive tennis life, starting when he was eight years old in the Ontario Tennis Association junior league: yips. Yips was the term for a sudden loss of fine motor skills in experienced athletes, usually brought on by nervousness or lack of confidence. They disrupted one's technique, timing, and mindset. Following Khalid's yips were always panic attacks.

Strengthening his grip on his racquet till his knuckles turned white, he took a deep breath, and repeated his go-to mantra in his head: *Just breathe and get the ball into the court.* He felt his shoulders slightly loosen.

Stefan hit the first ball to Khalid's forehand.

SMACK. A slight brush of wind.

Stefan blinked as Khalid's left-handed cross-court forehand return whipped back with lightning speed and force, jumping up with topspin but landing precisely in the left corner. Stefan hadn't had time to get his racquet on it, let alone move.

A screaming winner, as players call it. A shot hit so hard that it flew past the opponent without them touching it. With one forceful swing, Khalid had batted away his nerves.

Silence overtook all six courts of Torpedo Valley Park. The members stood still, surprised.

However, their expressions paled in comparison to the stunned look on Stefan's face.

Bibi turned to Ernest, astonished. "Sweet Jesus! We've got a brown Rafa here … he's amazing!"

Chapter 2: "Who let the straights in?!"

Since joining the Toronto Torches' league in 1997, Stefan, or "Queen Steffi," had enjoyed dominance over most players. Often bouncing between the two highest division levels that structured competition in those days, Open and A, there were only a couple of other players in Toronto who could beat him. One was Francesco Zappone, the league's president. But their rivalry—in which Stefan had been leading eight wins to six—was cut short when Francesco moved to Italy soon after the league folded in 2016.

Like Steffi Graf, the tennis superstar of his childhood, Stefan possessed the biggest shot in the league: his powerful forehand. From any position on court, and off of any shot thrown at him, Stefan would wind up his right arm with a dramatic circular backswing and fire that bullet for a winner, or put his opponent on the defensive.

The rest of Stefan's game was just as impressive. His serve, with an impossibly high toss, but timed perfectly to be spanked at the top of its arc, could be delivered heavy with topspin, slice, or flat, bouncing high or skidding low, precisely placed anywhere in the service box. His backhand was a graceful but sneaky slice that could skim the net and make his opponents bend low and hit back up, only for him to smash their reply with his forehand.

Stefan prided himself on being the perfect balance of distinct eras of tennis: dynamic modern tennis represented by his powerful forehand; traditional elegance of old tennis with his beguiling and effortless backhand.

He had rarely experienced losing, and never took it well. Not once did he speak of the painful loss to Peggy Bock when he was seven years old; but it was imprinted in his memory, haunting him before every tournament final for the last 33 years.

Perhaps that was why today—the inaugural day of the new gay

league in Torpedo Valley, and his first official day as president—wasn't such a great day for Stefan. After the first match with Khalid, he parked himself on the benches of court one, pretending to be speaking on his phone, but really watching Khalid play for the remainder of the session. A former two-time champion of the Canadian Gay Open—the league's biggest tournament In Canada—and the Toronto Torches' League Singles Tournament winner for four out of the last ten years, he wasn't supposed to lose that short practice match to Khalid, a mere newbie with bad taste in clothing. But he did lose, the score being 3-5.

For the following two and a half hours, Khalid had remained on court one the entire time, not losing a match. He beat Scooter, the loud jock of the group, who screamed, "you fucking loser!" to himself repeatedly while bashing his racquet to the side of his head. The score was 6-2, just as rain drops began to fall.

Coming off the court, Khalid was surrounded by the other members acknowledging his great play. The league, predominately white gay men, had a new star. And he was brown, masculine, and the hardest ball striker the league had seen in some time.

Following the crowd was Stefan, fuming over his loss, and hair dripping wet because he didn't bring an umbrella. *Umbrellas were for pussies*, he thought.

But Stefan was smarter than to wallow in defeat. He knew the only way to not lose to Khalid again was to practice with him as much as possible, access his game, identify weaknesses, and then use that knowledge to implement a winning strategy in a real tournament match. He knew he had to keep his enemy close.

"Khalid," Stefan called.

"Yeah, boss."

"Great play."

"Thanks. You okay Stefan? You sat out for the rest of the time."

"Yeah, a work thing came up. I'm a finance executive at Traders Inc., so I'm kind of a big deal. We were having system issues this morning and I thought I'd have to do some troubleshooting today, hence I was a bit distracted when I was playing. But I don't want to take anything away from you. You're a great little player."

"Thanks."

"We should play again sometime," Stefan said, forcing a smile.

"Definitely."

Bibi watched them approach, raising his eyebrows. "Oh you know she's pissed," whispering to Ernest.

Stefan grabbed his phone. "What's your number?"

He handed it to Khalid, who then entered his number.

"Great, let me send you a text to make sure," Stefan said, adamant.

Stefan shot a text to the number Khalid entered, to which Khalid's phone buzzed.

"Cool. I'll hit you up."

"Dat ho," Bibi said, "getting his number before any of us."

Khalid smiled, acknowledging Bibi and Ernest, and walked toward the parking lot just as a young woman in a maroon Toyota Camry pulled up. It started to rain heavier.

"How cute is he?" Bibi said to Stefan. "And super masc. Hello, I'm dripping."

"Please, he's not *that* masc," Stefan snapped.

"What does it matter if he's masc or not? That's such an offensive term," Ernest said, "just my opinion."

Khalid dumped his tennis bag in the trunk of the car, then got into the passenger seat. He and the girl chatted and smiled.

"Aw, cute. Maybe that's his sister," Bibi said.

The girl wiped his forehead, and then proceeded to shove her lips onto his. They rotated their necks while devouring each other. Bibi thought he saw some tongue, gasping dramatically.

"I don't think that's his sister."

Stefan, Bibi, and Ernest stood frozen, unable to look away.

"It's like a car accident," Bibi exclaimed.

When the kiss was done and the car began to drive away, Khalid looked up at the three and waved goodbye.

"What the fuck was that?" Stefan asked.

Scooter was walking by. "What, Stef?"

"The new guy. Khalid?"

Scooter looked at the car. "Bruh, I think that's his girlfriend."

"What?" Stefan said in disbelief.

"Yeah, Khalid's gay for play, Angelica told me," he giggled like a school boy.

"Gay for play?"

"Yup."

"What does that mean?"

"He's in our league, but he's not one of *us*."

Stefan raised his eyebrows, still confused.

"He's straight," Scooter's voice raised, "he likes the tacos, not the hot dogs. No homo!"

A bolt of thunder struck, lighting the dark grey sky.

Bibi screamed in horror, dropping his umbrella. "Oh sweet Jesus! Ernest, hold me!"

Ernest, whose eyeglasses were blurred by raindrops, picked up the umbrella and then wrapped his arm around Bibi.

Stefan's eyes grew wide and angry, his eyebrows caving in. "Straight? What the fuck! Who let the straights in?!" It wasn't the volume of Stefan's voice that frightened Ernest, but rather the cold intensity with which he yelled it.

Another crackling of thunder, this time lightning seemingly striking the ground. It began to downpour and the wind whipped through the rainbow of balloons, pulling them away from each other and snapping their strings. Stefan, Bibi, and Ernest watched the array of colourful bubbles fly away into the dark sky, eventually getting sucked into the clouds over Torpedo Valley.

Chapter 3: Executive Meeting 1 — "Locker Room Talk"

Three days later. Sitting at the head of the table of a Starbucks near Liberty Village, President Stefan sipped his black coffee, and then cleared his throat: "Welcome to the first council meeting of our new league, ladies and ladies. Ernest, part of your role with us is taking minutes. So start writing down everything I say in that little laptop of yours."

"Okay." Ernest pulled out his MacBook and pressed the on button, careful not to tip over his organic hibiscus tea.

"We don't have time for your gadget to power up, so take notes by hand."

"I don't have anything to write on. Trying to reduce the use of paper. How about I record everything on my phone."

Stefan sneered. "That could be incriminating. Just remember everything."

Bibi sat beside him, glued to his phone.

"You've met Scooter our events person, and Dakota, our treasurer and webmaster?" Stefan asked.

Ernest nodded. "Yes, we met at the opening day practice. Good to see you guys ag—"

Stefan, interrupting: "So B, what's on our agenda?"

"Well Miz Prez. We got a lot of things to go through. We can talk about the first social event at karaoke, the Canadian Gay Open, the summer barbecue, the year-end banquet ... should we just follow what they did in the old league?" Bibi said, reading off his notepad.

"I hate to throw us off track, but, speaking of that ... what happened to the old league?" Ernest asked. "Why did it end?"

Silence.

"Maybe you should ask Pika, here," Dakota smirked at Stefan. Ernest looked at them, puzzled.

"It was nothing, admin issues," Stefan snapped, and then changed the subject to party venues. "Sure B, we have to find an Italian banquet hall. That's what the burbs are good for right?"

"But you know we could totally do something different. There's an Argentinian steakhouse, I know I wouldn't mind a big piece of meat, ha!" Scooter exclaimed.

"Nah," said Bibi, "won't fly with the lesbians."

"We can't just assume all the lesbians don't eat meat," Ernest said.

"You're so cute, Ernest," Bibi chuckled.

Stefan looked pensive.

"What is it?" Bibi asked.

"Nothing."

"Bitch, spill."

"Calling people 'bitch' isn't really respectful," Ernest said to Bibi.

"Oh my," Bibi said quietly, rolling his eyes.

Stefan continued. "Anyway, so everything we say stays here right?"

Nods all around. "This is a safe space, girl. But I love me some tea, so spill," Bibi said.

Stefan: "Am I the only one who's disturbed by this new member?"

"Abby?" Bibi questioned.

"No, the dude ... Khalid ... the brown one."

"What about him?" Ernest asked.

"Guys, he's ... " Stefan hesitated.

"What?"

"You know, he's ..."

Bibi grew impatient. "Just cut the carbs and tell us!"

Stefan's voice landed in a thud. "He's straight."

The table went silent.

"Yeah? It was shocking at first, but so what?" Bibi said.

"So ... what? We're just going to let him join? What's next?"

Ernest thought it was a joke. "I'm sorry, what year is it?"

Stefan smiled condescendingly: "You're new. You know nothing about how this league works, okay?"

Bibi sipped his iced coffee. "Yes, it's a different situation, but Stef, there is no actual rule prohibiting them from joining."

Stefan already knew this, having looked up the league's rules the last two nights, which had been copied from the Toronto Torches' league policies. There was no mention of banning any type of person.

"But still, it's messed up. We don't know anything about this guy. Like how old is he?"

"Angelica told me he's 24," Dakota said.

"Exactly, he's young. What is he doing in a gay league? We don't know what he wants. We don't know what the …. straight agenda, or whatever it is, is!"

"Straight agenda?" Ernest asked, further appalled.

"Listen, I have no problem with them. I have some straight friends. But in our league? Relax Ernest. This is just locker room talk."

Ernest shook his head. "Us, them … we're not all that different. It's what we get labelled as that makes us different."

"Thank you Miss Teen Woke 2020," Stefan quipped. He turned to Dakota. "What if we were able to figure out if they were straight before they joined online? Maybe build a wall on the server to block 'em? Is that possible?"

"You want to build a wall? This ain't Mexico, Trumpy," Bibi said. "You're a little uptight Stef. Well, actually more than usual. You need to get laid."

Stefan couldn't remember the last time he had been with a guy. *Was it after the last time I won that tournament at Rosedale last year? Or was it the Torches' singles title the year before?* he wondered. There were so many titles, he got confused and went back to the argument. "Who brought him in? Angelica?"

"Yeah."

"Ugh, I knew we couldn't trust the lesbians. No offence," Stefan said looking at Dakota, who was unbothered.

Ernest noticed the more agitated Stefan got, the more noticeable his slight German accent became.

"By the way, Stef, you ever hear from Gabe?" Dakota asked. "Whatever happened to him?"

"I don't know."

She looked at her watch. "I gotta go, Beth is waiting for me."

Stefan didn't acknowledge her. "I knew my stray-dar was off. I mean, come on, who drives a Camry?"

"Me too … I gotta split," Scooter said.

Stefan took another sip of his coffee while Dakota and Scooter left. "We don't need them. We got each other. We're the holy trinity. Me, and Bibi, and now you, Ernest."

It was a nice feeling for Ernest. He hadn't felt a part of a close group since the environmental advocacy club he led at the University of Toronto. Even at his current job as a coordinator at World Vision Canada, he had few friends, and the ones he did have had gently warned him he'd have to break his habit of calling people out on what is and isn't politically correct. It was, as they said, "annoying as fuck."

"So you think the kind of car tells whether someone's gay or not?" Ernest asked.

Stefan: "Are you kidding? Of course."

"So Camry's mean straight?"

"Well duh." Stefan looked at Bibi, "Is this kid for real? What are you, on the spectrum or something?"

Ernest was so offended he couldn't think of a reply. *What the fuck?*

Bibi didn't look up from his phone. "Stef, don't be an asshole. That's just wrong. Ignorant."

"Okay, fine. So what does a big black pickup truck mean for an office worker?" Ernest asked.

Stefan: "I'm a finance executive."

Bibi put down his phone. "Ernest, let me tell you. Miz Prez here likes to appear like she's some big masc top with a big masc truck and a big d— ... come to think of it, why is the pickup truck black?"

Stefan dismissed Bibi. "Stop makin' up horse shit."

Bibi's eyes lit up: "Oh my God! It's black because you're envious of the brothas'," he said, laughing. He then turned to Ernest. "That's some kind of messed up racism, now ain't it, Ernest? You a brotha', you should know!"

Stefan: "I like my truck because I like it, okay?"

Bibi: "You're compensating for you know what."

"Shut up."

"Look at my car." Bibi said. "A Toyota Yaris! I am so confident with my masculinity that I don't have to compensate for anything!"

"You have that little junk box because you can't afford anything else."

"Meow meow." Bibi turned to Ernest. "See, I told you she's on her rag. Must be a heavy flow day!"

Stefan turned to Ernest. "And what do you drive?"

"I don't have a car." Ernest replied, looking down. "My mother lets me drive hers sometimes. But she has to be in it."

Ernest felt humbled; Stefan smirked. "Anyway, back to the league."

"Yeah." Ernest cleared his throat. "I don't mean to be challenging, Stefan."

"Ernest, you can call me Steffi. Stef."

"Ok. Stef. But isn't one of the tenets of our group to be a safe space for all?"

"Yeah ... all of *us*."

"*Us*, as in who?"

"As in you and me, and Bibi, and everyone who doesn't fit in that garbage straight world," Stefan said, locking eyes with him. "Straight guys have it so easy. This league is for *us*."

"That doesn't sound right to me. We need to be inclusive."

Stefan's eyes rolled. "You're one of those new age crazy liberals, aren't you? Are you upset or triggered right now? Need to call your therapist?"

Bibi looked up from his phone. "Listen to the kid, Stef. It is 2020."

Stefan got up, threw his cup in the recycling, and walked back to the table as Ernest watched.

"Coffee cups don't go into recycling. You need to put it in the garbage," Ernest said.

Stefan's eyebrows furrowed; he was perturbed. He then softened his face and forced a smile: "Fine, Greta Thunberg. We'll let the straight guy in … and see what happens."

***

Forty minutes later, the meeting—at which they confirmed that the theme colour of the opening social event should be coral, not salmon—had adjourned, Ernest sat on the edge of the curb outside the Starbucks, like so many times before, waiting for his mother Joy to pick him up.

"Can I wait with you, hun?" Bibi sat down beside Ernest before getting an answer.

"Is he always like that?"

"Stef? … oh don't mind her. She just really hates change of any kind."

"Oh."

"She likes to mansplain. Makes her think her dick is bigger. Don't let her toxic homosexuality get to you."

Ernest waited a few seconds, then timidly asked, "Bibi, do you know what happened to the old league?"

"No, sorry, hun. Stef is always so hush hush about it."

"Do you keep in touch with anyone else who was on it?"

"Apart from Stefan, no. He was part of that league for years. I know he had a BFF named Gabe Lamb, but he left the league years ago. There was also the league's president, Francesco. Stef and him didn't really like each other. He moved to Rome as soon as the league went tits up. There's rumours he did something messed up and that's why they had to end it."

"Really?"

"Yeah. Then, practices, tournaments, everything else … cancelled. We all lost touch with each other. Then a couple years went by and suddenly Stefan messaged me asking if I wanted to start a new league, but in Torpedo. And I was like, 'sure, I ain't doin' anything, and I ain't too good for the burbs—I already lived here.'"

"And what was up with Dakota calling him Pika? Some sort of nickname?"

"No clue, honey."

A fire engine red Mini Cooper pulled up. "Who's that handsome boy over there?" the driver, a beautiful and stylish woman with long blonde hair yelled out.

Ernest shook his head and looked down. "Alright, see you Bibi."

"Is that your sister?" Bibi asked. "Damn, she looks like Tyra!"

"Nope," Ernest then looked at the car, "Mother! God, you're so embarrassing."

"That's your Mom?" Bibi asked, in disbelief.

Ernest turned around, "Don't do it, Bibi. Don't."

Bibi's volume increased: "Momma Law, you're gorgeous, honey!"

"Ugh," Ernest grimaced. "Don't feed her ego, please!"

Joy didn't appreciate her son's comment. It was true, she was attractive, and she felt no hesitance to celebrate it. With glowing skin, long luscious hair, and a figure toned like a ballerina, Joy didn't look a day over 30 … although she was turning 45 later that year. She attributed her look to four things: running and teaching at her own yoga studio, unlimited wine, fire engine red nail polish, and the "biggest-ass" gold hoop earrings she could find at Ardene.

"Ernest darling, please! Your friend just knows beauty when he sees it!", Joy said, taking off her oversized sunglasses. "Well hello, you! You can call me J-Law!"

Bibi laughed. "Oh, I like her."

Joy blew Bibi a kiss as Ernest entered the car, slamming the door.

"Do you always have to be so extra?" Ernest said, lowering himself into the seat.

"You're so uptight. Your friends are *my* friends!"

"I'm not your GBF."

"What's GBF again? Why do you always say that? You're confusing mummy, dear."

"GBF. Your gay best friend. I'm not gonna be that token. I know it's very progressive and fashionable to have one, but it's weird."

"How is it weird?"

"Never mind."

"Well, you're even better than any GBF, okay? You're gay, and happen to be my son, and that's even better … you can't get rid of me. Bros over mos! Hollah!"

Ernest thought her little quips were annoying, but every so often, she had him laughing till it hurt. Sometimes, he'd even find her endearing. Ernest's father had left them before he was born, and Joy never talked about him.

She reached over and rubbed the top of Ernest's head with her palm. "Darling?" Her tone was sweet.

"Yes, mother?"

"Do you mind running into my friend's Dennis' house and picking up a bag for me?"

"No, mother, I'm not fetching your weed for you!"

"Oh my God! It's legal now."

"Then why aren't you buying it from the store? Can't you just go in yourself?"

"But darling, I don't have my push-up bra on. I can't get out of the car looking like this! What will everyone think of mummy?"

Ernest sank lower into the car seat.

PART TWO

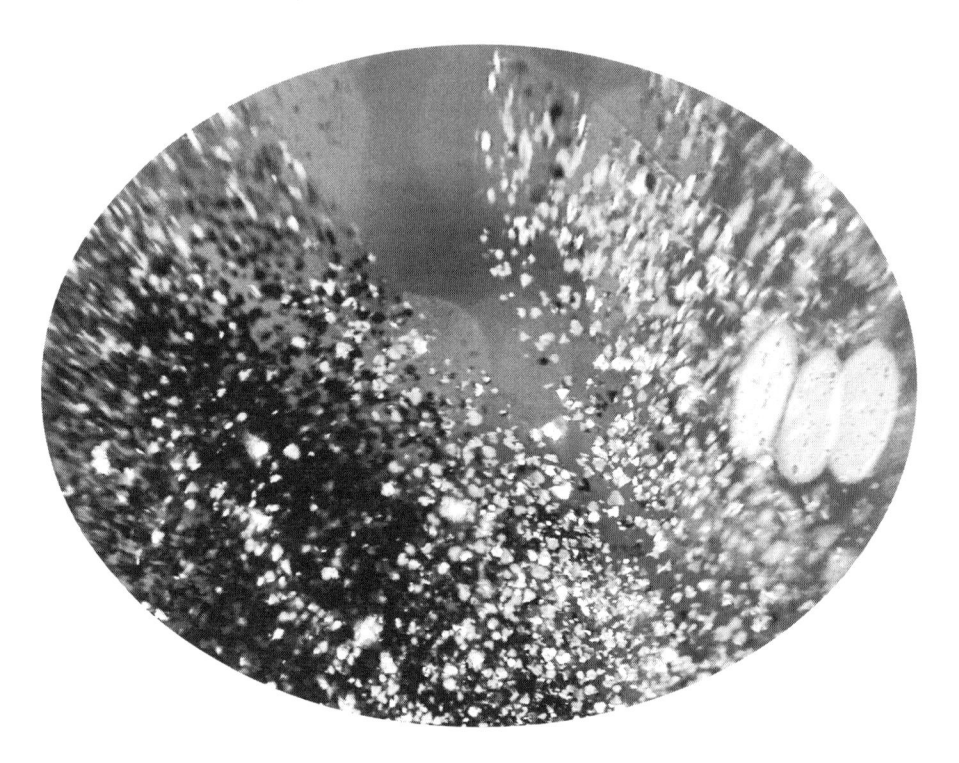

Chapter 4: Butterball and The Straw

Two days passed. Butterball Bibi Deveraux followed his Grindr from his small apartment in the pastel suburbs of Torpedo Valley to the overly populated neon urban jungle of Toronto, north past The Gay Village and in front of 120 Charles Street, East. The condo exterior was a smattering of black, red, and white squares. *This place looks like fucking Lego*, he thought. *I'm going to get fucked ... in a piece of Lego.*

Upon entry, the security guard unlocked the door. "Who are you here to see?"

Bibi realized in all his messages, he never got "Zeus'" real name.

"Hold on a sec," Bibi said to the guard, while texting *Whats ur name?* on his phone.

The response came back quickly: *I told u to call me Dr. Zeus, boy.*

Bibi giggled embarrassingly at the guard. He texted in a frenzy: *I'm in your lobby and the security guard is asking me for your name, sweetie-pie.*

The reply: *Oh. Jack Brown, suite 1705.*

Thirty minutes and two chocolate martinis later, Dr. Zeus had talked Bibi's ear off with stories about the office politics at his law firm.

Bibi's hookups varied. Some were short and right to the point: he'd meet the guy, no small talk, and body parts would be out and jiggling within minutes. This one wasn't like that. Finally fed up with waiting for Dr. Zeus to initiate, Bibi pulled out the small bottle of gamma-hydroxybutyrate, the drug that instantly relaxed people. It was common practice at gay hookups; Bibi couldn't remember the last time he hadn't used it during sex.

"Do you want a little G?" Bibi asked, "just a bit to loosen up. You don't have to. I'm not trying to pull some illegal shit on you."

"Okay sure," Dr. Zeus said. "Actually, I have something that would go perfect with that." He got up and turned on his television. "Here's my porn collection for you to browse while I get it," throwing him the remote and walking into his bedroom.

Bibi sat alone in the living room, unimpressed by what was on the screen. *My porn library is organized by category*, he thought to himself. He sipped his martini with a sense of superiority and crossed his legs.

Dr. Zeus came back with a glass pipe and a small Ziplock.

"You ever try Tina?"

"Tina?"

"Meth."

"Crystal meth? You want me to do meth with you? What do you think I am, some trailer park trash?"

"Yeah. I mean no! It will go perfect with the G."

Bibi was reluctant. "I heard that shit messes up your skin. Look at my face." Dr. Zeus got a closer look.

"Well not that close," Bibi lightly slapped his face, cheekily. "I am a lady."

Dr. Zeus took the slap in jest.

"It took years for my acne to clear up. I had to take Accutane. Hell no."

"Tell you what. You don't need to smoke it through your face."

"What do you mean?"

"Stay right there."

Dr. Zeus came back with a silver straw, looking excited. It was made of metal. "This sounds weird, but I'm going to blow it in my mouth, and then blow it up you ... down there."

Bibi's eyes widened, but his anus tightened. "Pardon me? With that? Up my what?"

"You'll love it. It'll just give you that something extra. You'll feel a rush."

"Extra? You mean a rush of extra gas! Dr. Zeus, are you kidding me? I'd rather eat green eggs and ham!"

"Just try it, just once, for me?"

Bibi felt a dramatic monologue come on: "You want to blow meth up my ass with a straw? I thought nowadays, it was all about doing it without a condom. But now you want to stick a straw there and blow it like a milkshake?" Bibi tilted his head and pondered: *Wait, is that what that song is all about?*

He shook his head and refocused. "Honey, I've had almost everything in every orifice possible! But I have never been asked something like this! What kind of slut do you take me for? What happened to good old-fashioned poppers? Where's all the romance gone?" he wailed, looking out the window, then dramatically putting his hand on his forehead.

Dr. Zeus' eyes suddenly looked like those of a puppy. A natural empath, Bibi thought about all the times Dr. Zeus' request must have been rejected. *I am Miss Congeniality, after all*, he thought to himself. *And it's good to keep an open mind.*

"Okay fine. Only one blow. That is all this ass is allowing today!"

"Awesome!" Dr. Zeus' eyes lit up like a child.

This made Bibi feel better. *If others are happy, then I'm happy.* "Why am I a fucking empath?"

"Whad'you say?"

"Nothing."

After the usual kissing, removal of clothes, touching and then oral play, Dr. Zeus then instructed Bibi to "lie down now and spread your legs."

Bibi did so, and was understandably anxious.

"Are you sure you just don't want me to sit on your face?" Bibi asked nervously.

"No. It'll be fine, I promise. I'm going to blow it in now."

Bibi waited for a few seconds, suddenly feeling a pinch. "Ow! That straw is cold! You keep it in the freezer?!"

"Stop clenching. Just relax." Dr. Zeus inhaled from the pipe, and then brought the straw near Bibi's buttocks.

Bibi shut his eyes, and took a deep breath as if he was in his yin yoga class. *You are doing this for the good of someone else. For the happiness of another,* he repeated to himself. *I'm basically a martyr.*

He heard a long blow below him. Dr. Zeus' face emerged, smiling mischievously: "Oh yeah, that's a good boy. Did you like that, boy?"

Bibi looked back sarcastically. "Yeah. Sure. Whatever floats your boat, buddy."

Dr. Zeus' smile grew.

"But that's it. One blow. Now the straw goes to the dishwasher!"

Dr. Zeus put the straw aside. "Okay, now, let's do something you want to do."

"Umm…" Bibi hesitated, "how about we just cuddle?"

"Nah, not for me dawg."

The effects of the crystal meth were minimal. Bibi didn't feel any of the exhilaration that Dr. Zeus promised. Furthermore, when it came time to ejaculate, nothing happened. Arms sore and sweaty from a rigorous hand job, skin chafed—and neither of them could produce the money shot.

"Damn, are we just dried up today? My arm is starting to hurt," Bibi wondered, stroking Dr. Zeus' shaft in a fury.

"No, it's probably the Tina. One side effect is that it can prevent you from cumming."

Bibi immediately let go of the penis, his voice lowering a couple of octaves: "Excuse me?!" What's the point of the drug if you can't shoot?!"

"It just comes with the high."

"What the fuck?" Bibi then hopped off the bed and started getting dressed.

On the way home, he berated himself for letting his empathy get in the way of his common sense and safety. *Meth up the ass? Really, you stupid bitch?* he repeated in his head.

Chapter 5: "No Homo!"

5a: Tops and Bottoms

The next morning, Bibi dragged himself to the Torpedo Valley Park tennis courts to practice with Ernest. Ernest was eager to play; he recalled Stefan telling him at the end of the first practice that the secret to improving was to "only play with *good* players. Ratings 4.5 and up. You can't be playing with people below that, or else they bring you down to their level."

Ernest also remembered Stefan's reply when he asked if they could practice together: "No I'm busy. I'm always busy because I'm very important," he sneered, then walking away to shoot the shit with the higher level players.

With that in mind, Ernest was happy that Bibi accepted his request to hit.

Despite headache and dehydration, Bibi still impressed with his tennis skills. It was April, and the bright sunshine was getting to him. He thought that if it was humid like in the middle of the summer, he might walk off the court and throw up.

With his height and long limbs, Bibi played with a graceful athleticism; his opponents remarked they felt like they were watching a curvy ballerina across the net. His sweeping strokes never looked hurried, always with adequate power and heavy topspin. It was a contrast to the laser-like speed that Stefan possessed, or the brute muscling of the ball by Khalid. Bibi had every shot in the book, and was comfortable playing from all positions of the court.

On the other side, Ernest, standing only five-feet, four inches, hit the ball early while it came up from the bounce—"on the rise", as it was referred to—to prevent Bibi's shots from spinning over his head. Obviously less skilled a player than Stefan, Khalid, or Bibi—and with a modest tennis rating of only 3.75—Ernest's groundstrokes were not as powerful. Primarily defensive, his biggest strength was his dogged ability to get every ball back and extend rallies until his opponent would make an error. Not a "pusher" or "junker"—players who hit with zero speed with or without various spins—or worse, a "moonballer," Ernest was no rookie dragging others down to his level. Although a strong baseline player, he never felt confident volleying, and was easily susceptible to a lob going over his head if he was forced up to the net because of his height.

"So how'd you learn to play, Ernest?" Bibi asked, as they took a short break on the side of the court.

"I kinda just watched Rafa on TV, although I don't really play like him. I just love him. We named our cat after him."

"You have a cat named Rafa?"

"Yeah. Then my mother had to be annoying and get another one and name it after her favourite player."

"No!"

"Yeah. Can you guess our other cat's name?"

"Is it …?"

"Oh yeah."

"No!"

"Yup. We call him Rodge for short."

Bibi laughed. "That's hilarious. Your mom seems really fun. She should join us sometime, hun. The gays would love her."

Ernest chuckled. "Everyone loves her … everyone loves anyone who proclaims themselves as fabulous."

"I need to sit for a sec," Bibi said, planting himself on the bench. The effects of the evening before were catching up to him.

"You okay? Your leg is shaking."

Bibi looked down to see his knee quivering quickly. "Oh sweet Jesus!" He pressed his hand down on it to try to calm it. "I may have slept wrong last night."

But that was a lie. He didn't sleep at all. After getting home from his date, he lay in bed staring at the ceiling, thinking about the metal straw. *That fucking metal straw.* He didn't know if the insomnia and shaking leg were caused by the crystal meth, or by the regret he felt for taking it. *You stupid bitch!* was the expletive on repeat in his head. He did eventually manage to fall asleep, but he woke up every 40 minutes or so absolutely drenched in sweat.

Suddenly the smell of Axe body spray floated onto the court. Ernest turned up his nose: "What is that?"

From a distance, a familiar figure, brown skinned with a bow-legged walk, in the same light grey sweats. It was Khalid. "Oh my God, it's the straight guy."

Khalid stopped in front of them, flashing a big smile: "Hey guys!"

Ernest again noticed his breath get shorter as Khalid got closer with each step.

"Well, hey there, Caaal" Bibi smirked. He always had that smirk—warm and inviting, but also a bit naughty. He had clearly watched too many *Sex and the City* reruns with Samantha's signature pre- and post-coital smile.

"Don't call him that," Ernest said. "Cal is for white guys named Callum or Calhoun."

"Oh that's right, we don't want to synthesize you," Bibi said.

"It's anglicize, not synthesize." Ernest clarified.

Khalid found this amusing.

"Who are you practicing with?" Ernest asked.

"Nobody yet. I heard you can just show up and there's always someone here, willing to play. Do you guys want to practice with me?" Khalid said.

Bibi perked up. "That's a great idea! Ernest here was tiring little ol' me out! Why don't you guys play a set?"

Khalid nodded and turned to Ernest. "Great. Ready, boss?"

Ernest's eyes widened at Bibi, as if to say, *what the hell are you doing!?*

"Uh, sure Khalid. But I'm not that good. I'm only a 3.75."

"The rating scale means nothing," Khalid insisted.

Bibi chimed in: "Ernest, I'm beat. And you said you wanted to assess your skills with the best ... here's your chance. I'll watch from here."

With a crushing combination of his jumping heavy topspin forehand and flat two-handed backhand placed in one corner after the other, Khalid beat Ernest soundly, 6-1, but the rallies were long due to Ernest's retrieving ability. As they headed toward the bench to Bibi, Khalid was encouraging: "Boss, you got a crazy scrappy game! You got so many balls back! I had to hit like three winners just to get it past you."

This made Ernest feel better. "Thank you. And thanks for hitting with me."

"You're like a wall! Awesome!"

Ernest beamed inside.

Rested now, Bibi popped up and began packing his stuff. "Wow, Khalid. You really play like Rafa. You really topped our little Ernest here!"

"Topped?" Khalid asked. "What does that mean?"

"Ignore him," Ernest said, then turning to Bibi. "Don't freak out the straight guy."

"No, I wanna know what that means. Tell me!" Khalid said.

Bibi and Ernest exchanged glances. "Shall I, or do you want to?" Bibi asked.

Ernest looked at Khalid. "It's like in tennis, one guy is the server—that's the top, and one is the receiver—that's the bottom."

"Makes sense, I think," Khalid said.

"Change the tennis ball to ... well, you know."

Khalid thought for another second. "Oh," nodding hesitantly at first, then opening his eyes bigger. It was the look of realization.

amazon.co.uk

A gift from Jeffrey Sotto

H[...] - *thank you so much! Hope you enjoy the read! From Jeffrey Sotto*

Gift note included with The Moonballers: A Novel about The Invasion of a LGBTQ2+ Tennis League ... by Straight People (GAY GASP!)

"Oohh!" He started laughing. "So I topped you Ernest! Ha that's awesome! I topped Ernest!" He laughed further, then turned to Bibi. "Next I'm gonna top you, Bibi!"

Bibi, deadpan: "Promise?"

Khalid let out a bigger laugh; a loud hearty one that reminded Ernest of the "bros" of his high school that used to bully him.

Bibi, sensing Khalid's delight in learning a new vernacular, said, "Khalid, darling. Ernest and I were going to have a kiki."

"A kiki?"

"We're just gonna hang out at my house. Care to make it a threesome?"

"Threesome? Oh…?"

"We're just having pie and some tea. Relax. No homo!"

"Of course. I knew that."

Bibi turned to Ernest. "Well, at least I tried, right?"

Ernest shook his head. "Miss Butterball, you're terrible."

5b: *An Ode to Bobbi Lee*

An hour later, Bibi sat across Ernest and Khalid in his apartment, still unable to stop his leg from shaking.

"Boss, what's with your leg?" Khalid asked.

"Oh, it's just excited that I have company," Bibi joked, then holding it down. *Damn metal straw*.

"You mind if I take a look around?" Ernest asked.

"Make yourself at home," Bibi replied, "I'm just so glad to finally have you both over for some girl time!"

"Sweet place," Khalid said.

"Thanks! I did all the decorating myself. I like to call it country bumpkin meets French can-can!"

Bibi's bachelor apartment was a mere 280 square feet, but he had made the most of it. A grey mid-century modern couch with a hot pink throw sat in front the television that had bunny ears made of wire on top of it. In between was a white IKEA coffee table. Beside the bed—which had a white satin cushioned headboard—was a large framed movie poster of *Moulin Rouge*. To the right, there was a vision board and a mood board, with various cut-outs and pictures tacked on, and scribbles everywhere. The kitchen was a tiny corner with a double hot plate plug-in, huge toaster oven, and fridge about half the size of a regular one.

Ernest's eyes stopped on a photo displayed on the nightstand; Bibi was holding a big trophy, in front of a pig. "Is that you?"

"Guilty!" Bibi exclaimed. "Miss Piggly Wiggly 2014. I gave my everything to raising that pig. Fluffy."

Khalid got up and stood beside Ernest. "Fluffy. Where's Fluffy now?"

"We ate her."

"What?"

"She got aggressive. So big daddy had to get the big axe out."

"Poor Fluffy."

"Poor Fluffy? Poor me! She almost bit my hand off when she didn't like the new feed we gave her. Plus she let herself go after winning that contest, she couldn't even walk anymore. So we roasted her. Even stuck an apple in her mouth. That's how we Filipinos roll! You guys should try it sometime!"

Ernest smiled. "I don't eat pork. Or meat. I'm vegan."

"Well of course y'are!" Bibi said, rolling his eyes.

"I didn't realize you were Filipino," Khalid said.

Bibi: "My momma is. My Daddy's as white as they come."

Ernest: "How'd they meet?"

"Funny story," Bibi replied. "Back in Tennessee, my Momma was the live-in maid and future nanny to Daddy's first child to-be while his first wife was still preggers. She then miscarried, and a hop, skip, and a jump later, my Momma snatched my Daddy up and they ran away together. People called Mamma a hussy, but I just say she's just opportunistic. A scrappy broad, ya know?"

Khalid and Ernest traded stares, giggling slightly. "Sounds like a telenovela."

"Yeah, it is a bit trashy, ain't it? Whenever people tell me about their family drama, like 'my parents are divorcing' and blah blah, I'm like 'boring!'"

"You ever miss the south?"

"Sometimes."

"When did you move here again?"

"End of 2016. Had to."

"Oh?"

"Yeah. Trump."

Ernest and Khalid grimaced.

Bibi continued: "A few days after he got elected, I was in line at a Dunkin' Donuts. Some hick customer started yelling at the brown cashier for no reason. When the cashier asked him to calm down, he screamed, 'don't tell me to calm down, you fuckin' brown piece of shit. This is our country again!' Then he turns around and looks at me 'You hear me, you dirty Mexican! This is our country now!'"

"Shit."

"I used to just get harassed because I was gay. 'Hey faggot!' they'd yell. But Trumpy brought the good ol' racism back. Well, there was always racism, but it was more subtle, you know what I mean? I'd just get looks here and there. Store clerks thought I'd steal. Ladies would clutch their purses harder when I'd walk past them. Same as with my Black friends. But they never said anything. Now it was okay to say those things out loud. People take their cues from their leader."

"I'm sorry to hear that."

"It's okay. I left, and it worked out for me. I mean, look at all those poor minorities shot by the cops. Canada ain't perfect—especially with Justin Trudeau doing Blackface—but it's a lot better than the States."

"You ever get lonely without your family here? You ever think about getting a boyfriend?" Ernest asked.

"Not really. I do think about getting a man every once in a while, but mainly when I can't afford shit."

Laughter.

Bibi continued. "I wanted to move to Toronto, but rent prices are just outrageous! So I found this place in Torpedo. Charming city, isn't it?"

Khalid read from Bibi's vision board. "You want to publish *another* book? You write, Bibi?" he asked, impressed, to which Ernest echoed the sentiment.

"Well don't be so surprised y'all!" Bibi said. "I'm not *just* a pretty face, you know? I went to college for creative writing. Even self-published a collection of short stories. It's on the shelves at the Glad Day Bookshop in The Village. "

"Wow."

"Yeah. They bought 25 copies from me. I'm basically J.K. Rowling sans the transphobia."

"Amazing!"

"Oh you millennials, so cute," Bibi chuckled, "you guys say everything is amazing. Anything to celebrate and get a gold star!"

"What kind of book is it?" Khalid asked.

"Poetry. I could be the next Rupi Kaur, you know? Diversi-tay! I've got to work my Asian 'otherness' now before some other ho takes that spot. Maybe I'll share some of my writing with you guys sometime."

"I'd love that. How about now?" Ernest asked.

Bibi turned his cheek. "Now you got me all bashful."

"Come on, just once!" Khalid said. "For me?"

Khalid's eyes suddenly looked like those of a puppy. A natural empath, Bibi thought about all the times Khalid had ever been told "no" in his life. *I am Miss Congeniality after all*, he thought to himself.

"Don't you be seducing me with those straight eyes? You sure you're straight?" Bibi smirked.

Ernest interrupted, sternly: "Stop that Bibi. We are not perpetuating the stereotype that all the gays are out to seduce or convert the straights!"

Khalid laughed. Bibi leaned into Khalid: "Don't mind Miss Woke here, she hasn't had her muffin touched in a long time."

"Bibi!" Ernest shrieked.

"You guys are hilarious," Khalid chuckled.

"Anyway, back to my poetry book—" Bibi pulled out a purple journal. "It's going to be called *The Iron Iris*, you know as a tribute to my absolute favourite movie of all time, *Steel Magnolias* starring *the* one and only Dolly Parton. Oh yeah, and the iris is the official flower of Tennessee."

"Can't wait to hear it."

He cleared his throat, and began reading dramatically. "This one's called *An Ode to my sweet Bobbi Lee*:

And now, may I say, my sweet Bobbi Lee,
there's no truer love than mine for thee;
as such, with tears, I shall depart
but with thee remains, my steadfast heart.

I promise this, a summer's kiss
when I see thee again in June;
In Tennessee blooms the blue iris moon,
But April will be too soon.
Autumn leaves fade, float to their grave
aye, September's too late;
may angels of snow, hold thee in glow,
for December's not our fate.

Till sparrows croon, in golden tune,
whilst in this heart, shall there be room?
I promise this, a summer's kiss
when I see thee again in June.

So wait, my sweet, my dear Bobbi Lee,
there's no truer love than mine for thee;
though time may flee, I'll dare intercede,
and, my sweet Bobbi Lee, time shall bend for thee."

Bibi put the book down.
Ernest and Khalid sat, speechless.
"That's ... beautiful. The rhymes, the images ... oh my God." Ernest said. Khalid nodded in agreement.
"Who's Bobbi Lee?" Khalid asked.
Bibi blushed. "Oh, this guy from my tennis club back in Tennessee. Bobbi Lee Moore. The undisputed Disney Prince of our league. Charming, wholesome, handsome ... perfect. And to make matters worse, he had an equally perfect boyfriend, Jeff. It was quite disgusting, really." Bibi sighed, then sounding a bit sombre. "I read him a couple of poems, he said I had talent. It's just nice to have that someone in your corner, believing in you, even if you don't believe yourself. Maybe I'll find someone like that one day."
"You will, boss," Khalid said.
Bibi suddenly got up. "Oh my heavens. The pie! I just get so carried away sometimes. You want some tea too? Or a cosmo maybe?" He pulled it out of the fridge, nuked it, and gave them each a slice on a plate.
"Do you have any beer?" Khalid asked.
The question horrified Bibi. "What? Beer? What do you think, I'm some straight hillbilly? No, honey."
"Tea is great."

Ernest took a bite. "This pie is amazing! What's in it?"

"Well, the secret ingredient is butter."

Ernest coughed.

Bibi raised his voice. "Swallow, hun, swallow! Don't you dare spit that out! What do you think this is? A hookup?"

"I'm vegan, remember?" Ernest said, sounding apologetic.

Bibi snapped. "Oh for God's sake! Is cum vegan?!"

Khalid's jaw dropped.

"Cause we all know every queen worth his socks has had to swallow it for the team, okay? Ha!" he laughed, raising his hand to high-five Khalid.

Ernest sat, flustered.

"Oh honey," Bibi said. "You'll have to excuse me, I get very intense about my pies. You don't have to put anything in your mouth you don't want to ... well until you get to the bathhouse."

Bibi turned on the television and then fiddled with his laptop. "Now while I get the drinks, you make yourself comfortable."

The laptop was projected to the TV. Folders of porn were lined up on the screen. Ernest quietly read out the folder titles: "Latino", "Gang", "Interracial ... straight?" Ernest read the latter folder again, puzzled. *"Straight?"*

Khalid giggled to himself.

"Yeah. Now don't judge me okay, Miss Woke! I like straight porn. Sometimes I get bored ... boys have fewer holes to work with," Bibi said. "Women really are the unsung heroes of ... well, everything!"

"I would never judge you."

"Plus, this just shows I'm being inclusive of all porn, okay? Isn't that right Khalid?"

"Sure," Khalid said. "Where's your bathroom?"

"See, I told you!" Ernest pointed his finger. "Now you've scared the straight guy."

"Oh jeez. You straight bros. We ain't going to jump you, okay?" Bibi said. "The bathroom's just beside the front door."

"Ha! No, I'm fine. I just really have to pee. Thanks," Khalid said, then walked away.

After the bathroom door closed, Ernest came closer to Bibi and whispered: "This is an impressive collection. Organized too. But you're nuts! Don't you think it's a little too much for him?"

"Oh hush, he's a big strapping manly man, he'll be fine. Now, what kinda porn are you into? Pick something to watch! "

Ernest paused. "I don't know." It was true. Ernest realized he didn't know what turned him on. "I don't have a fetish or anything. Is that bad?"

Bibi grabbed the pie and flowery tea cups. "Of course, not. You're just probably busy fighting the system and shit, it saps all your sexual energy! You woke millennials, pretending you're all oppressed and vegan and all that! Let me tell ya one thing, you're oppressed *because* you're vegan! When's the last time you had cheese? Honey, if you can't eat that, might as well be celibate!"

He went back to his computer. "Oh I have something perfect for you, my little social justice warrior!" He clicked on the interracial porn folder. "I bet you'll love this—an old white man in a business suit getting gang banged by a bunch of his Black coworkers. They're definitely sticking it to the man! So *very* woke!"

5c: *Why are all the good ones straight?!*

It was late afternoon now, and after downing the pie and gossiping like high schoolers—consequently forgetting to watch any porn— Khalid looked at his watch. "Sorry guys, I gotta get going. This has been fun, thank you Bibi."

"Girlfriend waiting at home?" Bibi asked.

Khalid: "No. I have a set to play tonight."
"A set?"
"Yeah. I spin around the GTA sometimes."
"Spin? Like you figure skate?"
"No. I mean I DJ."
"Oh!"
"Yeah. I make my own music too."

Bibi smirked and looked at Ernest. "Ernest darling, we have ourselves a fuckboy."

"Fuckboy? Hey, I find that quite offensive," Khalid said, grinning.

"I'm kiddin'. But you must have lots of pussy thrown at you like a mofo." Bibi then grimaced at Ernest. "Disgusting."

Khalid laughed.

"I should go too," Ernest said.

"I can drive you," Khalid offered.

"You don't mind? I was just gonna call my mother."

"Of course not, boss!"

"Okay. Thank you."

**

Ernest, looked down at the license plate on Khalid's maroon Toyota Camry. "DJKhal? I like it."

"Thanks. That's my stage name."

Ernest was surprised to find how neat the interior of the car was, until looking in the back seat: a microphone, a couple of speakers, and a bunch of flyers messily scattered on the floor.

Khalid turned on mellow electronic tunes, pulsing with a steady beat.

"Is this your music?" Ernest asked.

"Yeah. I know it seems conceited to listen to my own tracks, but I'm always looking for improvements."

"It's very chill. I feel like smoking a joint."
"Alright, boss."
"Oh God, I don't know why I said that. Was that offensive? I didn't mean to assume that you get high ... I was just trying to be cool."
"Haha, all good. It's called trap music, but with my own flavour."
"Okay. Trap music. Nice."
Ernest looked over at Khalid's arms on the steering wheel. His muscles and veins were popping out. Ernest turned his head the other way, trying to *not* be caught gawking. Realizing this was the first time they were ever alone, he suddenly felt nervous.
"Man, Bibi's been through a lot. I can't imagine it," Khalid said.
"Yeah, I know."
"You ever experience that?"
"Uh..."
"Shit, sorry Ernest. That's a personal question. You don't have to answer."
"No, it's okay. It wasn't quite as traumatic as Bibi's experience. I never got called the F word. I got other names though. People used to tease me ... 'Ernest the furnace! Here comes Ernest the furnace!'"
"Furnace?"
"Yeah ...because apparently I was so flaming, I was like a furnace." Ernest said, chuckling slightly. "It's silly, but I used to get hurt by that. Now it's funny."
Only Khalid wasn't laughing. He was actually frowning. "That's terrible. I'm sorry, boss. Kids are assholes."
"How about you? You ever get bullied?"
"Yeah. They'd call me Paki. Apu. Sand ni— I can't even say that last one."
"Brutal."
"My parents said everything changed after 9/11. Even years later, when I was 11, I used to walk home from tennis lessons. One night in October, when no other cars were around in my neighbourhood, I

remember an SUV driving by and throwing something. When it hit my head, I just heard a crack, and then I felt something dripping down my face. I ran home to my mom, panicking, 'Mom, is there blood on me?' She was like, 'blood, Khalid?' And I was like, 'yeah, some kids just threw glass or something at my head.' She said, 'it's not blood. Go to the mirror.' I did. There was egg dripping down my face."

"Oh my God."

"Yeah. I felt a little stupid. But the worst part of it was *what* they said when they threw the eggs. "Now time to drop a bomb on you, Paki!" Those were kid's voices. In Torpedo. A suburb."

"That makes me so angry."

"That's okay. My parents always used to say, 'forget those people. They don't hate you. They're just threatened by you, because you're different.'"

Ernest looked back to the windshield, shaking his head.

Khalid looked at Ernest, sensing his concern. "Ugh. Enough depressing stuff." He changed the subject. "So, do you have a boyfriend?"

Ernest raised his eyebrows. "Okay, you said you *didn't* want to talk about depressing stuff?"

"Haha."

"Let's say it's been a minute ... or maybe several minutes since I had a real boyfriend."

"Oh yeah?"

Suddenly a car came speeding past them, the male driver with sunglasses talking on his phone.

"Asshole, the speed limit is 60!" Khalid yelled out the window. His voice—lowering to a thunderous base—startled Ernest. "Sorry about that. I can't stand assholes who speed. Toxic masculinity."

Ernest's eyes widened. This was the first time he knew someone who wasn't a woman or gay man who deplored toxic masculinity like he did.

"Anyway, you were saying. You last had a boyfriend when?"

"Right." Ernest refocused. "Last time was when I was on the tennis team at university. We were doubles partners. Peter Winters. He looked like Pat Cash. Even had the little short shorts that were super tight in the front showing off the bulge. And when I called him on it, he'd play dumb and say, 'I don't know what you're talking about!'"

Khalid chuckled.

"Then after two years of playing together, he dumped me, first as a doubles partner—for Greg from his microeconomics class. He said he wanted a more powerful partner, and that my game wasn't big enough. Then I walked in on them getting it on in the locker room showers. And guess what—turns out Greg's game wasn't *that* big anyway."

"Ha! That's hilarious!" Khalid laughed, then catching himself and clearing his throat. He changed to a serious tone: "But sorry that happened."

"It's all good. I beat him in the singles final that year. I got a huge trophy. And you know what he had the nerve to ask me?"

"What?"

"He texts me, '*Hey Ernest, can I borrow your trophy?*' I'm like '*why?*' He's like '*I'm having a party tonight. Need to show off.*' I'm like '*no way!*' He's like '*Come on, I'll give you 20 bucks.*' And I'm like '*What the fuck?*' and then he's like '*Okay, I'll give you $25!*' and then I was like, '*Kay fine!*'"

Khalid burst into laughter again. "Awesome!"

Ernest suddenly felt self-conscious; "Sorry that was a lot of info. I didn't mean to get so into my silly gay shit."

"No, not at all, boss. I love it. You're a pretty cool dude."

"Okay. Thanks." Ernest smiled. "Well this is nice. Usually I'm terrified of straight guys. But you're like, a good one."

Khalid smiled. "What, were you stereotyping me, bruh?"

Ernest laughed.

It *was* nice. Ernest's memories—of being bullied at school by boys who said he talked like a girl, or moved his hands like a girl, calling him that horrible name, sending him crying and running home to his mother, and then being scared to go back to those boys the next day—felt a little more distant and hazy. Here was Khalid, a straight man, oozing of big manly manliness, who thought Ernest being gay was what *made* him cool.

The flutter in Ernest's heart turned into a full-on electric jolt.

***

Later that night, Ernest found himself in Khalid's car once again, and they had the same conversation, except it ended with Khalid moving his hand slowly toward Ernest's arm till softly holding it. Khalid then stopped the car abruptly, to which Ernest asked, "What's wrong?"

"I can't let you leave without doing this, Ernest," Khalid whispered, moving his face closer. Ernest's nerves melted quickly into exhilaration as Khalid pressed his lips to Ernest's mouth, lightly at first, then slowly increasing the pressure. Ernest stared at the street light peeking through the windshield, and then closed his eyes, focusing on the feeling of Khalid's full plump lips.

A second later, Ernest woke up, laying in his bed. *A DREAM. Fuck!* His heart beating as fast as if he was on a tennis court, he thought to himself in utter horror: *Shit! Why are all the good ones straight?!*

Chapter 6: The Night the Karaoke Stopped

6a: Pansies

About a week later was the league's first social event—hors d'oeuvres, drinks, and karaoke in the fancy party room of Stefan's condo in Toronto near King and Bay—with coral, not salmon—coloured decorations. Stefan was in his element. He loved talking at audiences, and being the host gave him many opportunities to indulge in his biggest pleasure: the sound of his own voice.

Standing in front of a group of league members including Bibi, Ernest, Scooter, Dakota, Angelica, and Abby was Stefan protesting the hassle of adhering to cultural diversity at the workplace: "I swear, if I have to pretend that I like the gulab jamun brought in by one of my coworkers in front of everyone one more time, I'm going to stab someone! Can't I just *not* like it *without* being racist?"

The league members laughed politely, then suddenly went quiet, looking behind Stefan's back toward the entrance. Khalid was standing there.

Stefan turned around: "Oh sorry, Khalid. Didn't know you arrived."

Khalid smiled politely. "Thanks for the invite. Sorry, for what?"

"Gulab jamun? Isn't that your people's thing?"

"I'm pretty sure that's an Indian sweet. My parents are from Syria, remember?"

"Oh. My bad."

Angelica, Scooter, and Abby glanced at each other, sensing the tension. "Awks,"

Angelica mumbled.

Bibi lowered his mouth to Ernest's ear. "Just between us girls … but, oh the drama, honey … I live for this shit."

Scooter gestured to Khalid with a pretend gunshot and winked an eye. "Bruh, come get a drink!"

Khalid came closer to the circle, soon spotting Bibi and Ernest.

"Give me a hug, honey," Bibi said. He and Khalid embraced. "Is that what you call a hug? I wanna feel your chest pressed against mine. I wanna drown in that sexy Axe body spray."

"Always with the jokes," Khalid laughed, hugging him again. "You know, I actually don't wear Axe."

"Then why do all straight people smell like that?" Bibi asked.

"Like what?"

"I don't know ... Walmart?"

Ernest, trying to forget the recent dream he had about Khalid, was slightly reserved. "Hi Khalid— Mr. Rafa DJ tennis star, good to see you."

"Boss, how are you?" Khalid said while reaching down slightly to hug Ernest. "When do I get to top you again?"

Ernest blushed. His face felt so hot he thought his glasses might fog. Everybody within earshot laughed. "Inside joke, guys."

Stefan watched with a scowl. While Khalid chatted with the rest of the group, he whispered in Bibi's ear, "what was that?"

"What?" Bibi asked.

"You hug straight guys now?"

"Oh shush. I'm just being friendly."

"Whatever. By the way, you didn't like my last Facebook and Instagram posts."

"Which one? I can't keep up with all your damn posts."

"I posted a selfie here tonight before people started arriving. There's only 20 likes so far. There's at least 50 league members at this party. This is a PR disaster."

"Oh lawd."

"Get your phone out now and like it."

Bibi pulled out his phone. "Done. I liked it."

"No, actually you need to love it. Click the heart. I need to maintain my brand."

"Okay, okay."

"Don't forget Instagram. And then get on Twitter and retweet that shit!"

Ernest came behind them. "Guys, I have some drinks for you."

"Thanks," Stefan smirked, "you're getting good at your job."

Bibi looked at the drink. There was a metal straw in the glass cup. He instantly jerked back. "What is that?"

"Vodka seven," Ernest said.

"No," Bibi said, shaken. "Is that a *metal* straw?"

"Yeah," Ernest smiled. "I brought them. Had a bunch from my environmental advocacy group at U of T. Less plastic, better for mother earth."

Butterball's face intensified. "You get that thing away from me!"

"Jeez, sorry," Ernest mumbled.

They turned their attention back to the group.

"So Khalid, you liking the club so far?" Dakota asked.

"For sure. Everyone's been real nice."

"Well of course everyone's real nice to you, Khalid. I wonder why," Ernest sarcastically said.

Khalid laughed. "Yeah. Well why are *you* so nice to me, then?" he asked, resting his hand on Ernest's shoulder.

Ernest blushed again, not being able to come up with a witty reply.

"It's because everyone wants to suck your cock, bruh," Scooter said, to which the members either howled hysterically or shook their heads in disgust.

Dakota noticed Abby; "Oh, how about you, Abby? Are you enjoying the league?"

Abby, although beautiful, had a real wallflower aura to her. In addition to her shyness, her voice was soft … faint. She was always around, but nobody really noticed.

She revealed a small smile. "Good. I li—"

Scooter interrupted, leaning in toward Khalid. "What did you think it was going to be like?"

"What do you mean?" Khalid asked.

"Bruh, you know what I mean. You know ... joining a gay club?"

The room got quieter; Khalid noticed people staring at him, eager to hear his reply.

"Oh. Actually, it didn't really cross my mind. I just wasn't getting enough court time at my current club." He turned to Angelica. "Right Angelica? The Forester Club has way too many members."

Angelica: "Yeah, they just wanna sell as many memberships as possible."

Scooter laughed. "Come on bruh. You didn't think, 'oh yeah, tennis with the gays, I'll beat all'em pansies to a pulp!'"

"No, not really."

"That's so straight," Stefan said.

"Straight?" Ernest asked.

"Well, not straight as in straight. Straight as in stupid." He turned to Khalid. "No offence. You know what I mean, right?"

Khalid forced a grin.

Stefan continued. "Anyway, that's what we all thought joining the league! Beat the nelly queens! Right guys?"

"A president probably shouldn't say that out loud," Ernest whispered to Stefan.

"Oh, it's just locker room talk, Ernest, relax!"

"Guilty!" Bibi said, "that's what I assumed! Turns out I was only half right!"

Ernest put his hand to his forehead, shaking.

"Hate to say it, but it's true," Scooter said. "I joined assuming I'd be the most butch of the bunch, well except for the lesbians, of course." He winked at Dakota and Angelica. "But shit, everyone in this league is good."

Ernest felt the need to chime in. "I never thought that when I joined," he proclaimed, earnestly.

"Well of course you didn't, Miss PC Police 2020," Stefan mocked him. "It's not politically correct or whatever! Gawd, nobody can have an opinion anymore."

"No, really." Khalid said, "I didn't assume that either."

Stefan rolled his eyes, then scanned the room. His eyes landed on members Jason Patterson and Aldwin Era, hosts of the *Ready Play Tennis* podcast, a popular program among the gay tennis crowd. He whispered to Bibi, "the podcasters are here. Gotta go schmooze. I don't know why these guys haven't asked me for an interview yet. Oh, Vong Show is coming later ... gotta see if I can get on that podcast too."

"You know they only interview real professional players, right? You ain't no Roger," Bibi replied. "As for Vong's podcast, it has nothing to do with tennis."

"Whatever." Stefan turned around, bumped into Abby without apologizing, and kept walking.

Suddenly, everyone turned to the entrance. Joy, Ernest's mother walked through the door, wearing a fire engine red dress that hugged her figure, her nails matching the colour. Trying to hide his embarrassment, Ernest pulled her to the corner. "Mother, what are you doing here?"

"Well, isn't this social open to all members and their significant others?" Joy asked. "And the wine's free, right?"

"You're my mother, not my significant other!"

"Well, Bibi invited me. He found me on the 'gram."

Ernest turned to Bibi, who had sneaked up behind them, "What?"

Bibi smirked. "You're welcome!"

Ernest frowned, to which Bibi remarked, "oh Ernest darling, don't be so uptight. The gays will love mummy!"

Bibi took Joy by the hand and led her to the main group. "Everybody, we have another straighty!" The group laughed. "This is Joy, Ernest's mom! Isn't she fabulous?" Bibi exclaimed.

"Hi everyone! You can call me J-Law!" Joy said, excited.

Ernest shook his head as he heard the cheers.

"You cannot be Ernest's mom," Angelica said, "you look like you could be his sister."

"Now, now, Angelica," Bibi said. "Stop hitting on her! We must not perpetuate the stereotype that all gays want to seduce or convert the straights!" Bibi looked at Ernest, "ain't that right Ernest darling?"

Ernest didn't think that was funny.

6b: *Truly Madly Deeply*

An hour later, the party was in full swing, with almost 100 people stuffed into the party room.

Ernest stood at the cheese board table, stuffing brie in his face while his mother chatted with a group of lesbians. Sensing his glare, Joy left the group and joined her son.

"I think your friend Angelica likes me," Joy said, giddy. "I mean, can you blame her? Look how hot I am! Hello?"

Ernest was perturbed. "Mom, she's just being friendly. She's taken. God, not everyone is in love with you."

"Oh Ernest darling. You always spoil the fun for mummy. Do you know for a fact that she's with someone?"

"Lesbians are always with someone! Don't flirt back with any of them. And don't hit on any of the guys. You'll be barking up the wrong tree."

"Okay, fine!"

Ernest stuffed another cracker with cheese into his mouth.

"Ernest, what are you doing?"

"What?"

"You're eating dairy! I thought you were vegan!"

Ernest grabbed a coral napkin and spat it out. "Crap! See Mother, this is what happens when you stress me out!"

Bibi and Khalid were approaching, Bibi whispering, "Khalid darling, you have to meet Joy, she's straight too. Yay straight people."

Ernest and Joy stopped bickering when Bibi and Khalid stopped in front of them.

"Joy, this is Khalid," Bibi said.

"Hi," Joy smiled, looking at him up and down.

Khalid returned the smile. "Hello."

Bibi stumbled a bit.

"Miss Butterball, are you drunk?" Ernest asked.

"Oh not at all, just warming up."

Joy subtly grabbed Ernest's arm. He glanced at her to see her mouth, "he's cute."

Ernest shook his head. "No."

He looked back at Khalid. "So, where's that pretty girl of yours? The one we saw pick you up at practice? You should have brought her."

Joy's eyes perked up. "What girl?" she whispered to Ernest.

Bibi turned to Joy. "They were making out in their car in front of everyone. Gross." Joy looked a bit disappointed while Khalid laughed.

"Yeah, that didn't work out. We're not together anymore. She actually ended it because I spent too much time working on my music," Khalid said.

Joy whispered to Bibi, "She? Did he say *she*?"

Bibi whispered back, "Yeah, he did."

"Or is he just referring to his ex-boyfriend as a woman? Or is she actually a woman? I know you guys like to interchange your genders in convo. Which I'm all for, you know— 'cause gender is fluid. Hollah!"

"Yeah, it was a woman. Khalid's straight."

Joy's face lit up. "Really?"

At the front of the room, Stefan stood with a microphone. "Okay queens, head over to the other room. It's karaoke time!"

Bibi shoved another chip with Jarlsberg into his mouth, shouting, "let's go guys!"

"What are you gonna sing, Bibi?" Ernest asked, walking behind him.

"A little Ri-Ri. *Wild Thoughts*. That's mah song!"

"*Wild Thoughts* by Rihanna? Really?"

"Yeah, why not?"

"That song is so misogynistic. I mean, come on, those lyrics? '*You know this pussy's for the taking?*'"

Bibi stopped and turned around to face Ernest, irritated. "Rihanna sings that line herself. If she wants to give her pussy away, just let her. It's consensual, for fuck's sake!"

Bibi turned around, bumping into Abby.

"Oh Abby honey, sorry. Didn't see you there. Come join us for karaoke."

"Okay."

Bibi marched toward the huge TV mounted on the wall, where Scooter held the remote control. He told him his song choice, to which Scooter giggled, and the song started.

Having too many tequila shots earlier in the evening, Bibi missed the first line, and sang the second in a deep slur: "*I know you wanna see me nekkid nekkid nekkid ...*"

The crowed laughed and hollered. Though Bibi wasn't able to hit every note or follow every word on the screen, he compensated by bending his body down forward while grinding his butt to the crowd. When the song finished, he high-fived Scooter, yelling, "and that my friends, is how it's done!", then literally dropped the microphone, causing a bang.

Stefan went up next. First blowing into the mic and asking, "can everyone hear me? Testing one two three," he cleared his throat and cued Scooter to play the song. "This is for you guys, from me. You're welcome."

The beginning of Savage Garden's *Truly Madly Deeply* started, to which Ernest heard some groans in the crowd. Angelica— standing with Ernest, Joy, Khalid, and Abby—rolled her eyes and said, "he sings this song every time. Like at every Karaoke night in the Torches' league."

"Oh," Joy nodded.

"Yeah, it's pretty terrible," Abby said.

"You've heard him sing this before?" Angelica asked.

"No, the song, I mean. Worst one ever," Abby replied.

"I'm going back to the bar. I can't hear this again," Angelica said. "You guys want a drink?"

"No, thanks."

Angelica nodded at Dakota to come with her; their exit catching Stefan's eye as he sang, and he glared at their backs with disapproval. *Surely, we're going to need to have a chat … you're supposed to be watching me*, he thought.

"This song brings so many memories back," Joy said.

"I think it may have been before my time," Khalid said. "Ernest, you know this song?"

"No."

"Y'all are just babies," Bibi said.

Joy watched Stefan sing and raised her eyebrows; "I think the song's supposed to be sung in a higher key, no? Or is Stefan lowering his voice on purpose?"

"Yeah, probably," Bibi answered, "cause deepening his voice makes him think he has a bigger di—, well you know what I mean."

As the last line of the song approached, Stefan signaled Scooter to lower something from the ceiling: a coral coloured paper lantern in the shape of a ball.

"Oh yeah. The good ol' ball explosion," Angelica said, having returned from the bar.

"An explosion?" Ernest said.

"Yep. Never fails," Angelica said. "And three, two, one ..."

As Stefan sang the last line, the ball exploded and fake coral rose petals floated toward the ground and into the drinks of the audience. A couple of obscenities were heard in between soft, courtesy claps: "Fuck, now there's petals in my drink!"

"Thanks Pika," someone else in the crowd said, laughing.

Stefan snapped, his eyes bulging. "Who said that? Come on, show yourself!"

Awkward silence.

"There it is again," Ernest whispered to Bibi.

Bibi shrugged his shoulders.

Stefan regained his composure. "Anyway, now it's time for a special treat. Let's see the chops of one of our new members. Stefan approached Abby, who looked terrified at the thought of singing. He looked past her and extended the microphone to Khalid. "Show us what you've got, bro. Everything seems so easy for the straight guy, so go ahead," he said, smirking.

Khalid's eyes widened. "Uh, okay." He slowly took the microphone and walked toward Scooter, quickly shuffling through the pages of the song selection book. A few seconds later, he made his choice.

"This is going to be good," Stefan smirked.

An old jazzy song seemingly from the 50s started to play. Khalid looked at the lyrics on the screen and raised the mic to his mouth. What he produced left the members' jaws dropping.

Khalid sounded like an old-fashioned crooner; his voice was smooth and deep as he snapped his fingers to the beat.

"Wow, what *can't* this guy do?" Bibi said.

Scooter walked over to Ernest. "Hey, straight dude's pretty hot, eh? He's gotta be bi-curious, at least?"

"No!" Ernest snapped. "You stay away from him! He's straight, okay? Don't you ever hit on him!"

"Okay, okay! God, Ernest, didn't think you could be so aggressive."

Stefan, recalling the feeling of Khalid's first forehand bolt past him in their opening practice, was furious.

Then, suddenly a memory entered his mind. "Do I know this song?"

"It's *Mack the Knife*," Joy said. "Frank Sinatra and Bobby Darin sang it."

"Right."

Ernest turned to Bibi. "Wow, I would have never thought Khalid sang! He didn't say anything about that at your place the other day."

Stefan glanced in Bibi's direction.

"I know. I was too busy blabbing about Fluffy and my poems. We should have just let him serenade us till we shot our loads," Bibi replied.

Stefan, eyebrows fully creased, then pushed his face into Bibi's: "We need to talk, right now." He then walked out of the karaoke room.

Bibi looked at Ernest confused, and then followed Stefan into the hallway, decorated with a giant coral bow hanging from the ceiling.

Stefan came out swinging. "Excuse me? You socialized with him?"

"Khalid?"

"Yeah, Khalid, the straight guy! Just cut the carbs and tell me the truth!"

"I just had him over for some pie," Bibi said.

"He was at your apartment?"

"Yeah. I had him and Ernest come over after hitting one day. I thought it would be nice."

"Wait, you hit with him?"

"He had nobody to hit with that day, so Ernest did and I watched. What's the big deal?"

"Liar! You played tennis with him, didn't you! That's why you said you were too tired to play with me the other day! You might as well have fucked him! I can't believe you're cheating on me!"

Bibi's face was a mix of disbelief and laughter. "*What?!*"

"No, it's fine. I guess next you'll be going to his tennis club and hanging with the other heteros? Gonna invite more straights into our league?"

"Well yeah, he did ask me to play some doubles at his club next week."

"You Günter Parche'd me!"

"Huh?"

"You stabbed me in the back!" Stefan's eyes bulged and a thick vein popped up from the side of his neck. "How dare you!"

"Stef, it's about time we hung out with some straight people, okay? We need to diversify! Our league is in the suburbs, for God's sake!"

"This is *our* space! You are *my* friend!"

Bibi raised his voice. "Have you lost your fucking mind?"

"I see you've fallen for it ... their straight agenda! I can't believe you let them get to you! We're done!"

"You're crazy!"

Stefan slapped Butterball across the face, the sound of a palm hitting a cheek echoing down the hall.

Bibi grabbed his cheek. "Oh my face! How dare you!" He then raised his hand and slapped Stefan back.

Stefan jerked to the side, then stood slowly back upright: "You know what? Forget it! Go be friends with him, I don't care! Go play tennis, drink a beer, go to Hooters, eat your Chick-fil-A, grab a titty ..." Stefan hurled, as if to throw up, but restrained and pulled his head back up, "... do all the disgusting things straight guys do! We are so done! You're cancelled, Bibi!"

"No, you're cancelled!"

"How can you be cancelled when you haven't even started?"

Bibi sneered. "That doesn't even make any sense!"

The sound of Khalid singing echoed into the hallway. Suddenly, Stefan realized something and begin mumbling to himself. "I know this song ... *Mack the Knife?*" Stefan said in a trance, his stare landing back on Bibi. "It's a German song about a man who comes to town to stab and kill everyone!"

Stefan turned around, yanked the coral bow from the ceiling, threw it at Bibi, and stormed into the back maintenance room. Khalid's song was about to finish.

Leaning back his head and shutting his eyes, Khalid began to belt the last line, *"because Mackie's ... back in ... —"*

Stefan opened the maintenance room's electrical panel, and before Khalid could sing the last word, pulled every switch to the off side.

The lights went out, the music stopped and the microphone cut; Khalid's voice was drowned in sounds of chaos and panic.

***

The abrupt stop of the final note changed the energy of the room considerably. There was the murmuring of gossip among the league members, wondering the same thing Bibi did before getting bitch-slapped and having a bow thrown at him: *Had Stefan lost his shit?*

But Stefan wasn't around to confirm or deny it. Immediately following his outburst, he disappeared, presumably to stew in his jealousy and anger in the comfort of his own unit in the building.

Bibi, still shaken after the altercation, found himself stuck to the table with the chip bowls and dessert platters.

"Ernest honey, I don't know about you but when I get stressed, I gotta get something in my mouth ASAP!"

"You mean dessert, or —"

"I gotta eat! The only way to solve problems in Tennessee is to eat' em!" He shoved a chip and a mini brownie in this mouth at the same time. "Sometimes you gotta just surrender and swallow everythang!"

People were beginning to leave.

"We better start cleaning up," Ernest said to the executives. Dakota collected plates, cups, and cutlery while Scooter picked up the coral petals off the floor.

Khalid had left, and Ernest was relieved to see Joy say goodbye for the evening, although not without embarrassing him in front of everyone. "Love you, Ernest darling. Come give mummy a kiss. This was fun—I just love the gays!"

"I can stay and help," said Abby, "Want me on dishes?"

"Sure! I'll wash, you dry." Ernest followed her to the sink, unable to avoid looking at her long athletic legs.

Ernest grabbed a platter and turned on the faucet. "Pretty crazy of Stefan to just yank the power like that and run, eh?"

"Well, I assume he's just pissed that he got upstaged."

"True."

Ernest realized that Abby was one of those people who would never start a conversation, and only speak when spoken to. But she didn't have a snobby vibe to her; it was more of a polite reserve. He decided to small talk.

"So, where are you from, Abby?"

"From Etobicoke, actually. I've lived in a lot of places though."

"Yeah? Whereabouts?"

"Everywhere. Here, then it was India. Thailand. Then Holland."

"That's cool."

"Yeah. I wanted to find myself. Very cliché."

Ernest chuckled. "So did you find yourself?"

"In a lot of debt, yeah."

"Ha."

"But I just had to get out of this city. Something wasn't right."

"What?"

"Everything. It took me a year and a billion hours of meditating in Mumbai to get that."

"I bet."

She continued. "Then I moved to Vancouver, worked there for a few years. It got better. Then I moved back here last year."

"Why'd you come back?"

"I missed my friends," she said, wiping a plate dry and setting it down.

Chapter 7: Butterball and The Mansion

Two days passed. Following his Grindr to a bar on the border of Torpedo Valley and Mississauga called The Undergroundo, Butterball Bibi Deveraux again found himself contemplating whether to go through with meeting the man on the other side of a profile called *"niceguyintheburbs."* Through their messages, Butterball learned his name was Fred.

The Undergroundo décor was subdued. Rustic benches and tables were aligned perfectly. A chalk board listed all the craft beers available; including pumpkin ales, hoppy IPAs, organic sours, and other drinks Bibi had no interest in. The waiters—whose name tags read "Caleb" and "Jethro"—had 70s pornstaches, and every waitress had a side ponytail gathered in a rose patterned scrunchie and thick plastic glasses. Bibi thought he may be in a bar on Queen Street West in Toronto.

What kind of hipster fuckery is this?

Bibi initially wasn't attracted to Fred's profile pic; hair thinning, a bit of a gut, he looked to be in his 50s. It wasn't that Fred was ugly; but rather he looked too wholesome. Like *not sleep with someone on the first date* kind of wholesome. Bibi had never been into that kind of man. Stefan often called Bibi's taste predictable, typical ... "girl, you are a basic bitch! You choose all your dates based on looks," Stefan would say. Bibi resented being called basic, but deep down, he knew there was some truth to it. In the last two years, Bibi's taste in men led him to a list of predicaments: a black eye from a bar fight where his testosterone "dude bro" date mistakenly punched him while trying to take out a shit talker at the bar who also happened to be half Asian and White; almost getting arrested when his date argued with the cops when they were caught speeding on a private racetrack that his date had illegally trespassed on; and most recently, getting a metal straw up his ass because his date was turned on by specifically blowing drugs up that way.

Bibi didn't get any of those vibes from Fred. Their text exchanges were a series of pleasantries such as, "*Hello, how was your day? The weather was beautiful today wasn't it?*" No naughty messages had been exchanged, and no random pictures of a penis showed up on Bibi's phone. Even the grammar in the messages was all proper. *Who does that? Perfect grammar = probable serial killer,* Bibi thought. But then he reasoned it out: *This is good. It might be time to date someone who is just nice.*

Their date started off well enough. Fred ordered a Heineken, and Bibi was relieved to find out the bar could make a chocolate martini for him.

"So …" Bibi said. "I didn't realize the suburbs had gay bars."

"Well this isn't a gay bar per se; but you'd be surprised. Torpedo is pretty hip and happening," Fred replied.

"*Hip and happening?" Who says that?* Bibi wondered.

They sat for the next 30 minutes making polite small talk. Fred ordered another craft beer, Bibi inhaling the martinis like candy.

"You play tennis?" Fred asked.

"Yeah."

"I have a tennis court at my cottage. You wanna see?" Fred asked.

Bibi perked up. "You do? Yeah, of course."

Fred shuffled through the pics on his phone. "Here," he said, holding it up.

The blue court was surrounded by flower boxes and benches.

"It's beautiful," Bibi said, "that's your place?"

"Yeah. It's my cottage"

"Is that a professional picture?"

"Yeah. It's from *Home and Garden* magazine—last July's issue."

"Your cottage was in a magazine?" Bibi asked, delightfully surprised.

"Yep."

Bibi leaned back and finished his martini in one gulp. *Is this dude loaded?*

"What do you do for a living, Fred?"

"I'm a business developer. Whatever that means," he chuckled. "I also do a lot of volunteer work with animals. Dogs mostly. What do you do, Butterball?"

"You can call me Bibi. Butterball's a little formal. I'm working as a server and also an Uber driver. You know, till I get something better."

"Butterball's your formal name, eh?"

"Yeah. You'll find out why," Bibi smirked.

Fred—wholesome as Bibi assumed—was puzzled by Bibi's reply.

"What do you want to do now? Wanna come over to my place for a drink maybe? I'm doing some renovations, but it's a lot more quiet than shouting over the table here."

Bibi looked at his phone. 9:15pm. He always noted how he'd get so sleepy earlier in the evening in the suburbs. "I'd love to, it's getting late."

***

Bibi sat in his Toyota Yaris and waited for Fred to come from the other side of the parking lot. Checking his Grindr, Scruff, and DudesNude to find no new messages, he noticed a navy blue Tesla drive up beside him. The window rolled down.

"I'm not too far from here," Fred said, "I'll drive slow."

"Wow. Nice wheels." Bibi nodded and followed him out of the parking lot. Ten minutes later, they turned on to Grand Garden Road, a wealthy neighbourhood. Bibi's eyes brightened as each house, with its well-manicured lawns and vibrant gardens, seemed to get larger the farther they drove. Eventually, they stopped in front of a massive grey cube with large windows framed in white, with a bright red door. There were lights turned on in the front porch and on the lawn.

"Whoa," Bibi whispered to himself as he got out of his car. Fred pressed a button on his keychain, turning the lights off.

"So remember I'm renovating, so don't mind the dust," Fred said, as he opened the front door and flipped on the light switch.

Bibi stood in the front hall and took in the sight: tall grey walls, a floating staircase, a sparkling chandelier, and black leather furniture. Beside Fred was a massive ball of golden fur, its tongue hanging below its button nose, staring back at him.

"Oh my heavens. Is that a lion or a teddy bear?"

"Her name is Gucci. She's a Tibetan Mastiff."

"Wow. She's beautiful. How much does she weigh?"

"Around 210 pounds."

The dog walked to Bibi, sniffing his pants. Bibi bent down, lightly running his fingers through the top of her hair. "Hi sweetie." He looked up at Fred. "She's not going to eat me, is she?"

"Not til later when she becomes friends with you."

"Aww, you're a lot nicer than most men, aren't you, doll?" Bibi said, plowing his face right in Gucci's mane and giving her kisses; she immediately jumped up and put her paws on his shoulders, causing him to fall backward to the ground. She climbed on top of him, aggressively licking his face. "Oh dear, she's quite forward, isn't she?"

"She likes you already," Fred chuckled, pulling Gucci off of him. "Noodle dog! Noodle dog! Relax Gucci!"

As Bibi got up and wiped his face, he noticed a large framed photo to the left of the staircase; he walked closer to it and read a handwritten note in the bottom right corner. *Fred, thank you for everything, J.*, the writing said. Bibi looked at the group of people posing for the photo dressed in tuxedos and ballgowns. There in the picture was Fred standing next to Justin Trudeau.

Bibi turned around. "Okay wait. Hold on for a second here, buster."

"Yeah?"

"You know famous people."

"I guess."

"You're like, rich. Like *actually*."

Fred laughed. "Well, yeah. Business is doing well, knock on wood."

Bibi turned around and scanned the room more. Crown moulding lining the 20 foot ceilings. Distressed greyish wood floors. Paintings with one dot in the middle that probably went for a cool million.

"Where's the dust?" Bibi asked accusingly. "You're a fucking liar!"

Fred laughed. "You're funny. Do you want a drink?"

Bibi thought for a second and then looked down at Gucci, who licked his hand once again. "I want the most expensive drink you have, Freddy-boy!"

Bibi sauntered gracefully behind Fred as he gave a tour of the house. With Gucci strutting beside him, Fred went from the living room, to the kitchen— with, as Bibi noted, stainless steel appliances and a double oven *(imagine how many fucking pies I could bake in here,* Bibi fantasized*)*—to the casual dining room, to the formal dining room, to the library, to the study, and then to the den, the last three rooms as big as a bowling alley. Bibi was pleasantly surprised upon entering the guest powder room: finally there was a room in this house that was smaller than his own apartment.

"Do you want to see upstairs? We don't have to if you don't want to," Fred asked politely.

Bibi finished his Virginia Black and put the glass on the bathroom counter. "Show it to me. I wanna see all of it. I'm calculating how much this place is worth."

"I hope you don't think I'm trying to show off."

"I prefer it!"

"Are you a little tipsy?"

"Yes. And I'm easy. Take me upstairs now!"

Fred took his hand and led him up the stairs and into the master bedroom. There was only a king size bed with a white duvet, and a side table with a candle.

"It's very zen in here," Bibi remarked.

"Thanks. I like things simple."

"You do?" Bibi asked, and then stepped close to Fred, their lips almost touching. "Well *I'm* very simple."

Fred broke into a giggle. "You kill me."

He then pulled Bibi's hands in gently, their bodies touching now.

"Are you having a nice time?" Fred whispered.

"Yup."

"Can I kiss you?"

"Like ten minutes ago, hello?"

Fred put his arms on Bibi's shoulders and pulled his face closer down, planting a big smack on his lips.

Suddenly there was a loud bark, followed by vicious growling. Bibi looked down to see Gucci beside him, but without the friendly welcome from before.

"Oh shit. She thinks you're attacking me," Fred said, signaling for her to leave the bedroom. "Noodle dog! Relax girl!"

"Um, Fred, is there a washroom up here?" Bibi asked, suddenly self-conscious.

"Yeah," Fred said. "Ensuite is right there."

"Thanks."

Bibi shut the bathroom door behind him and walked to the mirrored glass sink. Looking into his reflection, zeroing in on his eyes, Bibi's inner monologue raced: *Bitch, if you give the performance of your life, you can land this dude right here. Never drive Uber or have to wait tables ever again. Never have to think about starting an OnlyFans to upgrade your phone or car. Only focus on writing. Never only playing at tennis clubs during public hours, or subjecting yourself to the God-forsaken asphalt concrete public courts like a fucking animal. You can do this.* He pulled his shoulders back to straighten his posture and clenched his buttocks tight. *You got this.*

Bibi looked behind him and realized the toilet wasn't a toilet. It was a bidet. *A mutherfuck'n bidet, bitch.* He washed his genitals and between his buttocks and went back to the mirror one more time. *You got this.*

Bibi came out of the bathroom to see Fred sitting on the bed with a huge smile. He was holding the bottle of whisky with a glass. "More?" he asked.

"There'll be no need for that," Bibi said, determined to show off just his skills in the sheets. Bibi kissed Fred passionately, running his fingers through his thin grey hair and then down his slightly pudgy back. Fred grabbed him back, and they kissed and giggled until they were horizontal without shirts.

"Are you okay with this?" Fred asked.

"Stop being so polite. I want you to tear this bitch apart!" Bibi immediately replied, as he began unbuckling Fred's belt.

"Oh ... alright," Fred smiled, delighted.

***

Ten minutes later, Bibi lay beside Fred, trying to figure out what went wrong.

"Did I do something?" Bibi asked.

Fred was disappointed. "No, not at all. It's me. Sometimes it just doesn't work. I'm sorry. I don't know why. Please don't think it's you."

"Don't apologize honey," Bibi said, trying to sound cheerful.

But Fred continued to look down, despondent.

"Wanna just cuddle, or something. I could hold you?" Bibi asked.

"No, it's okay. I think you better go."

Bibi panicked slightly. *No! I haven't seduced this fucker yet. He hasn't fallen head over heels in love with me!*

"Are you sure?" Bibi asked, trying to hide his desperation. "We could watch the sun rise, or some other thing they do in the movies?

Or do you wanna sit on my face or something?"

"No it's okay," Fred said quietly.

"Um ... Fred, you didn't do any drugs did you?"

"What? No. I don't do drugs."

"No ... like ... meth or anything?"

Fred stared at Bibi, confused.

"I heard that can cause things to go ... dead," Bibi whispered.

"No, not at all," Fred reassured him.

"Just checking."

Bibi dressed in the bathroom quickly, trying to forget how a perfect evening was ruined in a matter of minutes. When he finished, Fred was waiting downstairs with Gucci, and they exchanged their courtesy goodbyes.

"Thank you for a lovely night," Bibi smiled.

"No, thank you. Maybe we can talk again soon?" Fred asked shyly.

"Of course!" Bibi said reassuringly. He looked down at Gucci and waved, "Bye Gucci-darlin'!" and turned around.

Driving away from the grey cubed mansion, Bibi shook his head, regretful of the chance he had missed this evening. *Oh well. Maybe I'm not meant to have a sugar daddy,* he sulked. Then a thought more terrifying and devastating than ever occurred and he grunted in anguish: *Maybe I'm supposed to ... be my own sugar daddy! No! Ugh! I'm no fuckin' Oprah!*

Upon arriving home, Bibi sliced himself a large piece of cherry pie he had made the day before. Taking the first bite, he opened his email on his phone, the one at the top catching his attention.

The subject line read: *Your Publication Submission,* from Silver Lining Publishers. Assuming it would be another rejection, he opened it anyway, reading:

Dear Butterball,
We at Silver Lining Publishers are pleased to inform you that based

on the sample you have submitted, we are interested in publishing your book of poetry, The Iron Iris.

Bibi instantly jumped up. "Yes! Yes! Praise Jesus! I'm going to *BE* fuckin' Oprah!"

His joy faded when reading the next few sentences:

We will be reaching out to you shortly to speak in person about the publishing process. Meanwhile, please note we will need you to submit the full manuscript as soon as possible.

Bibi worried. He only had about 25 poems written; a full book would at least start at 60 or 70.

Chapter 8: The Canadian Gay Open
May 2020

8a: Superstitions

It had been a month since the karaoke incident.

The Canadian Gay Open—or CGO, as it was often referred to as—was only days away. This was the first year it would be held in Torpedo Valley instead of Toronto due to the demise of the previous league. Being the largest queer tennis tournament in Canada, competitors based out of different city leagues could also enter and compete with Torpedo Valley's finest. This year's championships held more significance than prior years; the winner would likely be guaranteed a higher ranking—called a "seeding"—in the Pride Games to be held in Bonn, Germany, in August later that year.

Stefan was particular about his actions before tournaments. He'd make sure to have his small notebook in his tennis bag with back-up strategies he could use in the rare case he was losing.

In addition, prior to the first round, he would always post a selfie on his social media. His facial expression: pure blue steel. And always the same caption: *"<insert the name of the tournament> Let's do this. #tennis4lyfe."* If he made it to the finals, he'd do the same, but add the hashtag *#championshipmatchglory*. A trademark of his brand, and superstition.

Ernest's superstitions contrasted. He'd pay no particular attention to strategies or take selfies. Rather, it was in the way he'd interact with Joy before each match. During tournaments as a teenager, she'd come to watch him and have to force herself to not cheer for him loudly, as Ernest would discourage her if she did.

"You can't cheer for my winners, or even worse, cheer my opponent's errors, Mother. It's disrespectful to the other player, and it's bad tennis karma," he'd say.

Her response: "Excuse me, Ernest. But did the other player come out of my vagina? NO. I'll cheer for who I want. Kay, thanks."

During the summer when he was 15 and playing in the North York juniors league, Ernest had stumbled into a seven-match losing streak. Tournament eight, the last one of the summer season had started. Stepping to the line to serve the first point of his first round, Ernest realized Joy forgot to say "good luck" to him before the match—something she had never failed to do before. *Dammit. Loss number eight, coming right up*, he thought. *How dare she forget!*

To everyone's surprise—especially Ernest's—he won the match, 6-3, 4-6, 6-3. A stunning upset, as his opponent was the top seed of the tournament.

"It must have been because you didn't wish me good luck. That's it!" Ernest concluded.

"What?" Joy asked. "That doesn't make sense, Ernest darling."

Ernest reminded Joy not to wish him luck before the second round. However, he lost the match anyway.

After further thought, Ernest retracted his prior claim: "I got it! It must be because we thought about the superstition and tried to actively use it. You know what mother? Just say whatever you feel before matches, we won't pay attention to superstitions."

"Ernest darling. Now you're confusing mummy."

"The superstition is to forget about superstitions!"

From then on, the pre-match conversation between mother and son would be the same:

Joy: "Good luck, Ernest! Oh shit. I'm not supposed to say good luck. That's a bad superstition, right?"

Ernest: "Mom, how many times do I have to tell you? The superstition is to *not* think about superstitions!"

Out of the holy trinity, Bibi's superstition was the most plain and simple: Look fierce. "First, before every tournament I like to start with a mood board, you know, like retro, couture, skanky, whatever I feel." Then if he'd win his first few rounds, the mood always moved toward showing more skin: "Honey, the further you get into a tournament, the brighter and tighter the clothes get!"

Bibi was famous for playing the 2016 Toronto Torches end-of-year tournament final in a fluorescent orange halter tank top, and white spandex hot pants. "Even though I lost, I looked like a hot orange creamsicle that day. It was during my theme of dressing like desserts. You shoulda been there," Bibi beamed with pride as he told Ernest.

***

Entering the tournament venue was always an experience Stefan loved. He'd make sure to wear his sunglasses while entering the facility, and look aloof while walking past the rest of the players. He'd be careful not to walk too fast, however; this was so the other players could see him, yell his name hoping he'd wave back, to which he loved to not respond. As a two-time former champion of the tournament, he enjoyed being watched, and felt it wasn't on him to approach others to engage in conversation. Others needed to come to him, and if he deemed them worthy, he'd give them the pleasure of his reply.

One of the few Stefan believed was worthy was Tommy Trinh, the tournament director of the CGO for the last 12 years. Tommy met the criteria of someone Stefan wanted to acquaint himself with; handsome, muscular (he had never *not* had a six-pack of abs for the last twenty years) and great player in his own right, having won the title a few years back. It didn't hurt that he was a VP of one of Canada's big banks; Stefan was attracted by status in addition to appearance and tennis skills.

Stefan entered the Torpedo Valley Lawn and Tennis Club and slowly walked past the registration table where Tommy sat. But apparently not slow enough; Tommy didn't look up.

Turning around and pretending to have forgotten something in his car, Stefan walked back toward the entrance, his eyes peeking out of the side of his sunglasses to see if Tommy was watching. No luck.

Nothing irritated Stefan more than not being noticed. This time, he walked toward Tommy again while holding his phone to his ear, pretending to take a phone call.

"What do you mean?" Stefan said loudly, seeing Tommy's head finally up. "You know what, I can't do this right now, I'm busy. I have a tournament. Figure it out!" he said to nobody on the imaginary line.

"Hey Stefan," Tommy said. "Good to see you. Everything ok?," he asked, glancing at Stefan's phone.

"Just some issues at work. These guys would be completely lost without me—I mean I guess I'm kind of a big deal, but really I can't hold everyone's hand, you know TT?"

Stefan gave people he thought were important nicknames that he liked to say out loud so people would think he was close to them. Tommy always looked puzzled whenever Stefan called him "TT," and never returned the favour of addressing Stefan as "Steffi" as requested.

"So, I heard this new straight guy is pretty good, apparently very Nadal-like." Tommy said, "Bibi told me about the first practice. I couldn't believe he took you down."

"Well, he's not *that* good. Mind you, I was kind of distracted that day. You know, work stuff," Stefan said.

"But it's great that you're getting all these new members. I saw him earlier. He's pretty beefy—it's hot," Tommy's face lighting up.

Stefan rolled his eyes behind his sunglasses. "I hadn't noticed. He's not *that* masc, you know? Actually, I think he'd be a bottom if he was one of us, you know what I mean, TT?" Stefan smirked.

"Gotcha. So, I guess that wouldn't work out for you," Tommy said nonchalantly.

Stefan, offended, took off his sunglasses and said rather hostilely, "what? No! How could you even suggest that I'm a botto—!"

Just then, he turned around to see that the tennis podcasters were standing behind him. "Jason, Aldwin! Hi!" Stefan perked up.

"Hi," Jason said.

They awkwardly stared at each other for a few seconds.

Stefan was paranoid of what they had heard. He needed to confirm it, leaning in, and shouting, "I'm not a bottom!" at them.

"Ooh-kay, easy there," Aldwin said, taking a step back. "Thanks for the info!"

Stefan lowered his voice, mumbling, "you know, just in case that ever came up on the podcast."

Jason and Aldwin traded stares.

"Speaking of the podcast," Stefan continued, "if you guys ever want an interview, I can free up some time."

"We're fully booked for the season," Jason said, not missing a beat.

"Yeah. Sorry 'bout that," Aldwin chimed in.

Tommy ended the exchange. "I should get back to the registration desk. You all are on the next few courts, so better get changed. Good luck."

***

Meanwhile, Bibi, Khalid, Ernest, and Abby arrived earlier and were practicing some doubles on an outside court.

"You're playing great Abby! Love that one-handed backhand. You just need a little swagger to match your skills," Bibi said as they sat on the changeover.

"Swagger?" Abby asked.

"I think he means confidence," Khalid said.

Ernest nodded in agreement.

"So how do I get more swagger, then?"

"A grunt?" Ernest suggested. "Maybe a double syllable, like Monica? Or a high-pitched orgasm like Maria?"

"I don't want to draw attention to myself," Abby said.

"No, no." Bibi leaned in to the three of them. "Just between us girls … but when you get to the tournament, just pretend you gotta big d—."

"Oh God, Bibi, enough about the D! That's all you ever talk about. Dick dick dick," Ernest complained.

"Exsqueeze me, ugh," Bibi said. "Fine. We'll work on outfits. Abby darling, let me design you a mood board."

8b: First Round — *Why is nobody watching me?*

Like the entrance to the tennis venue, Stefan had to make sure people were watching when he walked on to the court. But other than the couple of American friends of his opponent from Boston, nobody was there.

Furthermore, Stefan found himself on a back court away from the centre viewing area. *Why is nobody watching me? Maybe because they can't find me,* he thought. He'd definitely need to talk about court assignments with "TT" later that day.

Refocusing on the match, Stefan easily won 6-0, 6-1 in just over an hour.

Walking back to the reception area to report his score, he noticed a small crowd gathered on the side benches of the more centrally located court one. Their heads whipping left to right trying to follow the tennis ball flying, whispering to each other in awe. He leaned in to see Khalid on court. He was serving for the second set 5-0, having won the first set 6-0.

"Hey Stef,"

Stefan turned around. It was Ernest and Bibi.

"Hi."

It was the first time Stefan and Bibi had seen each other since their argument. They avoided eye contact with each other, and focused on Ernest.

"How'd your first match go, Ernest?" Stefan asked.

"I won," Ernest said, in shock. "I still can't believe it."

"Who'd you play?"

"Edsel Colaco."

"What?" Stefan asked in disbelief. "You upset the number two seed? The one with the crazy forehand?"

"Yeah."

"Holy shit, Ernest. Well, look at you. Your first CGO and you're slaying the giants already. Way to go."

"Thanks."

Bibi decided to make eye contact first. "Yeah Miz Pres, you should play with him some time. Ernest is deceptively good."

"Yeah, I'd love to play you, Stefan," Ernest said.

"Um, yeah, sure. We'll talk," Stefan mumbled.

"Mmmmhmmm," Bibi replied cynically.

Stefan turned around and saw Khalid clobber a forehand topspin winner. The match was over and the crowd watched Khalid and his opponent chat while exiting the court. Walking in between Bibi and Stefan, he nodded at them: "Gentlemen. Good to see you."

Khalid's eyes landed on Ernest: "Ernest—boss! My bud! I heard about your upset! Congrats!"

Ernest blushed. The way Khalid's face lit up when seeing him was perhaps an even better feeling than the win itself.

But it was interrupted by another player blurting out behind them: "Who is that? He's hot?!"

"He even has a big manly grunt too," another player said.

Ernest's head snapped to the men talking: "He's straight! You stay the fuck away from him!"

"Meow!"

Stefan and Bibi struggled to restrain their laughter.

Khalid grinned: "Thanks for outing me, Ernest ... or in-ing me. You know what I mean," he chuckled.

8c: Quarterfinals — "You took the high road, bitch. How dare you."

The next day, Ernest found himself dreading his next match. His celebration of upsetting the number two seed in the first round, and then a solid player from Montreal in round two was short lived.

"Next on court one: Butterball Deveraux versus Ernest Law," Tommy shouted.

Bibi grabbed the can of tennis balls and strutted to the court, with Ernest walking behind him, staring at the ground. "Let's just get this shit over with, Ernest darling," Bibi said. "I hate playing friends."

"Ernest, Good lu ... I mean, break a leg ... oh, whatever," Joy said just as Ernest was about to disappear behind the court curtains.

He turned around, and said, "Mom, the superstition is to not pay att—"

"—attention to superstitions! Yes, son, got it!" Joy interrupted, ostensibly fed up, rolling her eyes. "Just ... you know what? YOU DO YOU!" was the most supportive and unsuperstitious phrase she could come up with.

The first set took about 35 minutes, with Bibi edging Ernest by one service break, 6-3.

"Good set, hun," Bibi said to Ernest during the changeover. "Just try to get your balls deeper."

Ernest wiped his face with a towel, "it's weird to get coaching from your opponent, but thanks. I'm so freaking nervous with all these people watching."

Bibi was nervous too, but for different reasons. At 3-2, while chasing down a sharp angle on his forehand, he smacked a winner up the line, but subsequently took a tumble. He got up, but then fell back to the ground, feeling the court was tilting inwards. He had felt dizzy a few times during that first set, and it seemed to be increasing.

The second set was similar; Bibi, nowhere near his best, still had too much game for Ernest. Ernest could do nothing but admire his opponents play; at one point, he looked at the crowd, to see Stefan look at him and cheer, "good try, Ernest" while giving a thumbs up. *Fuck, a pity-cheer. Must be bad if it's coming from that bitch*, he thought.

But then, serving for the match at 5-2, 30-love, Bibi felt an even stronger wave of dizziness take over. He tossed the ball up to serve, only to let it drop to the ground twice in a row. Walking to his chair with his hand up and saying, "sorry Ernest, just one sec," he stopped, hunched himself over the garbage can, and threw up.

Ernest ran beside him and put his hand on his back. "Oh my God, Bibi. You okay?"

"Sorry, I must be coming down with something. I'll be fine."

Bibi walked back toward the line to serve.

"You sure?" Ernest asked. "We can take a break if you want."

"No, thanks darlin'."

Bibi stopped at the service line, bounced the ball a couple of times, and hit an ace right in the middle of the centre service line. Ernest stood frozen, wondering how the shot was possible considering how Bibi was feeling.

It was 40-love. Triple match point to give Bibi the win.

Ernest turned and walked toward the ad side for the next point. He looked up and saw that Bibi had come up to the net with his hand extended.

"I'm done, Ernest. I don't feel good," Bibi said.

Ernest was confused. "What?"

"Good luck in the semifinals, honey."

Ernest reluctantly shook his hand, and before he could say anything further, Bibi hastily packed his bag and scurried off the court.

"Wait, what just happened?" Joy asked Abby.

"Something must be wrong with Bibi. He retired … forfeited. He just gave Ernest the match."

Ernest looked at Joy, who looked around to see if anyone was watching her. She turned back to Ernest, raising both thumbs up with a big smile. Ernest scowled, discouraging her celebration.

Stefan followed Bibi into the change room. "That was a nice thing you did for the kid."

Bibi turned around. "I didn't do that for him. But thanks."

"What's wrong then?"

"I actually just feel sick. I think I have a fever."

"Oh. You want me to drive you home?"

"No, I think I can manage."

"Okay." Stefan turned around to walk away, then looked back. "I'm sorry I was such an ass at karaoke."

Bibi's face softened, "It's okay."

"You know how I get sometimes."

"I know."

Silence. They smiled.

"You apologized," Bibi smirked. "You took the high road, bitch. How dare you."

Stefan reached down to hug Bibi. "I love you, you stupid bitch," he said affectionally.

"I know. I love you too. Now should I post some corny pic of us on IG?"

"Love means never having to post you're sorry, B."

8d: Semifinals — Ego Injury

The final day of the tournament had arrived; trophies were to be awarded. For the first time since 2006, the CGO semifinals were all Canadian.

The first semifinal had Ernest against Scooter. Joy had to teach classes at the studio, and Bibi was still feeling ill and couldn't come to watch. Ernest, feeling alone, lost quickly, 6-1, 6-1. Furthermore, he got perturbed by increasingly loud and obnoxious "COME ONS!" and fist pumps from Scooter the closer he got to victory. It was odd; although a bit rough around the edges, Scooter was a nice person off-court. When shaking hands at the net after match point, Ernest politely said, "good match", but tried to telepathically say what he was thinking for the last hour: *Like really, do you need to cheer like that when you're beating me this easily? Asshole.*

The second semifinal was the match everyone was anticipating: Stefan versus Khalid.

Khalid had jumped through the second round and quarterfinals making tonnes of friends along the way. For the last two days, all Stefan could hear in the locker room or in the viewing areas was everyone proclaiming "how nice the new straight guy was," to which he'd walk away immediately. Even Abby, after being served a double bagel—a score of 6-0, 6-0—in the second round, still swooned about Khalid: "To put it simply, what a lovely man."

Such sweet sentiments, plus wanting to exact revenge from their first meeting, fuelled Stefan's resistance—the need to remind Khalid that this match, this tournament, this league—was not for people like him. He was psyched.

But he didn't get his revenge. No matter how hard Stefan hit and how many times he ran around his backhand to clobber a forehand, Khalid would absorb the pace and return it with interest. The crowd watched in surprise; the usual gasps or applause which accompanied incredible shots were silenced. Everyone was stunned to see Stefan get demolished in the first set, 1-6.

Stefan rummaged through his bag to get out his tennis notes, and ultimately stumbled on tip number 7: *If all else fails, junk your opponent. Win ugly.* It was an embarrassing way to play, but an effective one, as a small number of players were able to do that to him.

Serving the first game of the second set, Stefan mixed his shots up—"junked"—as best he could; he chipped, looped and hit short and then deep; but Khalid was too skilled. He stepped in, driving his shots for winners or putting away volleys.

At the changeover, Stefan realized he needed to do something to throw Khalid off rhythm. Mess with his mind. Take "winning ugly" to the next level.

Through the tournament, it became apparent what Khalid's superstition was; for every match, he'd have three water bottles—one of some orange liquid, the two others water—lined up perfectly on the ground in front of his chair. As Stefan walked to the other side of the court to start the next game, he casually kicked Khalid's bottles over, pretending not to notice.

After the first point of the game, Khalid stopped and was distracted, noticing his bottles lying horizontally and out of line on the side. His eyes immediately shot to Stefan, who purposely was looking away. Khalid quickly ran to realign them, and then ran back to serve the next point.

It didn't matter. Khalid continued to dominate the match. Furious, Stefan smashed his racquet into the court, its frame mangled and strings twisted.

Now down 0-4, accepting the fact that he was going to lose, Stefan made a decision. He hit a backhand long on purpose, and then with his right hand, grabbed his right thigh and calf and started stretching it. He limped in between points, stopped trying to run for balls, and swiftly lost the second set and the match, all while continuing to rub his leg. Some players were explicit in blaming their losses on injury and would retire, as Bibi had done the day before. But Stefan was more cunning: he appeared injured, but finished the match half-heartedly, then brushed it off and eventually gave his opponent the credit for winning.

"Yeah, I felt something in my leg. But it totally didn't take away from how great Khalid played," he said after to someone watching.

That way, people would think he *did* lose because of injury, despite the fact he didn't say it. A clever way to look like a stand up and noble competitor.

The truth was Stefan had faked the injury. The leg pain he claimed to have suffered was a lie to hide something that was of a completely different nature: a full-blown shot to his ego. Losing because he wasn't good enough was too much to bear. He had done it numerous times before in the old league, notably to Francesco Zappone in one final in 2010.

The title was to be battled between Khalid—the new "lovely" straight guy, and Scooter—the gay and toxically masculine "bruh" who constantly shouted "COME ON!" obnoxiously to himself like an over-juiced ape.

Meanwhile, Stefan would be forced to watch from the sidelines, trying to nurse his self-pride.

To make matters worse, he noticed Khalid talking to the podcasters after the match.

"Would you maybe be interested in doing an interview on our podcast, Khalid-sweetie?" he overheard Aldwin ask.

"Wait, how about my podcast, Khalid?" Vong Show, the other host said. "Do mine first!"

Stefan felt like smashing another racquet.

8e: Finals — The Glitter Bomb

"Get him for us, Scoot," Stefan whispered to Scooter.

"Us?" Scooter asked.

"Yeah. Send this guy back to Costco."

Scooter chuckled, then leaned in with intense eyes; "bruh, this is for me."

Scooter had never won the CGO before. It was such a grand occasion for him that he invited his mother to watch the final. Wearing a peach coloured cardigan and bright white New Balance walking shoes, Scooter's mother—who in her looks and mannerisms channeled Betty White—sat quietly in the viewing area beside the court. She brought a pillow to put on the chair in which she sat.

Leading up to the match, Scooter closely guarded her. Then, as he was about to head on court, he spoke to the group of the spectators, including Ernest, Stefan, Dakota, and Abby.

"Don't talk to her!" Scooter said intensely, far enough away for his mother not to hear.

"What?" Ernest asked. "Don't talk to your mother?"

"Yeah. And don't be so loud and, you know ... gay."

The group looked puzzled, and then pissed.

Stefan stood up from his chair, trying to assert authority. "Don't be so gay? What the fuck is that?"

Scooter looked back at his mother, then turned again to Stefan; "she doesn't know this is a gay tournament."

"Does she know that *you're* gay?"

"No."

The group was shocked. A few laughed. Stefan shook his head. "Has she met you?"

"Shut up! Look at me ... hello? I'm not obvious." Scooter asked again: "So don't say anything, okay?"

Confusion and nods.

Scooter ran from the lounge and toward the court.

Ernest turned to Stefan. "That's so messed up."

"Ernest, look at his mother," Stefan said. "She brought a pillow to sit on. Obviously, she's a smart woman. I'm sure she knows her son likes cock."

The first set was tense, with Scooter sending most balls down the centre of the court, and Khalid rifling shots corner to corner, inching his way to the net to cut off any short balls. Finding himself on the defensive too often, Scooter lost the first set 5-7. He often shouted at himself, and as expected, bashed his racquet to his head.

At 3-3 in the second set, Scooter took an extended bathroom break, claiming his contacts were drying out. Upon return, they had a 40 shot rally that included a dropshot, a lob, an overhead, and a couple of near splits retrievals. The last ball landed on Scooter's side and bounced on the bottom right side line and baseline corner, right in front of Ernest, Abby, and Stefan seated nearby.

"Out!" Scooter screamed, and turned his back on Khalid, then cheering himself on.

Khalid did a double take, wrinkled his eyebrows, and went to the ad side to serve the next point. "30-40." Break point.

After missing his first serve, Khalid spun in a short second serve. Scooter chipped his backhand and ran to the net, with Khalid replying with a topspin lob. Scooter turned around and immediately pointed up his right index finger, indicating it was out before the ball bounced, this time completely inside the baseline.

"YES! Come on Scoot-Dawg!" he screamed, and ran to his chair.

Khalid slowly walked toward the next; "uh, are you sure about that call, boss?"

"Yeah bro. Way out!"

Ernest stood up, hands on his hips, and shook his head. "Scooter, that was way IN."

"Not your call!" Scooter snapped.

Khalid raised his hand and looked at Ernest as if to brush it off.

Thrown off, Khalid hit the ball off his racquet frame four more times for errors over the next two service games, allowing Scooter to win the second set 6-3.

Khalid regained the momentum in the deciding third set super tie-break, with a hard service return and then serving two aces. 3-0.

Scooter responded with an underhand serve drop shot, catching Khalid by surprise and drawing a long response. The crowd silently looked at each other, some shaking their heads. The underhand serve was, for lack of a better term, a "dick move", a cheap shot. 3-1. Then, he followed it up with a hard flat ace. 3-2.

As Khalid prepared to serve, he noticed his beating heart got faster and harder, to the point he could hear it ringing in his ears. His feet suddenly felt like bricks, and the grip of his racquet felt like a cold steel rod. He tightened his hand around it to try to squeeze the sensation away, but to no avail. He tossed the ball up to serve far too forward into the court and swung his racquet, sending the ball to the back wall. He tried again, but his arm felt heavy, and hit his second serve into the bottom of the net. Double fault. *The nerves were creeping in.*

Changing ends at 3-3, Khalid stopped at his chair, and reached into his bag to grab another water bottle. Slightly shaking from exhaustion and nervousness, his hands fiddled around the bag until he felt an unfamiliar object in one of the deep pockets.

Then:

A LOUD EXPLOSION.

The spectators watched a rainbow of glitter burst out of Khalid's bag and into the air. Ernest saw it like it happened in slow motion; the sparkles shooting up and hitting Khalid in the face, then creating a cloud of colourful dust into which Khalid disappeared. It landed on his hair, body, and the entire bench, and Khalid emerged from the cloud like some sparkling multicoloured creature. The players on other courts stopped. Complete silence filled the tennis centre. Already frazzled by his nerves, Khalid's butt fell on the bench, and he tried to compose himself by dusting the glitter from his eyes and face.

Ernest jumped from his seat and ran to Khalid's side. "Oh my God! Are you okay? Are you bleeding?" he asked as he scanned Khalid's body.

"I think I'm okay. I don't know what that was," Khalid said, confused.

Scooter approached the bench slowly, dumbfounded. "Bruh. What's up? You having some sort of coming out parade?"

Tommy then came on to the court. "Khalid! Shit! What happened? You alright?"

While they tended to Khalid, Abby had crept up from behind, and after inspecting Khalid's tennis bag, screamed in horror. "AHHH!"

"What?"

"I think … I think someone planted a glitter bomb in your bag, Khalid!" Abby said, horrified at the words coming out of her mouth.

They all looked at Khalid in shock and sympathy.

Meanwhile, Stefan watched all this unfold from his chair, then took a phone call and walked away.

"Do you think you can continue, Khalid?" Tommy asked.

"Uh, yeah, I think I can. I just need a minute or two to get this stuff off me."

Ernest accompanied Khalid to the bathroom and helped him clean up as much as possible. As Khalid frantically splashed his face over the sink, Ernest swept his shoulders and back clean, all while his eyes watered.

"Boss?" Khalid said, noticing. "Why are you about to cry?"

"No, it's nothing. It's just … it's just so disturbing," Ernest whispered.

"I'll be fine. It's just a little glitter. Maybe now I fit in."

Ernest looked unimpressed.

"Okay," Khalid said. "Bad joke."

"I can't believe someone would do this. We're supposed to be better than this," Ernest said.

Khalid went back to court to finish the match, but it proved to be in vain. His eyes irritated from clearing the glitter out, he couldn't see the ball as clearly, and netted the first two shots. Then, he double faulted twice. 3-7. He was three points from losing the match. The anxiety and panic had elevated to a new level.

During the next point, Khalid tried to swing his nerves away as hard as he could, but didn't make contact with the ball, and it passed him and hit the back wall. Dumbfounded, he looked down at his racquet to see if the strings had magically vanished to leave a giant hole; but the strings were there; he had missed the ball completely. 3-8.

He looked over at Ernest, widening his eyes. All those memories from Khalid's past—losing the under-12 boys Ontario provincial finals, and the Forester club tournament playoffs, and countless others he tried to forget—came rushing back; he was having the yips.

Or could this be PTSD from a glitter bomb?

Two points later, Scooter was jumping up and down, having won the tiebreak 10-3, and the championship. After quickly shaking hands with Khalid, he ripped off his shirt from the collar, pounded his chest, and screamed the loudest and longest "COOOMMMEEEE ONNNN!" while falling to his knees. In the middle of his roar, he felt a sharp tear at the bottom of his neck, like a string in his throat had snapped. Projectile shots of blood then landed on court. Blinded by his elation and ignoring what was coming out of his mouth, Scooter fell on to his back and continued to celebrate as the blood kept oozing down the sides of his mouth.

Scooter's mother—seconds earlier cheering her son's win—looked concerned at the blood on his face. But as he screamed to the ceiling in victory à la Novak Djokovic, she became shocked and then embarrassed at her son's behaviour. She sat back down, clutching the pillow beneath her. The realization was shattering. *Oh my God. My son is ... an asshole?*

Stefan, relieved that Scooter won, ran back to the registration table; "TT!"

Tommy, staring down at his phone, didn't look up.

"TT!" Stefan said again. Tommy's face remained down.

"Tommy!"

He finally looked up. "Yeah, what's wrong?" Tommy asked.

"Toxic homosexuality, basically."

"Huh?"

"Scooter! This idiot thinks he's won a UFC fight. He cheered himself so loud and must have popped some vein in his throat. Blood on the court everywhere."

"Blood? First glitter, now blood? Guys, we don't want to get banned from this club too!" Tommy remarked, as he went to get the janitor.

***

After prizes were handed out and photos were taken—with Scooter's mouth stuffed with gauze while hoisting the winner's trophy—Stefan made sure to bid his courtesy goodbyes to the important people.

"Congratulations on another tournament well done, TT," Stefan said while giving a hug.

Thanks Stefan. And guess what?"

"What?"

"We're shortening the name of the tournament from the Canadian Gay Open to just the Canadian Open next year. Removing the *gay*."

"Oh?"

"Yeah," Tommy smiled, "you know, to make it more inclusive. It's not just for the gays anymore."

Stefan suppressed an eye roll. "Right."

Chapter 9: "I'm going home and polishing my trophies!"

Later that evening, while waiting at the bus stop near the parking lot of the Torpedo Valley Lawn and Tennis Club, Ernest saw a shiny black Ram pickup stop in front of him, its windows rolling down.

"Where's your mom?" Stefan shouted.

"Teaching at the yoga studio," Ernest replied.

"Get in."

"You sure?"

"Just get in."

Ernest reluctantly placed himself in the passenger seat, fascinated by the number of controls on the dashboard. He peeked around further; like the exterior, the car was impeccably clean inside. Black leather seats, way too much legroom. Very sleek and modern for a pickup truck.

"So today was a shit day for both of us, eh?" Stefan said. Suddenly he grabbed his right calf. "Fuck!"

"What's wrong?" Ernest asked.

"Just some cramps. They always make me feel nauseous. Was constantly squatting like a bottom trying to get Khalid's shots."

"Oh."

Silence.

"Well at least we didn't have a glitter bomb explode in our bag," Ernest said. "That was so messed up."

"Yeah, crazy," Stefan said. He changed the subject, trying to sound chipper: "Well you had a good tournament, Ernest. Semifinals! Gold star for you Miss Woke 2020!"

"Thanks."

"Today sucked for me. I can't imagine anything worse than losing," Stefan said. "But you know what I'm going to do that always picks me up after a loss?"

"What?"

"I'm going home and polishing my trophies!"

Ernest laughed.

"What? Are you laughing at me? What do you do for a pick me up? Go online and sign some petitions? Get into some online war on Facebook about going organic?"

Ernest scoffed. "No, I go home and play with my cats. They're called Roger and Rafa."

"That's funny." Suddenly, Stefan grabbed his right calf again, grunting louder. *Now my leg is actually cramping. Fuckin' ego injury karma.*

Stefan slowed the car down, eventually stopping on the side of the road while grabbing his thigh. "I can't drive. My leg cramps when I step on the pedals. You got any pickle juice?"

"What?"

"Pickle juice. It stops cramps."

"No, I must have forgot it at home," Ernest said sarcastically.

"Whatever. Can you drive?"

"Me? No way. I don't have my license."

"What? What are you, 20, 21? How can you not have your license?"

"I'm 25. And you don't need a car if you live in the GTA."

"Well you're about to learn."

"No!"

Stefan winced again. "I can't drive. Didn't you say you drove with your mom in the car?"

"Yeah."

"Done."

"Nope."

"Listen, I didn't renew my CAA. Let me text Bibi."

Five minutes passed by; no reply from Bibi, and Stefan's cramps intensified.

Stefan put down his phone. "Okay, you're driving."

"Stefan, I failed the G2 test twice!"

"Did you fail it by crashing the car?"

"No."

"Then we're good! Listen, my leg is spasming, I can't drive. All you have to do is push the pedal. I can help you steer."

Stefan got out of the driver's seat and hopped around the front of the Ram to open Ernest's door: "don't worry, my car's not a stick shift. I know you're not a top, so there shouldn't be a problem."

Ernest rolled his eyes and got out. After seating himself in the driver's seat, he looked down at his feet. They didn't reach the pedals. "Crap. I'm too short."

Stefan grinned. "That's kind of cute." He reached over to the dashboard to press the seat adjustment button. Ernest felt himself moving forward, and took a deep breath.

"Listen. Ernest. Look at me," Stefan said.

"Yeah, yeah," Ernest seemed to brush him off.

"Ernest. Eye contact!"

Ernest turned to his right, stopping on Stefan's deep blue eyes, like the ocean.

"You have your G1. You know all the rules. You've driven before. You can do this."

Ernest felt a sense of calm. "Yes. Yes, you're right."

He looked forward, noticing the pearl rosary hanging from the rear-view mirror.

"Are you religious?"

"No, I'm spiritual. I just feel like a little faith can be really helpful." Stefan said, feeling slightly vulnerable. "Now don't go telling me on how corrupt the church is, now's not the time for a lecture."

"I wasn't going to. Actually, we'll need it now more than ever." Ernest took a deep breath. "Jesus, take the wheel."

Ernest turned the ignition and took the gear out of park. The car jerked forward. "Crap. Sorry."

"That's okay," Stefan said, resisting the urge to change his mind.

Ernest eased his foot off the brake and made way onto the road. They both felt like they were holding their breath.

"You're going to be fine. We're going to be fine," Stefan said serenely, then suddenly feeling another shooting pain in his right leg. "Shit!" *Fuckin' ego injury karma.*

As the distance travelled went from feet, to meters, to finally kilometers, Ernest grew more relaxed, letting out a sigh.

"See," Stefan said, "you totally got this."

"Thanks," Ernest smiled, quickly looking over to catch Stefan's eyes once again.

Suddenly, Stefan moved his hand from rubbing his calf to pointing ahead, "You're drifting to the right. Keep your eyes on the road," then placing it on top of Ernest's, nudging the wheel back to the left.

Ernest jumped slightly at the touch of Stefan's hand, to which Stefan let go.

"Sorry," Stefan said.

"It's okay."

They remained quiet for the next few minutes while Ernest concentrated. Stefan noticed the drivers around passing them by, and then looked at the speedometer. 30 km per hour. 20 km per hour slower than the speed limit.

Ernest's eyes bounced from the road ahead, the side mirror and then the rear-view, just like the teacher at Ultimate Drivers a couple of weeks ago said. "I'm not too bad, eh?"

"Uh, yeah. You could go a little faster if you want, you know," Stefan said.

"Do I have to?"

"Whatever works for you, my friend."

Ernest saw Stefan's tennis bag sitting on the back seat in the rear-view mirror; the racquet he broke was sticking out of one of the pockets.

"You're gonna have to replace the racquet you smashed?" Ernest asked.

"Yeah."

"You know what I have in my tennis bag?"

"What?"

"A wooden racquet. In case I get so upset on court I feel like I need to break something. It's cheaper than having to replace racquets."

Stefan grinned. "Smart."

Ernest returned the smile. "I saw you and Bibi made up today."

"Yeah. No matter how much we argue, she's quality. I would do anything for her."

"That's nice."

"You sound surprised?"

"You don't seem too close to anyone."

"Thanks, I know you think I'm an ass."

"No, I didn't mean it like that."

"I'm sure. No, but it's different with Bibi."

"How so?"

"I lost a match—this super close match—one time at Davisville. I was gutted. Bibi came and watched, cheering me on. And you know what she said to me after I lost? 'Winning or losing a tennis match doesn't measure your self-worth.'"

"That's a great philosophy."

"Yeah. I know. She's wise. I try to remember it but sometimes I forget. Tennis is everything to me."

Silence.

"Bibi's the only one who can get me out of my head by making me laugh like an idiot," Stefan added, sighing.

Ernest's eyes were stuck on Stefan. Stefan's eyes bulged out as he looked back at the road.

"Ernest! Watch out!"

Ernest looked forward to see two glowing balls coming toward the windshield. He quickly slammed on the brakes and saw the outline around the yellow circles: two small ears, body crawling, with a big bushy tail. It disappeared under the car.

Stefan couldn't tell the difference between the screeching of the breaks and Ernest's screaming. A large thud was heard from the driver's front tire and the car swerved right, going over the sidewalk and just stopping in front of a tree.

"Fuck! Oh my God! My car!" Stefan screamed while running out to check the damage.

"Shit! I'm so sorry!" Ernest said, running up beside him.

Turning on his phone flashlight to inspect for dents, Stefan breathed out a sigh of relief. "Thank God! No damage. I think it's okay."

Ernest lowered his head and exhaled. "Oh good."

They continued to follow Stefan's flashlight around the car, eventually stopping on the front left tire. Blood was dripping from the rim and in front of the driver door.

"Oh shit."

Stefan pointed the light toward the road to see an animal body ripped open at the belly and flattened with tire marks at the neck. Ernest took a step to his left and noticed his foot touched something on the ground. The glowing balls—the eyes on the decapitated head of the raccoon—were staring back at him, just like he was staring into Stefan's eyes mere seconds before.

"Oh God oh God oh God!" Ernest screamed while running to the other side of the car.

"Calm down!" Stefan shouted.

"I killed it! I killed it!" Ernest panicked.

"It's just a raccoon!"

"It was a living thing!"

"Who cares? It's a rodent!

"How can you say that? You're such an asshole!"

"Fuck, Ernest! Not only are you annoyingly self-righteous, you're one of those snowflakes who gets offended by everything!"

"Shut up!"

"No, you shut up!"

Ernest felt his jaw clench. "You know, it is people like me who really make a difference. Unlike others who are so self-absorbed they have no idea about what's going on around them."

"You're calling me self-absorbed?"

"Did I stutter?"

"You people sit there with your organic vegan lattes and shit, spewing out your wokeness like diarrhea."

"My wokeness? Whatever! It's about what's right! For example, I don't know, allowing straight people to join our league! You're the president but you're a fucking bigot!"

"You know, as the president I can throw you out of the league!"

"You're the president for God's sake! People look to you as an example!"

Stefan's voice lowered. "Before you wave your useless liberal arts degree in my face, it's because of people like me that allow people like you to have your say."

"What are you talking about?"

"Faggot!"

"What did you call me?" Ernest said, outraged.

"Faggot."

Silence.

Stefan looked away and then back at him. "Don't act like you've never been called that before. When I said this league was for us, I meant it was for all of us who have been called that. This league, my righteous friend, is to protect us from that."

Ernest struggled with a reply. *Was that a valid point?*

"People aren't like that anymore," Ernest said.

"You're young and you still have hope. It's sweet," Stefan said sarcastically. "Let's see you if you still have that at my age."

They stood for a couple of seconds, staring at each other.

Stefan grabbed his leg again. "Shit! These cramps are making me nauseous." He put his hand over his mouth and ran closer to the tree. Bending over, he vomited.

Ernest walked slowly behind him. "Stefan, you okay?" he asked quietly, the venom gone from his voice.

Stefan hurled again.

"Ernest," Stefan whispered.

"Yeah?"

"Can you do me a favour?"

"Yeah."

"Do you mind just coming closer and rubbing my shoulder?"

Ernest paused, unsure if he misheard. "What?"

"Please, just rub your hand on my shoulder," Stefan muttered.

Ernest slowly moved his hand down and gave Stefan a pat.

"No, a bit more."

Ernest moved his hand lower again, pressing his palm into Stefan's right shoulder.

"Yeah. Keep going," Stefan said.

Ernest continued as Stefan vomited a few more times, finishing off with a last surge that lasted about five seconds.

"Wow," Ernest remarked. "That was a good one."

When the feeling passed, Stefan reached up and put his hand on Ernest's. "Thank you. I just need some water."

***

They re-entered the car—Ernest headed to the driver's seat without hesitation. Stefan noticed a text notification light up on his phone, which had fallen on the floor of the passenger's side.

"Bibi replied," he said.

Ernest started up the engine.

Stefan read the text. "What the fuck?"

"What is it?"
"Bibi's at the hospital. In the E.R."
"What?"
"It's okay, I should be fine to drive after we drop you home."
"I'm going with you."
"It's late. Your mother will kill me."
"No, Stefan. I wanna go with you."

Chapter 10: Executive Meeting 2
— "My biggest strength is now my biggest weakness!"

As Stefan—drinking from a plastic water bottle to rehydrate from the puking—and Ernest walked toward the entrance of the E.R. of Torpedo Valley General Hospital, they saw a giant Tibetan Mastiff tied to the entrance gate. It was Gucci, the dog belonging to Fred.

"A plastic water bottle?" Ernest commented. "Really? You know how bad that is for—"

"Ernest, not now!"

As Stefan walked closer, Gucci growled, and then barked loudly, causing him to swerve and bump into Ernest. "Stupid dog," he muttered.

When they entered the stark white hospital room, they saw Fred standing over Bibi, lying in the bed with an IV attached to his arm.

"B. What's wrong? You okay?" Stefan asked. He then looked at Fred suspiciously. "Who are you?"

"This is Fred. He's my friend. You didn't reply right away, so I texted him," Bibi said.

"Hello," Fred said warmly.

"Can you excuse us, Frank?"

"Fred."

"Right. Felix. We just want to talk to Bibi alone for a sec."

"Sure." Fred walked past Ernest and left the room.

"What happened?" Stefan said.

Bibi began to ramble: "You know what, girl? I'm so sorry I just panicked and didn't know who to call. I was feeling a little woozy during the tournament—not that you didn't deserve that win yesterday Ernest, cause you did—but I went home after and was feeling like my head was spinning and I felt like throwing up and first I thought it might be from overextending myself on the court and taking the extra hours at work but no..."

"Whoa, whoa B, what are you rambling about?" Stefan interrupted.

Bibi continued. "So yeah and then I got this call from the hospital this morning and they said they wanted to see me, and I was like 'now?' and they were like 'yeah, the sooner the better,' so I came in and saw Dr. whatever-his-name is and then all of a sudden I was like, 'what... what are you talking about?' and then next thing I knew, I was here.'"

Stefan looked back at Ernest, with a questioning look as if to ask if he understood what Bibi was talking about. Ernest's face indicated he didn't know either.

Stefan turned back. "B. Eye contact. I don't understand. What is it?"

Bibi looked away. "The HPV shot."

"The what?"

"I should have taken that HPV shot three years ago. My doctor in Tennessee advised me to get it, just in case. But that shot is like $300 each and there's three of them. I couldn't afford it. So I didn't get them. I thought PREP would be all that I needed."

Ernest walked a step closer, now standing beside Stefan. Stefan looked at Ernest in panic.

"HPV ... what does that mean again?" Stefan asked cautiously. "I thought that only affected women."

Bibi's eyes began to well. "Men get it too. HPV makes you susceptible to getting stuff." He looked down and buried his face into his hands and began to sob. Wiping his tears, he looked back up. "At first, I just thought I had IBS or something. Sometimes I'd see blood when I took a shit, but then I thought it was because the guys I was meeting were pounding me too hard. Then I started waking up in the middle of the night drenched in sweat. I lost a few pounds without trying and then thought, *'Oh good, I can go to Dairy Queen and get a large now.'* Then I started getting dizzy on court. That was the last straw. So last week, I went and got a physical." Bibi wiped his tears again. "They found a tumour in my rectum. They called me in this morning to tell me it's cancerous."

Stefan felt the life draining from him. "No. No, that can't be right."

"Oh my God, I'm so sorry," Ernest said, reaching over to put his hand on Bibi's arm.

"Do they know that for sure? How can they be sure?" Stefan questioned.

"I don't fucking know!" Bibi burst into tears again. Stefan hugged him, trying to stop himself from crying. Ernest stood, watching; the silence broken by sniffling noises and sobs.

Bibi grabbed a tissue and wiped his face.

A pause.

"You know what the funny thing is?" Bibi asked.

Stefan and Ernest leaned in. "What's that?"

"My biggest strength is now my biggest weakness." Bibi began to laugh hysterically. "Who would have thought this booty would be dangerous for another reason?! Ha! Isn't that funny?" He laughed again, louder and maniacally this time.

Stefan and Ernest smiled awkwardly, even laughing too, until Bibi's laughs became sobs again, and he wailed, " I don't know how I'm going to fix it!"

"Don't you worry. We're going to fix it. Don't you worry," Stefan whispered as he gently held Bibi again and rubbed his shoulder. Ernest watched Stefan's bottom lip quiver and a single tear rolled down his left cheek.

***

On the way out of the hospital, Stefan and Ernest passed Fred, who sat in the hallway with Gucci sleeping at his feet. Opening her eyes, Gucci immediately jumped up and began barking at Stefan, to which Fred restrained her. "Noodle dog! Relax!" Fred commanded.

"I'm sorry," Fred said. Stefan ignored him and kept walking with Ernest behind.

"Stefan," Ernest said softly as they walked toward the car. "You okay?"

"This isn't happening," Stefan mumbled. He stopped and crushed the plastic water bottle in his hand.

Ernest, sensing Stefan's despair, tried to make a joke. "You still have that stupid plastic water—"

"Not now!"

"Okay, okay, sorry."

Stefan's voice intensified: "This isn't happening! He's my best friend, my family, for fuck's sake! After Gabe left, I had nobody." He turned around and threw the bottle into the branches of a tree hanging over the parking lot, which scared the chickadee birds to flee the area in one large flock.

***

It was well after midnight now and Ernest, still driving Stefan's truck, pulled into his driveway. There was a car parked behind Joy's Mini Cooper.

He turned Stefan. "Thanks for the driving lesson tonight."

"Thanks for coming to the hospital."

"You sure you're good to drive home?"

"Yeah, I'll be fine."

"Can you text me when you get home please?"

"Yes, mother," Stefan smirked.

Ernest got out of the truck and watched Stefan drive away, shyly lifting his hand to wave goodbye, to which Stefan saw but did not reciprocate.

Turning around, Ernest walked closer to the car behind his mother's. It was a maroon Camry; its familiarity slightly unnerving him. Through the backseat window, he peeked in to see a microphone, a couple of speakers and a bunch of flyers messily scattered on the floor. Outside the car, there were speckles of glitter on the ground near the driver door.

Ernest backed away from the car slowly, looking down.

The car's license plate read "DJKhal."

PART THREE

Chapter 11: "Extend beyond your reach!"

It started with good intentions. Joy thought if she learned how to play tennis, she could get closer to her son. True, she overshared many personal things with Ernest that made him uncomfortable. Downright horrified him at times. But she always thought, since he was gay, it was like she had a little sister she could girl-talk with.

She never told Ernest about his father though; that he was just as much of a social justice warrior as his son; that she met him at a spoken word poetry reading in late 1993 as he was articling at a tiny law firm; that sadly, dates and calls became fewer and far between, until he disappeared. Albeit, he hadn't escaped her completely; by January of 1994, she found out she was pregnant. So when Ernest was born in September that year, she got a little piece of his father back. Joy said she would always be open and honest with Ernest about anything; but Ernest never asked, and so she didn't feel the need to tell him.

The karaoke night at Stefan's condo party room a little more than a month ago presented her with a chance to get into her son's sport. As the party was recovering from the power cutting out during Khalid's song, Joy swooped in.

"So, Bibi tells me you're a really good player. Like really good," Joy said to Khalid.

"Thanks. Bibi's being kind."

"Maybe you're just being humble."

"Maybe."

"You know I always wanted to learn how to play tennis."

"Oh yeah? You mean Ernest hasn't taught you?"

"Yeah right. He has zero patience for me."

"Oh." Khalid grabbed another cracker from the cheese plate.

Joy moved in a bit closer to him. *This guy's probably half my age, but damn, he's hot. A little flirting never hurt anyone.* "So, do you teach at all?"

"Not since I was 18 and had my teaching certification. It's been forever," he replied, crunching another cracker.

"I'd love some lessons."

Silence, except for more crunching coming from Khalid's chiseled jaw.

Joy grew impatient. *Ugh. This guy is dense as fuck. Definitely, definitely straight for sure.*

She moved in and rested her finger to his chest, close enough so she could slightly feel his pec beneath. "Well I want to learn. And I want *you* to teach me!"

"Oh," Khalid said, surprised, "of course, Miss Law," he smiled shyly.

Bibi came, noticing her touching him. "Is this how straight people flirt? Do you have to flaunt it in our face? Keep the PDA to yourself! Gross!" he mumbled, and walked away.

***

A week later, Joy found herself panting, drenched in sweat, chasing tennis balls slowly fed to her from Khalid across the nets at Torpedo Valley Park. Though completely missing shots with every swing, Joy found herself getting a little jolly while Khalid yelled at her repeatedly: "harder, push harder!" She'd then start easing up, hoping his screams would intensify.

Then a few days after, as Joy warmed up in her yoga studio preparing to teach a class, she smelled a familiar scent—Axe body spray. She turned around to see Khalid standing in the front row, in Speedos and nothing else; she couldn't help but gawk at his light brown skin glistening over his bulging chest and six-pack, with the perfect amount of body hair.

"Hi Miss Law!" he waved with a big smile, like a little boy.

Joy half smiled quickly, then signaled to him that there was no talking. "Welcome class! Let's get started."

During strenuous poses in which the 40 degree room caused most to be standing in puddles of sweat, Joy found herself inching closer and closer to Khalid as she instructed each move. They kept catching each other's eyes in the mirror and then looking away, until she made a point to adjust his posture. Pressing her fingers into his flexed biceps and adjusting them slightly, she felt her jaw clench.

Then other parts of her clenched.

As she looked him dead in the eye, lowered her voice and said, "You need to extend beyond your reach. Exxxteennnd."

Forty-five minutes later, class had ended, but her fingers were still pressed into him—in the back seat of her Mini Cooper. "Extend beyond your reach, boy! Extend!" she screamed as he thrusted himself in her.

When it was over, Khalid reluctantly spoke: "Um ... Miss Law."

"Oh Khalid, I told you already. You can call me Joy."

"Right, Joy. Um. Should we have done that? I'm friends with Ernest ..."

"Ernest is a big boy. He's 25; he can deal with it," she said. "Wait. Khalid, how old are you?"

"24."

She howled. "Oh shit! Our age difference is almost as big as your age!" He found that funny too.

"Any friend of Ernest is a friend of mine," she said, giggling again.

"I really like him. He's so smart, and a real stand-up guy. You did an amazing job with him.

"Thank you. I'm so proud of him. But he's too annoyed with me all the time for me to let him know."

"He was telling me about some asshole ex-boyfriend of his from university. Poor kid."

"Peter Winters? That piece of shit who dumped him for some guy named Greg from his microeconomics course? He told you about that?" Joy asked.

"Yeah, he did. I'd say we're pretty good friends."

Joy worried, for she knew her son's pattern when it came to boys. Ever since Peter Winters broke his heart, Ernest only developed crushes on boys unavailable to him. Not the ones with boyfriends, in jail, or underage. It was worse.

Straight boys.

Joy believed it was a defence mechanism. Ernest could not get hurt by straight boys not reciprocating not because they weren't into him, but because they were not his type—in every sense.

Joy shared this belief with Khalid.

"What? You think Ernest might like me? Like *like* me?" he asked.

"I'm afraid so. I should have noticed it before. He mentions your name all the time," Joy said. "His face lights up when he talks about you."

"Really?" Khalid smiled, feeling touched. "But shit! ... Oh, I'm sorry for swearing Miss Law."

"Oh my God! Stop calling me that."

"Sorry."

A few seconds of silence.

"What do you want me to do?" he asked, "I don't want to hurt his feelings."

Joy kissed him on the lips. "You know what, nothing. Let's just not tell him about this right now."

***

Fast forward to the present night, after the finals of the Canadian Gay Open in which he drove a pick-up truck, decapitated a racoon, comforted Stefan while he puked on the side of the road, and found out that Bibi had a cancerous tumour in his ass, Ernest stood on his driveway, looking at Khalid's car. Everything he saw in the driveway seemed to be accompanied by a loud screech, like in a horror film: the DJ flyers in the back seat, the license plate, the glitter on the driveway near the driver's seat door.

What is Khalid doing here?

Ernest quietly opened the front door and entered the hallway; suddenly something clicked that had been bothering him recently; *Axe body spray; That's the shit I've been smelling in this house for the last few weeks!*

Putting down his tennis bag, he heard yelling coming from his mother's bedroom, and felt his heart sink. As he walked closer to the door, the words were loud and clear.

Joy's voice was heard yelling out, "Extend beyond your reach, boy! Extend!" Then, Khalid grunting.

Ernest stomped and knocked on Joy's door. "Mother, get out here!"

The yelling stopped.

"Ernest? You're home? I thought you were getting dinner with Bibi and Abby? Uh, I'm sleeping!"

"Open the door now, Mother!"

"Hold on, honey!"

She opened the door slightly, only sticking her head out.

"I thought you were teaching at the studio tonight," Ernest asked.

"Last minute cancellation. I'm really tired. How'd the match go? Actually, you can tell mummy tomorrow. I'm gonna go to sleep. Goodnight darling!"

Ernest put his hand on the door, preventing her from closing it. He looked at her intensely, and raised his voice. "Mother."

"Yes, darling?"

"There's glitter on your face."

"What?"

Ernest spoke slower, glaring at the sparkles around her cheeks and mouth. "There's glitter on your face ... open the door. I know who's in there."

Joy looked down, then back at Ernest. She let the door open, to reveal Khalid standing there with a guilty look on his face, holding bedsheets in front of his genitals.

"I was going to tell you, Ernest," Joy said, "I just asked him for a tennis lesson, and one thing led to another..."

Ernest looked furiously at Khalid. "You mother-fucker!"

Khalid looked back awkwardly. "Um, bad choice of words, boss."

Ernest ran to his bedroom and slammed the door. Throwing himself on his bed, he saw something equally disturbing out of the corner of his eye; in front of his closet was his cat Rafa, on top of the back of his mother's cat, Roger, both letting out violent moans simultaneously. Everyone seemed to be getting some action that night.

Chapter 12: *Call Me Maybe*

Stefan remembered getting into his truck for the first time. It was Spring, 2011. A time of joy for him: tennis-wise, he had just won a provincial tournament at the Green Hills Club, defeating his nemesis, Francesco Zappone in a tense final. On the work front, he had been promoted to director of finance at Traders, Inc., upping his annual salary to $98K. Leaving his office that day and walking toward his compact 2005 Volkswagen Golf, he thought, *I'm a big fucking deal. I should have a big fucking truck.*

Three days later, Stefan sat in his new black Ram in the parking lot at the Dodge dealership in Toronto, with Gabe Lamb, then, his best friend, in the passenger seat.

"This is amazing, Stef. But really? Do you need a big car like this?" Gabe asked.

"Come on, I need to make an entrance wherever I go." Stefan put on his Ray-Bans, stared into the vanity mirror while running his fingers through his hair, and then turned on the engine.

The first ride on the Don Valley Parkway was memorable. Windows down, wind blowing, sun shining on their smiling faces. Stefan's delirium heightened as he pressed the gas pedal harder, making their way to the Rosedale Club for a practice match. Later, Stefan didn't care that Gabe had beaten him that day. It didn't matter; he was on top of the tennis league and his work. And, most importantly, there was Gabe—with his hazel eyes, slow and graceful manner in which he spoke, his striking handsome features—his very best friend that he stared a little too long at sometimes ... often, beside him.

Stefan was in love with Gabe.

After devouring sundaes at the nearby Summerhill Market, Gabe cautiously asked, "Hey, you think I could drive the new truck?"

"Are you kidding me?" Stefan scoffed.

"Come on! Just for a bit. We don't have to take it on a highway." Gabe widened his hazel eyes, and Stefan looked longingly back.

He sighed and gave in. "Fine."

As the sun was setting and they cruised along Bloor and then Church street, Gabe fiddled with the buttons on the steering wheel, accidentally switching on the radio station. Stefan could hear the introductory beat of Carly Rae Jepsen's *Call Me Maybe* faintly, to which he exclaimed "Turn that up! This is my jam!" Gabe did so, and they continued riding through the village with the song blaring as they sang along and giggled like teenage girls.

Stefan gazed into Gabe's face, alternating focus between his hazel eyes and big smile shining in the last lights of the orange pink sky, and thought to himself, *this is happiness.*

As that memory faded, Stefan hopped into his truck to go to the practice courts. He thought for a second and realized that he had only ever let two other people drive his truck: Gabe, all those years ago, and Ernest, just the other evening.

Chapter 13: The Song Sparrow
June 2020

"The standard treatment for anal cancers that cannot be removed without harming the sphincter is external beam radiation therapy—also called EBRT—combined with chemo, called chemoradiation. The two treatments are given over the same time period. The chemo is usually 5-FU with mitomycin. This combination is typically given twice a week for five weeks or so. The EBRT is given daily, Monday through Friday, for five to seven weeks. We'll reassess the size of the tumour before we consider any surgery."

Bibi didn't understand much of what Dr. Agarwal, the oncologist, was saying.

"Okay, Doc," Bibi said passively. "Did you get that babe?" turning to Fred, sitting beside him in the doctor's office.

"Sort of, I guess," Fred replied.

"Okay good. At least someone knows what's going on." Bibi turned back at the doctor. "You know what, doc? Just tell me where to put my ass and go right to it."

Silence.

Bibi giggled; "You know I've said that before, but never in this situation."

***

The chemotherapy room at Torpedo Valley General Hospital was not what Bibi imagined.

"Aren't there supposed to be old people getting chemo too, and we all sit in comfy chairs and talk shit over pot brownies?"

"No, I'm sorry," the nurse said. "It's just you today,"

Other than the large leather recliner facing the window, the room was bare.

"We are trying to get a T.V. in here though," she added.

Bibi nodded.

The quiet time staring out the window as the medicine flowed through his veins was good for him. Bibi brought his notebook and worked on his poetry every chemo session, regularly updating the publishing house on his progress when he got home. As most writers do, he had always struggled with procrastination, or worse, writer's block. But during chemo, when he felt stuck, he'd just look out the window at the tall maple tree and watch the leaves blow in the wind, or the clouds roll by, for hours at a time. Oddly, on the maple's branch closest to the window, Bibi always saw this one kind of bird; tan and grey with bold streaks of white down its chest. A Google search revealed it was a song sparrow. This made sense; it always seemed to be singing at him, he believed. At one point, he opened the window to listen, amusing himself thinking it may tell him the lines for his next poem. After seeing it in the same place day after day the second week, Bibi began talking to it: "Are you the same damn bird coming to visit me all the time, sweetie?" He'd chuckle to himself and then go back to his writing.

Fred encouraged Bibi and asked, "what's inspiring you this time to get all this writing done?"

"Impending death."

"Not funny."

"No, I'm serious, babe. Something magical happens at chemo. The more I sit there thinking about dying, the more motivated I am to write my best shit," he smiled.

The radiation was a different story.

"So you're going to remove your gown and lie in the pod. Then we'll do the front and then the back," the radiologist said.

"The front? Nobody told me you were going to do the front too," Bibi replied.

"That's how it works. Just relax, it'll be fine."

Bibi got used to his body—including his manhood—getting poked and adjusted into different positions by various hospital staff over time. They'd then walk back to the control room divided by a protective glass, leaving him alone.

Bibi's eyes followed the green laser traveling over his body, eventually stopping on the shaft of his penis. Then, the most terrifying sounds as the green light flickered: noises similar to a television screen blurring, sounding on and off. Bibi panicked and looked at the control room. "Um, are you going to burn it off, Doc?!"

"It's fine, Bibi, just hold still or I'll zap the wrong spot. Just relax."

"Yeah, I'm totally relaxed, especially after you said that!" he said, then kissed his teeth.

The radiation treatments were every day, and Bibi developed a routine. He'd close his eyes, think about what he'd write next, or about returning to tennis, or about Stefan or Ernest. Sometimes his head flooded with questions and answers of how he got to be in this pod, in this situation, in this moment. The warning signs the months prior—which included the pain or itching around his anus; the blood in his stool which he assumed was because he had gone "too hard" the night before with his hookup; the feeling of a lump inside his rectum that he assumed was a big hemorrhoid.

He'd berate himself often. *Why didn't I get that injection? Fucking HPV.*

The side effects of the radiation were more severe than chemotherapy. Bibi got accustomed to staring at the blue juice he would often vomit in the toilet after chemo, or being greeted by handfuls of his bleach blonde hair on the pillow in the morning; but that was mild compared to the itching, peeling, and burning skin on his butt and pubic area weeks after radiation.

"Shit! My dick looks like burnt bacon ... I'm crispy as fuck," Bibi whined, sitting on the bed beside Fred.

Fred looked down. "It's not that bad, babe. And the doctor says it'll heal."

Bibi nodded, trying to encourage himself. "Right... you're right, it'll come back."

Fred reached up and put his hand on Bibi's shoulder. Bibi held on to it.

"Um, honey, I wanted to talk to you about something," Bibi said.

"What's that?"

"I just want you to know how much I appreciate that you're here for me through all this."

"Of course, I wouldn't be anywhere else."

"You always say the perfect thing."

Fred grinned.

Bibi continued. "But this is a lot. Way too much. This is only going to get worse and you don't have to—."

"Stop," Fred interrupted, "I'm going to stop you right there. You're not getting rid of me, whether you like it or not."

Fred grabbed Bibi's other hand and squeezed it a couple of times.

"Thank you. But—"

"Shut up."

They kissed.

Bibi's tone shifted to upbeat. "And you know when this treatment cycle is done and I'm all better, I can go to Germany for the Pride Games in August. You know, have fun, and forget about all this for a bit."

"What? You can't travel and compete. You'd still be too weak to play," Fred warned.

"No, I'm not gonna play. I just want to be there. To support my girls. Stefan and Ernest need me. And the cute straight one. He's definitely going to need support."

Fred shook his head, "I still don't think—"

"And *I need them*, babe," Bibi interrupted firmly. "I need them, and

I need tennis. I need something to look forward to. I have to go to Germany."

Fred's face loosened. "Okay. Then Gucci and I are going with you."

***

Week four of treatment, with all of his hair gone, and his face gaunt from losing approximately 20 pounds, Bibi sat in the leather recliner of the chemotherapy room, trying to squeeze out the last couple of lines of another poem. He looked out the window at the maple tree; as always the little song sparrow sat perched on the branch, staring back at him. Bibi put his notebook aside and opened the window, resting his arms and head on the sill. Looking into the eyes of the sparrow, he asked, "You *are* the same bird. I recognize you, sweetie." The bird chirped.

Bibi smiled. "But how can you recognize *me*?"

Chapter 14: *Real* Tennis

"Thanks for asking to hit. I definitely need the practice before the Detroit and Montreal tourneys. And Germany of course," Abby said to Ernest. "I thought you'd be busy hitting with Bibi or Khalid?"

"No. Bibi is too weak now. You know..." Ernest said.

"Yeah. I've been praying for him."

"Thanks. And Khalid ... we're not really talking right now."

"Oh sorry. Do you wanna talk about it?"

"Thanks. Maybe another time."

The Torpedo Valley courts were busier than ever. Despite the league having permits for designated times reserved for members, many still had to wait to play. It was 30 degrees Celsius, exacerbated by 60% humidity.

The day was notable for Ernest. Not an instinctively aggressive player, he surprised himself by how much he was dictating play. An hour in, Ernest found himself up 6-3, 5-1, only four points away from the win. Abby hadn't played a terrible match; she just made errors when she tried to match Ernest's pace.

This was a good sign, he thought. *I can carry this confidence into the Detroit and Montreal events, maybe all the way to the games in Bonn.*

After a cold service winner, and then a sharply angled backhand forcing Abby to miss the next shot, Ernest was up 30-love. Two more points for victory.

Ernest served, and then saw a different racquet path on Abby's return; she swung her racquet low to high over her head, sending a moonball that caused Ernest to look up in the blinding sun. It drifted slowly to Ernest's side of the court, landing a couple of inches inside the baseline with massive topspin. He wound up his forehand and threw himself into the shot. The ball blasted off his racquet and hit the back wall.

"Out."

The slow pace of the shot had thrown him off.

Every ball Abby hit after that had varying spins, speeds, lengths and heights, to which Ernest repeatedly replied with a shot out or into the net, until he was broken. 5-2.

Abby continued testing Ernest's consistency and patience, and then surprising him with flat hard shots to end the points with winners. Eventually, she caught up, 4-5.

Ernest had completely lost his rhythm and his confidence, and inevitably the second set, 5-7.

During the changeover, Ernest, annoyed, couldn't look Abby in the eye, mumbling, "nice set."

"Thank you," she replied, not looking at him either.

"Super tiebreak to end?"

"Yeah, sure."

Walking back to the baseline, they noticed some spectators. Stefan and Khalid were watching, standing about 20 feet apart.

Khalid nodded to Ernest, offering some encouragement, but Ernest pretended not to see.

Perhaps it was the added pressure of being watched, or the extreme heat. Ernest seemed to unravel completely, giving Abby errors for free points. On the last one, she hit a looper which pushed Ernest about ten feet behind the baseline. He hit a shot back too short. Abby then chipped a drop shot winner. 10-1 in the super tiebreak for Abby—a most dramatic comeback win.

"I'm sorry," Abby said as they shook hands at the net.

"Sorry?" Ernest said, hiding his disappointment, "for what?"

"She junked you to death," said a voice behind them. They turned around; it was Stefan, who was approaching.

"Yeah. About that," Abby said, looking back to Ernest. "It's ugly, I know. But I had to. Desperate times call for desperate measures."

"I get it."

"Plus, every player loves hard shots. Think of everyone as big greedy bottoms! They eat that up! But give 'em no speed, they don't know what to do," she said.

Despite frustration, Ernest chuckled. "You sure know a lot about bottoms for a girl. But you're right. I'm gonna have to learn to deal with all types of players."

"God, I hate junkers," Stefan said, "junkers, pushers, moonballers ... no offence Abby ... but is that even tennis?"

"Tennis is getting the ball into the court, isn't it?" Abby replied.

"No, I mean like *real* tennis."

"Well, I'm sure even *you've* lost that way."

They stared at each other awkwardly.

Abby turned away and began packing her tennis bag on the side bench. The humidity seemed to have increased. She noticed her shirt was drenched; beads of sweat dripped from it on to the court. "Sorry, guys, do you mind turning around for a sec?" she asked.

She pulled her shirt off and quickly shuffled through her bag for a new one. Stefan turned around slightly, stealing a look to see her green polka-dot bikini covering her perky breasts catching the sunlight. She was stunning. Without thinking, he whistled.

"How dare you objectify her!" Ernest said with disdain.

She laughed. "It's okay, Ernest." She put on a tank top, the sides of the polka-dot bikini still visible.

"So who you playing with today, Stefan?" Ernest asked, "Want me to warm you up for a bit? Maybe you can help me get my timing back?"

"Sorry, Scooter should be here any minute."

"Oh."

Abby and Ernest gathered their bags and walked toward the exit. Khalid was still standing there.

"Hi Khalid," Abby smiled.

"Hey Abby, nice comeback. Smart play," he replied.

He then turned to Ernest, who refused to make contact and walked past him. "Ernest, how are you doin', boss?"

"Fine."

Ernest sped up. He wanted to go home. He had just lost a match in which he had a massive lead, and didn't feel like making chit-chat with the guy he thought was his friend who had been—dating, seeing … or who knows what it was—his mother for the past month.

Gross.

But as Ernest walked faster, he still heard Khalid behind him.

"Ernest … Ernest? Can you stop for a sec?"

Ernest turned around. "What do you want?"

"I … I just wanna make sure we're cool."

"I don't have time to talk right now."

"Listen, I have a gig. I'm spinning at The Cave next week."

"The Cave? The straight club?"

"Yeah. You should come. Um… your mom is gonna be there. We want you to be there. *I* really want you to be there, boss."

Ernest paused, suddenly feeling guilty for his hostility. *Am I being unreasonable? Is this anger unwarranted?*, he wondered. He looked back at Khalid, whose eyes seem to plead; Khalid's handsome face looked sweet in its desperation, and Ernest remembered why he had a crush. Khalid's friendship made him feel less lonely. He felt hurt all over again, and brushed Khalid off stoically. "I don't know. I'll see if I can make it."

Chapter 15: The Cave

15a: "Get back in the closet!"

"The Cave? Sorry honey, I don't do straight clubs, especially in the burbs. It's against my religion," said Bibi firmly, as the nurse attached his IV to his hand.

"Bibi! Please!" begged Ernest, "Khalid's been trying to make nice since I found out about them. My mom will kill me if I don't show any effort. It's been so awkward ignoring her at the house. I'm starting to feel bad."

"But a straight club?"

"Yeah, he's got a gig there."

"Kid, you visiting me during these hospital treatments is supposed to calm me. Now you got me all stressed out, and you know what that means!" Bibi raised his voice and his hand.

"What?"

"It means the tumour in my ass is going to win! It feeds off stress!"

Bibi dramatically flailed his hand, causing the trolley holding the chemotherapy bag to move and swing back and forth.

The nurse came back. "You're gonna have to relax, okay darlin'? Or else that needle's gonna come right out of your hand." She held the bag steady, and walked away.

Bibi leaned back into his chair, took a deep breath, and closed his eyes.

When he opened them, Ernest still stood there, eyes bigger and sadder than a small child. "I can't go alone."

"A straight club? Ernest darling, I'm dying of cancer. Don't you think I've suffered enough?"

Ernest looked like he was about to cry.

"Darlin', don't make that face at me," Bibi mumbled.

***

The next day at Bibi's apartment, Stefan had a similar reaction when Bibi asked him to join them at the club. "Did you say The Cave? In Torpedo? You're kidding, right?"

"No," Bibi replied, "Khalid and Joy invited Ernest, who invited me, and now I'm inviting you. But you know as well as I do that the gays can't go alone to a place like that. Look, we can make fun of straight people! Judge them! You're so good at that."

"Why would I go to a straight club to listen to this bruh play bad music?"

"It's for Ernest, we need to support the little shit. Remember, he drove when you were cramping that night."

"Isn't knowing me enough for him?"

"Oh lawd," Bibi said, shaking his head. "Hey, if you go, you can post it on your social media. Steffi goes to a straight club. Hashtag open-minded!"

"Nah. Can't you just bring Fred?"

"No, it's not his thing. Plus he can't be away from Gucci for too long."

Stefan cleared the dinner table and began washing the dishes. Twice a week, he would bring Bibi dinner and help tidy up his apartment the day after a chemotherapy treatment. Those were the days that Bibi felt the weakest and only got out of bed to puke in the toilet when Stefan or Fred weren't there.

"Sorry. Can't do it," Stefan said.

"You want me to go alone to the straight club? I'm dying of cancer. Don't you think I've suffered enough?"

Stefan rolled his eyes and sighed.

***

"ID, kid," the bouncer at The Cave said as Ernest approached. After holding Ernest's G1 to the light, he handed it back and tilted his head toward the entrance. Behind Ernest was Bibi and Stefan.

"Bet you I'll get ID'd and you won't," Stefan mocked Bibi.

"Whatever."

Bibi took a step forward. "ID please," the bouncer said. Bibi smirked back at Stefan and proudly handed it over.

Stefan then moved toward them as slow as possible, but the bouncer didn't flinch. Then taking half a step backward and locking eyes, Stefan desperately uttered, "Bro, you sure you don't want to see my ID?"

"Nope." No hesitation.

Stefan looked down and joined Ernest and Bibi at the door.

"Those lines around your eyes. I told you, yo ass is spending too much time in the tanning bed," Bibi laughed.

"Shut up."

On the wall behind the cashier was one of Khalid's flyers, with an image of a man in a ski mask with the heading "Catch the Bait … DJ Khal."

"Oh, our little fuckboy is a kind of a big deal," Bibi said.

Ernest looked anxious. "I'm gonna need a drink as soon as we get in."

***

With every entrance he made, Stefan carried a confidence inspired by Jennifer Lopez music videos; within each one is the recurring motif of J-Lo entering a club surrounded by other hot—but never hotter than her—girls, to which the crowd takes notice. All others are deemed inferior, mere spectators, to J-Lo's untouchable fabulousness. Stefan saw himself the same way.

But tonight was different. Eyes did not flock to him as he strutted in with Ernest and Bibi through the entrance of The Cave. Stefan, as well as Bibi, felt something they hadn't since they were in the closet; they felt like outsiders.

"Girl, just relax," Bibi said to Stefan. "You look tighter than my ass."

"I don't remember the last time I was surrounded by so many straight people. I'm feeling nauseous."

Ernest spotted the DJ booth. "I guess we should say hi."

They approached the area, which had another giant poster of Khalid's flyer behind it. Khalid, wearing a black t-shirt and black baseball cap, nodded his head to the beat of the music while holding his large headphones.

There were some people dancing in front of the glass that separated Khalid. Stefan and Bibi, noticing the crowd of baby faces obnoxiously smiling and laughing, lowered their heads in fear of being noticed as the "older" people in the club.

There was one woman dancing a little more enthusiastically than the rest. Gold hoop earrings, short red dress, a glass of water in hand spilling slightly as she bopped around uncontrollably. Fire engine red nail polish. She turned around. Ernest was not impressed.

"Ernest darling!" Joy screamed, "You made it! Yay!" Feeling relieved that Ernest might be warming up to her again—it felt like forever since he had spoken a word to her—she reached in for a hug, to which he begrudgingly reciprocated.

"Gawd Mother, what are you wearing?"

"What do you mean?"

"And the lipstick? Your mouth on fire?"

"No, Ernest, *she's* on fiya!" Bibi interjected, grabbing Joy by the waist and spinning her around with excitement.

Joy then looked at Stefan, politely smiling and sticking her arm up as an acknowledgement. Stefan forced a grin.

"Haha, she really Nazi saluted you," Bibi said to Stefan.

"So good to see you all!" The group turned around to see Khalid, who had come out of the DJ booth.

"I'm so glad you came, boss," Khalid smiled cautiously at Ernest.

"What kind of music is this?" Stefan asked.

"It's a bit of a mix of things, but it's basically trap music."

"Trap music?"

"Yeah."

"Is it called that because you gotta trap people to listen to it?"

Bibi turned to Stefan, "What the fuck is wrong with you?"

Looking back at Joy and Khalid, Bibi tried to clear the tension. "Stefan gets a little uneasy around the straighties. We need a drink."

Joy smirked. Khalid put his arm around her and softly kissed her head, then gestured that he had to get back in the booth.

Thirty minutes and three drinks later, Bibi and Stefan leaned on the back walls, arms crossed, watching people on the dance floor.

"Pitiful," Stefan said.

"Shall we?" Bibi asked.

"Why not?"

They made their way to the dance floor as the same electronic thuds repeated.

"What do we have to do to get a little Dua Lipa in here?" Bibi said, bopping back and forth.

Stefan stood stiffly. *What am I doing here?* He then noticed that Bibi had started to find his rhythm, swaying and then sashaying his hips left to right.

"Bibi, no!" Stefan leaned into Bibi's ear, "you can't dance so … you know, fabulously! Dance like you're straight. Try to go off beat. Pretend you're a stiff zombie!"

"You mean like you?!" Bibi replied.

"Listen, we can't stick out here! Get back in the closet!"

But it was too late. Despite how flamboyant Bibi seemed, there was a girl behind him, gyrating her hips close to his butt. Bibi's eyes widened with concern; he mouthed, "kiss me!" to Stefan while trying to avoid facing her.

Stefan backed away slowly; instead of finding the situation funny, he was jealous: *Why aren't any girls hitting on me?* Everything was a competition.

Bibi glared at Stefan in desperation. The girl put her hands on his shoulders and then down to his hips; he felt violated. *I do not consent to this!* he thought.

Suddenly, Ernest stumbled near, holding a martini glass and shaking his head up and down, side to side.

"Ernest!" Stefan said, grabbing him by the arms, "Oh God, you're plastered!"

"I'm fine," Ernest said, breaking free of his hold and walking toward Bibi, who was gesturing to him to come over.

Bibi grabbed Ernest close, yelling, "honey, am I glad to see you!" and firmly planted a kiss on Ernest's lips.

The girl immediately took her hands off Bibi; "oh, are you gay?"

"Yes!" Bibi screamed back, "I like dicks. So guess what? I'm allergic to you!"

She then laughed and hugged him. "Oh my God, I love you even more!"

"Bibi, what the hell are you doing?" Stefan said angrily.

"What?"

"Ernest is trashed! You can't just stick your dirty mouth on him like that!"

"Since when do you care?"

"Hello?! Consent is a thing in straight-land!"

"Relax, it's okay," Ernest said. He looked at the DJ booth and saw his mother and Khalid kissing. "Actually I could use another drink." He looked at Stefan; "go get me one!"

Bibi laughed. "Haha! I like drunk Ernest!"

Stefan was taken aback. "Ernest, what's wrong with you?"

"What do you mean?" Ernest said. "I'm fucking fabulous! I'm in a straight club and watching my mother make out with someone younger than me! Whoop-di-fucking-do!"

Bibi and Stefan watched as Ernest continued to bizarrely dance around, spinning in circles and bumping into others on the dancefloor.

"Be a swan, Ernest darling!" Bibi said, trying to be encouraging. "Be a swan!"

Eventually, Ernest crashed into Joy and Khalid, who had made their way down from the booth.

"Ernest," Joy said with concern. "You okay? You know how dizzy you get when you drink."

Ernest scoffed. "Pffftt. Please!"

"I'm going to get you some water."

"Don't bother Mother! Just take care of your other child!" Ernest said as he raised his voice and stumbled, looking at Khalid.

"Boss, maybe you should sit down," Khalid said.

"Bro, fuck you!" Ernest shouted.

Joy: "Ernest!"

Ernest: "Yeah you heard me! Fuck you, Khalid! And fuck you too, Mother!"

Joy stood furious and hurt. Ernest always bantered with her, but never talked back like this.

Bibi came behind and put his hands on Ernest's shoulders. "Honey, you're kinda wasted right now."

"No!" Ernest shouted. He turned back to Joy. "You took him away from me!" he said, spilling his martini completely.

Bibi interrupted again: "Ernest, stop!"

"No Bibi! I hate you Mother! I hate you because I love him!"

Stefan shook his head, "Ernest, shut up!"

Ernest continued, letting the words spew out like vomit; "I don't care! Yes, I love you Khalid, even though you're fucking straight and fucking my mother! You motherfucker! HA! You're right, bruh, bad choice of words! I love you, you motha-fucka!" suddenly throwing his head back and laughing like a madman.

Until Joy's next words next made him stop.

"Ernest," she stepped forward and put her hand on his shoulder. "I'm pregnant ... Khalid and I are having a baby." Khalid held her hand.

Bibi and Stefan gay gasped, but no sounds came from their mouths. The most dramatic gasp type, like in a silent horror movie.

Ernest smirked, shook his head, and looked down at the floor.

"We didn't want to tell you like this," Joy said. "I'm sorry."

A flood of emotions hit Ernest; he wasn't sure if the music had slowed down, or if a strobe light had caught his eye and temporarily blinded him, or if his hands and feet had suddenly turned into bricks. He turned to Stefan and Bibi, who were still in shock; "I just need a minute alone."

"Ernest, let me explain!" Joy said. But Ernest turned and walked toward the exit, until they could no longer see him in the doorway.

Khalid and Joy slowly walked hand in hand back to the booth, finding the farthest corner where they thought nobody could see them. He bent down, putting his arms around her waist and slowly rocked her back and forth. "It'll be okay," he whispered.

She shook her head slightly, her eyes flooding. "Will it? I don't know."

"It will. I promise," Khalid said, holding her tighter.

15b: Pleasantries

Two hours later, Stefan and Ernest found themselves in the parking lot of The Cave, laughing with Stacey—the girl who tried to dance with Bibi earlier in the night—and her friend Kelly.

"I cannot believe you thought he was straight," Stefan said to her.

"Excuse me?" Bibi said.

"No, really," Stacey said, "I had no idea!"

"Come on! He's as flaming as it comes!" Stefan said.

"What? You saying being flaming is bad?"

Stefan paused. "Of course not. I'm just saying that if one of us was going to give off the straight vibe ..."

Bibi interrupted. "Oh lawd!" He turned back to the girls. "Excuse him, his manliness is being threatened."

They all, except for Stefan, found that to be funny.

"We really don't go to straight clubs to be honest ... not that we don't like straight people. Just not our thing, you know. But we like straight people, don't we Bibi?" Stefan said.

"Oh yes! We love the straights! Y'all are just adorable!"

***

It was 12:30am now. Stefan and Bibi climbed into the Ram.

"Why did we exchange numbers with these girls?" Stefan asked.

"I don't know. Isn't it just a thing people do? It's like saying, 'let's get together soon!'... 'gimme your number!' ... 'have you lost weight?' Pleasantries. They mean nothing. Whatever."

"Well that was enough breeder time for me." Stefan looked down at his phone, and then over at Bibi's. "Did Ernest reply?"

"He did. Said he got too stressed out and took an Uber home. Ordered Taco Bell."

"I thought he was vegan?"

"Well, he must have been shaken up."

Bibi swerved slightly as Stefan began driving. "You okay?"

"Yeah. Just tired."

Stefan reached to turn on the radio but Bibi raised his hand. "Girl, my head is spinning a little. Do you mind if we keep the radio off?"

"Of course."

Bibi quietly chuckled. "You know my parents would have killed me if I talked to them like Ernest talked to Joy?"

"So would mine."

"I bet."

"Have you told your parents yet?"

"About what?"

"Being ... sick."

"I told my mom. She cried, of course. I think she told my dad. But I haven't heard from him."

"Still?"

"Yeah. He's a southern religious man, you know? And I'm his only son. I don't think he'll ever forgive me, or forgive himself for the fact that his boy would rather play with dolls than go fishing with him ... Anyway, you heard enough of that before."

"I get it. People don't change, B."

"I know. I couldn't have gotten through all that if I didn't have you to talk to. Thanks girl."

Stefan kept his eyes on the road. "Of course. All dads are assholes. Isn't that the rule for us?"

Suddenly Bibi dry heaved. "Oh shit. Stef, I'm gonna be sick," he said, rolling down the window.

"Oh God. Not in my car!"

"Can you pull over?"

Stefan stopped on the side of the road, not far from the spot where Ernest previously took the head off a raccoon. Bibi hopped out and hurled his head toward the grass, letting out a good amount of what he had just drank. Stefan came behind him, rubbing his shoulder. "Take your time."

"Thanks."

Ten minutes later, Bibi felt better, and they got back in the car.

Bibi stared at the streetlights and the passing cars as Stefan remained fixated on the road ahead. He was driving slowly.

Bibi looked at Stefan. "When's the last time you talked to him?"

"Who, my dad?"

"Yeah."

Stefan had to think. "About eight years ago, when my mom ... you know."

"Oh."

"But I'll probably see him when we go to Bonn for the games. Should be interesting. We'll exchange pleasantries. Whatever."

"Maybe it won't be so bad."

"People don't change, B."

As he continued to drive, Stefan heard his father's voice echo in his ears: *"All this time, I tried to make you something you were not. All this time, I knew something was wrong with you. Now I know."*

Chapter 16: *STAY IN YOUR LANE!*
July 2020

16a: *The Straight Man Bending the Gay League!*

The Pride Games, to be held in Stefan's hometown of Bonn, Germany, was approaching quickly. Like the Olympics, the Pride Games were held every four years with athletes from the LGBTQ2+ community from all over the world competing in over 30 sports. The event was organized by the International LGBTQ2+ Tennis Association (ILGBTQ2+TA), the overarching organization in which each queer league belonged to.

The winner of the singles gold medal for tennis was equivalent to the Ladies gold in figure skating at the Winter Olympics, or the Gymnastics all around champion at the summer games. Steffi Graf. Katarina Witt. Simone Biles. Immortal inspirations for the mostly gay men competing.

In the months leading up to the games, the yips—or paralyzing nerves that left his game in ruins—which plagued Khalid in the CGO final against Scooter disappeared. Khalid won the leagues' tournaments in Detroit and Montreal in July; his ranking in the International Gay League rose, guaranteeing a high seeding and favourable draw in Bonn. His success gained attention overseas; pictures of him were splashed on the ILGBTQ+2TA's Facebook page and Instagram with the heading, *The Straight Man from Canada Bending the Gay League!* Not every comment under the posts was positive however; other gay tennis purists commented, *This is an abomination to our league! Kick the straight man out!* with the hashtag *#outwiththestraights!*

Nevertheless, Khalid continued to make friends among the players he met and defeated, reinforcing his reputation as "the super nice/cool/chill/amazingly talented/hot-as-fuck straight guy."

As Khalid's star ascended, Stefan's saw the opposite. He descended in tennis performance and morale. He had only made the semifinals in Detroit, losing to a lesbian named Olive Yakamoto (*who knew there were Japanese lesbians living in Detroit?*, he thought, *that must have definitely thrown me off*) and then falling in the quarterfinals of Montreal to Scooter, to whom he had never lost to previously. Mindful of Stefan's sensitivity to losing, Scooter restrained himself from over-exaggerating his cheers for himself and breaking a blood vessel in his throat from screaming victory; he was completely silent.

A pleasant surprise, Abby advanced to the fourth round of both tournaments, her combination of consistency, placement, and craftiness—including her moonball—driving her opponents to madness.

Eager to distract himself from Khalid and Joy, Ernest threw himself into tennis and his budding friendships with Bibi and Abby. He made the quarterfinals in Detroit and the semifinals of Montreal, earning the same results as Stefan. However, despite his improvement, Stefan never could find the time to hit with him. But it didn't matter to Ernest, who was happy to hit with anyone except Khalid.

The preparation for Bonn was intense; everyone wanted the chance to capture the elusive gold; its glory only up for grabs every four years.

Everyone except for Bibi, who—while too weak to compete—would still be going along with Fred and Gucci, to play devoted cheerleader.

16b: The Apollo Spa

Pre-Pride Games PAR-TAY!, the caption read on the Facebook event invite Khalid received from Bibi. *Come join for a relaxing gurls night at the Apollo Spa before we jet set to Germany for the Pride Games! Friday, August 14, 2020, 8pm*. Also invited were Ernest, Stefan, Fred, and Scooter.

The flight to Germany from Toronto's Pearson airport was the next day at noon. Khalid didn't have to DJ that night, and Joy had an appointment for a new weave. *A spa?* Khalid thought. He had never been to one before, not even for a manicure. *Maybe I could get a massage? It'll help relax before the tournament.* He accepted the invite.

The Apollo Spa was in the gay village of Toronto. Since joining the league, Khalid had visited the area a few times for dinner. But he didn't recall seeing a sign for the spa before.

Parking his Camry on the corner of Church and Maitland, Khalid followed the building numbers past a few bars and a coffee shop. His phone indicated the entrance was at the side of the building. Standing in front of the barely visible sign, he texted Bibi. *Hey, I'm here at the Spa. Where are you? Should I meet you at the entrance, or inside?* Five minutes went by without a reply and the soft spits from the sky turned into full on rain; Khalid walked inside into the entrance.

"ID please," said the cashier behind a window.

Khalid stood in the tiny lobby. *Doesn't look like a spa.* He slid his driver's license under the glass.

"I don't know if my friends are here yet. Should I give you their names?"

"No, you'll have to find them yourself."

"Oh."

The cashier glanced at the card, looked at Khalid and then slid it back out of the window. "You want a room or a locker?"

"Uh ... for what?"

"Your clothes."

"Okay. I guess I'll get a locker."

The cashier placed a coil wrist band with a key on the counter. "The locker number is on the key. Towels are in the change room. $35.25. How will you be paying?"

"That's it? Are the services extra?"

"I don't know what you're talking about."

Khalid didn't find Bibi, Ernest, or any other familiar faces in the changeroom. Confused, he took a cue from another man and followed: he undressed, put his clothes in the locker, wrapped a towel around his waist and proceeded to the dimly lit hallway. The man in front stopped, turned around to stare at his body and smirked, "hey. Wanna go to the back area together?"

"No thanks, boss. I'm meeting a few friends here actually," Khalid replied.

"Okay then." The man raised an eyebrow and turned away.

Khalid looked down at his phone; still no reply from Bibi. *Odd.*

He then wrote a message in the event invite. *Guys, I'm here. Where are you?*

There was a hot tub nearby. As he entered, the two men sitting and talking stopped their chatter; their eyes following as his jacked body disappeared into the bubbling water. Khalid saw their heads move up to get a better look at his crotch when he took his towel off.

He nodded and smiled shyly.

"Where are you from?" one of them asked.

"Torpedo Valley," Khalid replied.

"No, I mean, what is your background?"

"Oh. Syrian."

The men nodded their heads in unison. "Mmm," one grunted.

Khalid looked away. *Where's Bibi?*

"I've met some really nice guys from Iran," the other man said. "But nobody from Syria."

Khalid nodded. "I'm just here to meet some of my friends. Not sure where they are though."

The man's tone suddenly changed. "Relax kid, I wasn't trying anything. Jeez, these young cocky shits," he said, shaking his head.

Khalid grabbed his towel and got up from the tub.

Circling the hallways, he suddenly stopped at a peculiar sight before him: a set of twins, the same height, body, and man bun standing at the end. Steam swarmed around them as the pale light flickered slightly above their ominous faces. Khalid squinted to get a clearer look. Then came their voices. Deep, and in sync.

"Khalid. Come play with us, Khalid."

A chill came over him. He stopped walking; his arms tensed. *How do they know my name? What's the name of that horror movie again?*

"Khalid? Khalid is that you?"

Suddenly a voice was coming from behind him. He turned around: Scooter stood with a grin on his face. "Bruh! I thought that was you!"

Khalid turned back to the end of the hallway. The twins were gone.

"Scooter! Good to see you, boss," Khalid said, suddenly upbeat.

"I knew it!" Scooter said, slightly raising his voice. "I knew my there were definitely some vibes around you! I wasn't sure if it was gay, or bi, or whatever."

"Um, okay?" Awkward pause. "So where are the others?"

"Who?"

"Bibi, Ernest … Stefan? Have you seen them yet?"

"Not sure what you mean?"

"Didn't you get that invite on Facebook? We were supposed to have a pre-Pride-Games spa night here tonight?"

"Sorry—I didn't get that invite. Sounds like a hell of an orgy."

"No, that's not what it is."

Scooter leaned in. "Bruh, don't act like you don't know where we are. I know this ain't your first rodeo!"

"Huh?"

"Look at you, playing all innocent. Nice strategy." Scooter winked. "Here, come with me. I got a room."

Scooter walked down the hallway and entered his room. Khalid looked back at the empty hallway where *The Shining*-ish twins once stood, and turned back to follow him.

Khalid entered the doorway and found Scooter, completely naked, laying on the bed, stomach down. Khalid felt his phone buzz and then looked down.

A text from Bibi. *Sorry, what are you doing at the Apollo Spa? Pretty sure that's not your scene. Lol.*

"Shit. Scooter, I think this is a mistake," Khalid said. He realized ... he was in a bathhouse.

Scooter looked up from the bed. "Yeah, I know, everyone assumes I'm a top. But whatever, fuck 'em, right bruh? Now ... come over here."

Khalid panicked. "No, I mean I'm not supposed to be here."

"Bruh, come on! It's not really gay if you're the top!"

Khalid left the room, walking a couple of laps in the maze-like hallways, then finding the change room. He threw on his clothes and ran out the entrance while tossing the locker key at the front cashier, who barely looked up.

It was pouring rain outside now; he was soaked as he rushed to the parking lot, fumbling through his pockets for his keys.

Approaching his car, he noticed there was some paper folded underneath the windshield wiper. He picked it up and slowly unfolded it to read the angrily written words in red block letters, the ink running:

GET OUT. THE STRAIGHTS DON'T BELONG

Attached to the paper was a membership form; Khalid looked at the top left to see a red Costco Logo. More red ink running beneath, it read, *STAY IN YOUR LANE!*

PART FOUR

Chapter 17: Willkommen in Bonn
The Pride Games—Bonn, Germany
August 2020

"Canada!" the speaker announced.

The Canadian flag, waving from a 30 foot pole, was held by Mark Tewksbury during the opening ceremony. Whereas the other countries' competitors gathered behind their flag bearer in no particular order or form, the Canadian contingent marched four athletes at a time, perfectly in line.

The group—Stefan, Bibi, Ernest, Abby, Khalid, and Scooter—entered the Stadion von Bonn stadium from the northeast side of the runners track.

A firecracker launched into the sky with every country's entrance, eventually bursting into a champagne-coloured waterfall of sparkles. Giant video screens in each corner of the stadium zoomed in on the athletes; everyone was ecstatic seeing their big smiles plastered. Cheerleaders scantily clad in rainbow uniforms and holding neon pom-poms scattered on the centre of the track; some doing cartwheels and flips, others a synchronized dance, and some just bouncing up and down, giddy like cartoons. Camera flashes blinked among the sea of spectators, which included Joy and Fred. However, of the three levels of seating in the stadium, only the bottom one was full.

Still, Ernest was awestruck.

"Try not to look too high in the stands. It's depressing," Bibi said. "It was the same when I went to the games in 2016."

"What's Mark Tewksbury even doing here?" Stefan asked.

"Whatever bro, he's like a hundred years old, but he's still hot as fuck!" Scooter said.

Ernest nodded. "I'd have to agree with you on that one." Suddenly, a feeling of anxiety washed over him; he looked around. Mark Tewksbury wasn't the only attractive face. It appeared that every athlete was ridiculously good looking, tall and muscular; he felt himself shrink a little.

Bibi was out of breath; "Guys, can we just take the speed down a notch, you're walking too fast for me."

The flight had tired him out. He had only been out of chemoradiation for two weeks before the trip. Thankfully, his appetite returned; he was even able to keep the plane food down, a feat which seemed impossible during treatment.

He turned to Khalid, recalling the last night in Toronto at the bathhouse. "I still don't know what happened that night. Someone must have hacked into my Facebook. Who would have lured you into the Apollo?"

Khalid shrugged his shoulders; "I don't know, boss."

Scooter howled. "Well if you ever want to *try* again," saying "try" while making air quotations with his hands, "you let me know, bruh. HA!"

"Jesus, Scooter! He's fucking straight, just stop!" Ernest snapped.

Khalid looked at Ernest, "Thanks, boss."

Ernest didn't look at Khalid, or acknowledge his comment.

"Guys, look up! We're on the big screen!" Abby shouted, pointing up.

They raised their heads to see Ernest and Bibi smile and wave at themselves, only to be shoved aside by Stefan, who, once he got the frame to himself, served his signature blue steel expression and snapped a photo of himself on the jumbotron.

***

An hour later, the group stood at the end of the track gathered with the other countries.

"Okay I'm over this," Scooter said. "When is this done so we can go eat?"

The countries had been announced in alphabetical order, and they had finally arrived at Z. First came Zambia. Then, Zimbabwe followed a minute later.

"Zambia? Zimbabwe? There's gay people in Africa?" Stefan joked.

"I know, right?" Scooter laughed.

Ernest rolled his eyes. "Shhh! People will hear you and think Canadians are dumb assholes."

"We're trying to break the stereotype," Stefan snarked.

"Lawd," Bibi shook his head, then changed the subject. "So, when are we meeting your dad, Stef?"

"Tomorrow morning."

"How are you feeling about it?"

"Good ... I think. You guys are still coming with me?"

"Of course."

The crowd cheered as the lights dimmed.

"Now to welcome our main act! Introducing ... international Billboard superstar and Grammy nominee ... Carly Rae Jepsen!"

Fireworks exploded again; the stadium got louder.

"Holy shit!" Stefan exclaimed. "Oh my God! It's Carly Rae fucking Jepsen!" looking around him to find a mutually enthusiastic fan.

But there was no one to be found, only Bibi, with his arms crossed and a look of judgment. "No, bitch."

Stefan dismissed them. "Whatever! You guys are lame!"

Carly Rae Jepsen ran to the front of the stage in the middle of the field; "hey guys! So happy to be a part of the Pride Games!" The close up of her face on the jumbotron revealed a lot of makeup.

"Honey, you look like a drag queen!" Bibi yelled. "I love it!"

Then a familiar tune. The opening sounds of *Call Me Maybe*. Stefan jumped up and down, screaming uncontrollably.

Ernest turned to Bibi; "I've never seen Stefan be so ... "

"Flamey. You can say it, sweetie. A flamey nelly femme queen.

She pretends she's some big manly top, but underneath it all she just wants to bend over," Bibi cackled.

Stefan found himself in a delirium; back in his hometown to compete in a sport he loved, amidst the spectacle of the opening ceremony, and watching his favourite singer perform his all-time favourite song. He danced and shouted the lyrics with unabandon, closing his eyes to savour it.

Then suddenly, he felt his shoulder hit something; he opened his eyes and found Abby had fallen on the ground beside him.

"Sorry, Abby!" he said, extending his hand to help her out. "I hope I didn't bump you too hard! I get into a trance when I hear this song!"

"No, I'm sorry … I love this song. "

"You too?" Stefan said, pleasantly surprised.

Chapter 18: "Hallo, Vater"

Stefan had not seen his father since the passing of his mother in 2012. Even then, Stefan quickly hopped off the plane from Toronto to Bonn, attended the service and burial, accepted condolences after, and then promptly rushed back to his hotel, telling his father that he "didn't want to inconvenience him by staying at the house." He caught a flight back to Toronto two days later, citing "a very important work meeting he could not miss."

This didn't mean he wasn't sad or didn't care; on the contrary, he was devastated. He had kept a close relationship with his mother after he moved to Canada in 1999. Once a week, every week, he would call her to talk about his fabulous new life in North America: the exciting people, the diverse culture, the sense of rush and adrenaline. And possibilities. Mother Porsche didn't speak much, just content to hear that her boy was happy. To her delight, he'd often promise her he'd buy her a ticket to come visit him in Toronto one day. But that day never came.

One thing they didn't talk about was Stefan's father.

"What happened with your dad?" Ernest asked as he, Stefan, and Bibi rode in the cab to Father Porsche's house the morning after the opening ceremony.

Stefan explained: "So, you know I used to compete in junior tennis a lot? My father was a pro player back in the day—not a highly successful one, mind you—but he still got to play some big names. Anyway, he was obsessed with me winning. All I heard growing up was, 'Stefan, you have to win, and not just win, but beat everyone … pound them!' he'd say, 'like a goddamn schnitzel.'"

Bibi giggled.

Stefan glared at him. "What?"

"Sorry, I just think it's funny he said that, when all you want now is to *be* pounded! HA!" Bibi howled, then putting his hand up to high-five

Ernest.

"You would think the chemo would've killed your funny cells," Stefan retorted.

"How dare you!", Bibi said, air-slapping Stefan.

Stefan looked back at Ernest. "So, as I was saying, I got a sponsorship with Nike when I was 15. The old man was proud. He'd always brag that his boy was sponsored and all that. A year went by, my results in juniors weren't so great, and Nike pulled the plug on my deal. He wasn't too happy with me. Then a few years later, I finally came out. Long story short—things just got worse between us."

"Did he freak out?"

"No, worse. He was ashamed," Stefan said. "I needed to get away. So I moved to Toronto for university."

"Whoa," Ernest said. "That's rough. I'm sorry, Stef. But maybe he's a lot nicer now."

"People don't change, Ernest. He doesn't go for that 'everyone gets a gold star no matter what' crap. Honestly, neither do I. That's besides the point. This is why I wanted you guys to come with me today. I'm not taking any negative energy from him this time."

Ernest looked back out the window, taking in the scenery: the classical architecture mixed with the simple light orange and yellow buildings; the cobblestone sidewalks, the big beautiful oak trees; the groups of people riding bikes; the absence of skyscrapers; the bright and glittery lights and rainbow décor specifically put up for the games, the pockets of retail areas with popular stores.

"Wow, Bonn is more current than I thought. I just saw a Sephora!" Ernest said.

Stefan and Bibi smirked at each other, realizing that Ernest had probably never been out of Canada before.

***

After the cab dropped them in front of Stefan's childhood home, Stefan had a request. "Okay guys, so don't act too—"

"Oh no," Ernest interrupted, "too gay? Please don't say we can't act or talk *too gay*!"

"No, not that … otherwise you'd both need muzzles."

"Meow," Bibi said.

"Well, maybe don't bring the gay thing up. What I was going to say was, just don't be so … you know … woke, and annoying!" Stefan said. "If he says something stupid or offensive, just let it slide. It's easier that way."

"Yeah, but that's not right," Ernest said. "How's he gonna know he's wrong if you don't say anything?"

"You know, Ernest, sometimes being the bigger person is just letting the other person win. You just have to let it go every once in a while," Stefan replied.

Bibi was impressed. "Look at Miz Prez. All philosophical and shit."

Ernest was resigned. "Fine."

Stefan rang the doorbell. About a minute went by, and the door opened. Father Porsche, now with white hair and eyes sunken into his face, looked smaller than Stefan remembered.

"Hallo, Vater."

"Stefan," his father said. Noticing Ernest and Bibi, he spoke in English: "Why do you look so orange?" his accent heavy.

"What?"

"Orange. You look like that Trump idiot."

Bibi and Ernest laughed. "See I told you Stef, you gotta stop with the tanning."

"Come in, boys," Father Porsche said, "I just picked up some weisswurst from the market."

"Weisswhaa?" Ernest asked.

"It's sausage, white sausage," Stefan replied.

"Oh, I'm vegan," Ernest said.

"What?" Father Porsche said.

"I don't eat meat."

Father Porsche turned to Stefan. "What is he saying?"

"Never mind," Stefan replied.

"Girl, isn't white sausage what we came for?" Bibi joked.

Stefan's father was warmer than Bibi and Ernest had imagined. He asked the boys about themselves and their lives in Canada, and was glad to hear Stefan's career was going well.

"What car do you drive, son?"

"A Ram. A big black one," Stefan beamed with pride, holding up his phone with a pic.

Father Porsche nodded with approval. "Very nice. Too bad it's American." He turned to Bibi and Ernest. "You know, a strong man needs a strong car."

Stefan reached behind his chair and handed his father a large gift bag; "this is for you."

"Oh, you didn't have to."

"Yeah I did."

"What?"

"Nothing."

Father Porsche reached into the bag and pulled out a red and white box; there were decadent pastries under the cellophane window. "What is this?"

"They're called BeaverTails."

"It looks like you ran over a cake with your American car and put sugar on top."

"I know you like your sweets. They're a big thing in Canada."

"I'm diabetic now."

"Oh. Sorry. Well there's more in the bag. Look."

Father Porsche took a black box out of the gift bag. "Virginia

Black?"

"Yeah. It's Canadian whisky. The best."

"It says American Whisky on the box."

"Yes, but it's really a collaboration between Drake, you know that Canadian rapper, and some American guy."

"Who? Brake?"

"Drake."

"Bake?"

"Drake!" Stefan raised his voice, then catching himself and lowering the volume. "I hope you like it."

"Danke, son," his father looked pleased.

"You're welcome," Stefan said, smiling. He then looked at Bibi, as if to say, *this is oddly going well, isn't it?*

Bibi nodded back with an encouraging grin.

Father Porsche put the whisky on the table. "Stefan, I could have used this watching your matches when you were a kid."

Stefan knew it. At some point, the tennis putdowns would start.

"You know boys, my son would drive me and his mother crazy watching his tournaments."

"Vater!"

But his father would not be interrupted. "He had so many chances to win all those matches. He even had a Nike sponsorship, you know? But Stefan … was just too weak in here," he said, pointing to his head, "such a waste. With all that talent."

Ernest tried to keep things upbeat. "You know, I'm sure he tried the best he could."

"I don't think so, young man," Father Porsche said.

"Of course he tried his best."

"I disagree with you. And not because you are Black."

Ernest and Bibi stared at each other, stunned.

His father continued. "Listen, okay? I'm not a bad guy. I'm not racist. I treat everyone the same, Black, White, purple, whatever."

"Uhh…" Ernest mumbled.

Stefan interjected; "Ernest, don't bother."

"Such a waste of talent, my son." Father Porsche mumbled.

Stefan stood up. "We should be heading back now."

"So soon?"

"The tournament starts tomorrow."

"Good. What time should I be there? It's at the nationales Tenniszentrum von Bonn, ja?"

"You're coming to watch, Daddy Porsche?" Bibi asked.

"Yes," he said, "I'm going to see my son win the gold!"

Stefan shook his head. "Don't go putting pressure on me again. There are a lot of amazing players here."

"There's even some straight ones," Ernest said, curious to see his reaction.

"Straight ones?" Puzzled, Father Porsche looked at Stefan. "I thought this was the games for gay people?"

"Yeah, it's the Pride Games, most of the players are gay, but some are straight. Technically, anyone can enter."

His father raised his eyebrows, concerned. "Listen, I accept the everyone. You know that now, right Stef?"

Stefan raised an eyebrow. *Really?*

Father Porsche continued. "But the straight guys are going to kill you! You boys will get slaughtered! Might as well go home now!" He reached over to the plate and tossed a piece of sausage in his mouth.

Stefan stood up. "We gotta go."

***

A few hours after returning to the hotel, Stefan heard a knock at his door. He opened it to see Ernest standing with a wooden racquet.

"This is mine. I was thinking maybe you could use this, you know, if you need to release some anger on court. So you don't have to break your racquet … you could smash this instead." Ernest said. "Or, in case you feel like your dad is stressing you out."

Stefan grinned warmly. "Thanks."

Chapter 19: Pity-fuck

That evening was the tennis tournament welcome party, held at a bar near the hotel. Eager to forget about the earlier visit with "Vater," Stefan bought everyone—including Khalid—a round of Jägerbombs.

"Relax Ernest," Stefan said, "you need another shot?"

"No thanks," Ernest replied, seemingly unable to shake his anxiety.

"Ernest darling, what's wrong?" Bibi asked.

Since the opening ceremony, Ernest's belief had grown stronger: every athlete in Bonn was irritatingly good looking, all over six-feet, gorgeous, and ripped. Their incredible jawlines with a five o'clock shadow and pronounced cheekbones anchored by dazzling smiles; their V-shaped silhouettes framed by bulging arms and veins; the perfect amount of chest hair peeking out of their plunging V-necks. More men poured in, drowning Ernest—only five-feet four—in a sea of hot "masc" energy, barely able to see over their shoulders.

"Fuck. Is there anyone here that *isn't* hot?"

Stefan sensed Ernest's insecurity. "Just ignore that."

Ernest then caught a reflection of himself in the bottom of a mirror. "Oh God. I'm the ugliest— ...I don't belong here. I'm gonna go."

"Blasphemy, honey. Europeans love the chocolate. They will eat you up like the dutty ho you are! Ha!" Bibi said.

"You're just saying that."

"Ernest darling, I have an affirmation that is tried and true."

"Yes."

"Take a deep breath, and repeat after me."

"Okay."

"Black cocks matter," Bibi said with a giant smile.

Ernest gay gasped. "Oh my God! I can't believe you just said that! You're mocking a real social movement!"

Stefan, shocked: "Wow, B. Just wrong. This is my cue to leave the conversation," he said, walking away.

"Oh fuck, sorry Ernest. You're right, that was too far," Bibi apologized.

"There's some things you can't joke about."

Awkward silence.

Ernest then leaned into Bibi's ear and whispered, "even so, I heard they can be racist here."

"Excuse me, Miss Woke, are you assuming that Europeans are racist? Honey, *that's* racist."

"You know what I mean. And if I was an exception, I'm no fucking Michael B. Jordan!"

"Relax, be a swan, sweetie, be a swan. No boys will talk to you if you look like you're clenching. You wanna save that for later, okay?"

"Fine. Yes, I'm a swan. I'm a swan."

But as the night went on, Ernest's concern increased. The Canadian contingent seemed to be catnip that night. He saw Scooter make out with a blue-eyed blonde in the corner, and then eventually leave together toward the hotel. Stefan seemed to be looser than usual, laughing and flirting with some men from Austria. Joy had to swoop in and save Khalid a couple of times from some overly friendly guys. Even Bibi, who despite looking gaunt and holding Fred's hand the entire evening, was invited for a foursome with an apparently very wealthy couple from Monaco.

"They're staying at the Grand Castle Hotel 20 minutes away from here. It's a six star!" Bibi exclaimed, excited.

"So, you guys gonna go?" Ernest asked.

"Yeah, but only just to see it. They're in the penthouse! After we get a tour, I'm gonna say I'm feeling sick and we have to go. Gotta pull the cancer card when I can! Why, I can't put out when I'm dying. I need to save my energy."

"Well, have fun, be safe."

Bibi suddenly felt guilty. "Oh, do you want me to stay with you, honey? No problem at all."

"No, go ahead. You and Fred should go wild."

"Okay. Well, just message me if anything." Bibi and Fred then followed the couple out of the bar.

Ernest sat at a booth in the corner, inhaling croquettes and other nibblies from the appetizer table, looking longingly at the crowd. This reminded him of why he rarely went to bars. He always got attention whenever he led rallies, fundraisers, or social justice events, but never at purely social settings. Though he'd never say it out loud, he felt regular bar goers were superficial and stupid ... "basic." He decided that as soon as he tasted some of the desserts, he would go back to the hotel room to join Abby, his roommate for the trip. Maybe catch a reality show on TV where he could judge people to cheer himself up. He looked down at the table while devouring a cracker with a big piece of brie on top.

"I thought you were vegan."

Ernest looked up to see Stefan standing there.

"Oh shit," Ernest said, "I keep forgetting and keep shoving everything in my mouth. I thought you were getting it on with those Austrian guys?"

"I did, but they started talking smack. They said all North Americans are shit on clay and all we're good at is bashing the ball on hard courts. That we aren't good enough to grind matches out. I disagreed and they laughed at me. Fuck'em."

"Oh."

Stefan sensed that Ernest was overwhelmed in self-consciousness. He felt bad for him. "How are you doing?"

Ernest shook his head, shoving another croquette in his face.

"Maybe you should talk to people," Stefan said.

"Nah, guys that look like them usually don't pay attention to me."

"What? No."

Stefan noticed that amidst the crowd of athletes, one figure—a

Caucasian slender man with brown hair and very tight shorts, more than three inches above his knee—slowly approached them. "Ernest, I think this guy is into you. He's coming toward us."

Ernest looked up. "Oh my God. Peter."

"Who's Peter?" Stefan asked.

"My ex from university. Fuckin' asshole," Ernest mumbled.

"Ernest? Ernest Law? Is that you?" Peter said, stopping in front of them.

"Uh Hi. Hi Peter," Ernest said. "What are the chances?"

Peter Winters. Ernest's former tennis doubles partner and ex-flame from university, who dumped him for Greg from his microeconomics class. The guy who would wear the shortest, tightest shorts, and then would deny doing so on purpose. The guy who broke Ernest's heart.

Stefan looked Peter up and down, scowling slightly.

Ernest gazed at his ex's shorts, still as tiny as hot pants. "Well, you haven't changed a bit."

"I thought I might run into you at one of these gay tennis thingys!" Peter said. "I moved to the New York. We've got a great league of queens there! Are you still in little old Torpedo?"

"Yeah, still there." Ernest said. "New York? Sounds fancy."

Peter pointed to another man at the bar. "My husband's over there. He's competing in the decathlon."

"You're married now?"

Ernest and Stefan glanced at Peter's husband, whose body resembled that of Thor. He looked at Peter and waved, to which Peter enthusiastically yelled, "this is Ernest, my little old friend from Torpedo!" His husband nodded and then smiled at them.

Stefan looked at Ernest's face; although Ernest had put on a smile, Stefan knew he was sad. Even more than sad. In addition to the insecurities Ernest felt that night, running into his ex-boyfriend was like a stomp on his heart.

Without thinking, Stefan put his arm around Ernest's shoulder and moved closer, their bodies touching. Ernest turned to Stefan, puzzled. Stefan extended his hand. "Peter, nice to meet you. I'm Stefan, Ernest's boyfriend."

Ernest's eyes widened.

"Oh. Nice to meet you," Peter responded with a firm handshake. "You from Torpedo too?"

"I live in Toronto. I'm an executive at one of the biggest financial institutions downtown." Stefan tilted his head and rested it on Ernest's, his hand now slow rubbing Ernest's shoulders.

Peter awkwardly stared at them. "Well ... good for you, Ernest.

Ernest didn't know what to say. "Yes, uh, good for me. I mean, thank you."

"Babe, we should get going," Stefan said to Ernest. "Juan Carlos invited us to drinks in his hotel room, remember?"

Ernest nodded. "Yeah. Okay."

"Our friend Juan Carlos from Brazil is the heavy favourite in the wrestling event," Stefan smirked at Peter. "He's got some V.I.P. hotel room set up. Wants to show us some of his moves," Stefan concluded, winking at Peter.

Peter nodded. "Oh, okay. Nice meeti—"

"Bye!" Stefan interrupted, quickly whisking Ernest away to the other end of the bar until Peter couldn't see them.

"I can't believe you dated that guy," Stefan said.

"Who's Juan Carlos?" Ernest said, chuckling.

"Oh never mind that."

Ernest turned to Stefan, locking eyes. "Hey, just so you know, thank you. I really appreciate that."

"Don't mention it."

Ernest looked out at the crowd. "Well, you don't have to stay with me. Go, do your thing."

"Well what are you going to do then? I told you, you should go socialize. Don't be so self-conscious."

"I already said, bars are not my thing. Look, Scooter hooked up with some Norwegian guy. Bibi and Fred got invited to a foursome. Khalid even got approached, but my mother shut that down quickly." Ernest looked down. "I'm gonna head back to the hotel now. Have fun."

Stefan knew all that already, having seen everyone in the group leave to presumably hook up with their new acquaintances.

"Look, I'm sure someone here will be into little guys. And you got that Black hipster thing going on—pretty rare!"

"Thanks." Ernest forced a smile and turned to walk away.

"Ernest, wait." Stefan fidgeted. "Have another shot with me."

Ernest continued toward the exit. "Thanks, but I don't wanna be hungover for my match tomorrow."

"Right … Why …" Stefan hesitated, "why don't you just come to my hotel room tonight?"

Ernest stopped. "Huh? Is that a joke?"

"Just come with me," Stefan said casually, as if it wasn't a big deal. "I'm not sharing my room with anyone."

"I'm sorry?"

"Yeah … I got you. It might be fun." Stefan smiled hesitantly. Now he was feeling insecure. *It felt weird to be vulnerable.*

Ernest was dumbfounded. Stefan looked sweet, warm. Even … *charming?*

"Um…I don't think that's a good idea."

"Come on, I feel bad—" Stefan suddenly stopped himself.

Ernest's face sank, his voice faint. "Thanks. But that's okay."

He walked toward the exit, eventually feeling Stefan's hand on his shoulder.

"Hey, I'm sorry, I didn't mean it that way. I just want you to have fun too," Stefan said.

"No worries. That's nice of you. But I don't want to be a pity-fuck, Stefan." Ernest walked away.

Stefan shut his eyes and shook his head. *Shit.*

***

Abby didn't regret skipping the player's welcome party; she found herself glued to the TV, howling at a Spanish telenovela while sprawled on the hotel bed. Plus, she felt socializing was too exhausting.

The door opened; Ernest entered.

"How was it?" she asked, turning down the volume.

"Meh."

"Really?"

"I should have just stayed here with you."

"How come?"

"Nothing, it's stupid."

"Stupid's my favourite. Come on, you can tell me. This is a safe space, my friend."

Ernest took a breath and sat on the bed. "Ugh. I know I shouldn't care about this stuff but … everyone there was so hot. And like, big and ripped. Everyone seemed to be connecting and then leaving together to hook up. While I ate, like, 12 croquettes."

"But aren't you vegan?"

"I know. When I get upset, I forget." Ernest rolled his eyes and continued; "anyway I just felt so … you know, ugly. Invisible."

"Like you don't belong?"

"Yeah."

"Like everyone was invited to this special club, but you weren't because of something outside your control?"

"Exactly."

Abby nodded; "I understand."

"And then Stefan … he …"

"He what?"

Ernest lay on his bed. "So everyone was hooking up, right? And … he offered to bring me to his hotel room—because he felt bad. A pity-fuck. Can you believe that?"

Abby sat beside him. "Don't feel that way. I went to the games in 2012 and all those guys looking to hook up are idiots. You're the full package, Ernest."

Ernest was unconvinced.

She continued; "and Stefan. I'm sure he means well. He's not ... well I assume he's not always great about articulating it."

"How do you know that?"

"I'm a good judge of character." She smiled, then grabbed the remote. "Wanna watch this telenovela with me? It's ridic! This girl's in love with the evil twin of her baby daddy's daddy, whom everyone thought was dead. It's like an Almodóvar movie."

Ernest chuckled, "sure."

"And I picked up some pretzels stuffed with ham. They're in the fridge. Fuck veganism!"

"Bring it on!"

As they settled on their beds munching on pastries and chocolate, sounds slowly started to emerge. It wasn't coming from the television.

It became louder and clearer.

Ernest, repulsed, put his hands over his ears.

Joy's voice, yelling, "Extend beyond your reach, boy! Extend!" over a squeaking mattress could be heard from the other side of the wall.

"Turn up the volume! Turn up the volume!" Ernest screamed at Abby. He then pounded on the wall behind him: "For fuck's sake, I can hear you guys!"

Chapter 20: "All Straight People are Cancelled!"

The top two seeds of the tennis singles division were Margaret Fork from Australia, and Igor Off of Russia, respectively. In the year leading up to the games, they had been dominating the gay tennis scene in their areas of the world. Margaret won three tournaments in her native country and one in Thailand. Due to her spectacular skills at net, and—as constantly pointed out by most gay men in the league—the fact she was a rather masculine presenting lesbian, she was nicknamed "The Iron Fist." Almost as impressive, Igor scored wins in the Czech Republic, Spain, and at home in St. Petersburg; he also was the reigning gold medallist from the last Pride Games in 2016.

Margaret and Igor were also devoutly homosexual; like Stefan, they both expressed disgust at the thought of anyone outside the LGBTQ2+ community joining the gay leagues. They had written hate comments under one of the many ILGBTQ2+TA Facebook page posts about Khalid, one in particular called, *New Groundbreaking Straight Superstar Khalid Adam wins Detroit Tourney!* Margaret's response: *An absolute disgrace and slap in the face to the sanctity of gay organized sports!*, to which Igor clicked the heart emoji.

After realizing they were of the same opinion through the chain of combative pro and anti-heterosexual player posts, Margaret and Igor began direct messaging each other, sharing vitriol and conspiring to drive straight people out. When the tournament draws were released and Khalid had stacked up enough points to be seeded eighth, they saw their opportunity; the heterosexual needed to be put in his place.

***

The opening day of competition was beautiful. 22 degrees Celsius, sunshine with a bit of cloud cover, and hardly any wind. Humidity was low, which was a good sign for the North American players; the less humid it was, the more similar the European red clay courts would feel to North American true hard courts: fast and suitable for flatter, powerful shots. Since clay absorbed topspin so easily, it was common knowledge that the European players' main tactic would be to try to spin their opponents off the court.

Khalid and Joy walked through the tennis facility to get to his first round match. Holding hands, she could feel a little sweat coming off his palms. "You nervous, babe?"

"Maybe a bit. There's always that fear of travelling all this way to lose in the first round. But winning's not all that matters, right?"

"Whoever said that was a loser," she laughed. "Kidding! I'm just glad it's not me out there!"

He chuckled, and lifted the back of her hand to his lips, giving it a soft kiss.

As they neared the court, Joy noticed two shadows behind them, getting closer with each step. The figures reached the corner of her eye, then eventually cut in front. It was Margaret and Igor; Igor was holding his phone up and filming them.

"You guys have a lot of nerve!" Margaret shouted, her eyebrows arched, nostrils flaring.

"Excuse me?" Joy said. "Who are you?"

"Holding hands like that in public. You straights are disgusting! Flaunting your twisted love in our face like this!"

Igor moved in with his phone. "We're filming this and posting it everywhere. It will be viral! You'll be ruined! Cancelled!" he shouted, with his hard Russian accent.

"What are you talking about?" Khalid asked.

Margaret sneered. "You don't belong here! We want you out of these games! Go back to where you came from!"

Igor chimed in; "Yeah, go back to Walmart and eat your McDonalds or whatever you people do!"

Joy backed away; "You're crazy! Get that phone out of my face!"

The number of onlookers grew. "Girl, that's some drama, honey! Get me some popcorn," one of them quipped.

Khalid stepped in front, his face close to Margaret's. "You need to back up, ma'am! She's pregnant!"

"Oh my God! Fuckin' breeders!" Margaret said.

"Yeah, what you gonna do next? Have a gender reveal party? Project the binary crap on them? And guess what? Your baby's probably gonna be trans! Then look at all the time and money you wasted on pink confetti, assuming their sex! So there! HA!" Igor mocked.

Khalid tried to take the high road; "look I'm just here to play tennis. I'm not looking for any trouble."

"That's how it starts," Margaret replied. "You people invade our sports, pretending you're allies. Then it becomes all "Straight Lives Matter!" and shit. Then you'll have your own parade! Can you imagine? Straight pride?"

Igor laughed maniacally. "It would be the most boring parade ever! Excuse me while I nap! HA!"

Some giggles from the crowd.

"That's enough. Get out of my face!" Khalid said, raising his voice.

"Oh my God, I love it when straight guys get mad. So hot," a voice from the bystanders said.

"No, you get out of our face!" Margaret yelled. "*YOU* GET OUT OF *OUR* SPACE!"

Silence.

Margaret moved closer to Joy. "This life you have chosen is going to send you to hell! That child in there is the devil spawn!"

"Are you for real?" Joy said. "Is this some sort of joke?"

Khalid put his hand on Margaret's shoulder; "step away now!"

"Excuse me! Get your hand off of me! Someone call the police!"

"This ain't the States, bitch!" Bibi said, suddenly emerging from the crowd, Fred walking beside him with Gucci on a leash in one hand, and his phone filming the incident with the other. "Back off! Or I will break your big lesbian fist! No more tennis—or dates—for you!" Bibi shouted.

A gay gasp from the crowd.

"Stay out of this, traitor!" Margaret said. "And get that camera out of my face!"

"No, you fuckin' muncher, we're filming you, and *you'll* be ruined!" Bibi yelled.

Fred stuck his phone in Igor's and Margaret's face; Igor then shoved his phone in front of Fred's phone.

"You're cancelled!"

"No *you're* cancelled!"

"No *you're* cancelled! All straight people are cancelled!" Igor shouted.

The two men circled each other, thrusting their phones in each other's faces.

Gucci barked viciously, her large teeth on full display, causing Margaret to move back.

"You get that bitch under control!" Igor yelled.

"She's *your* friend!" Bibi shouted.

"What?"

"I'm not talking about the dog!" Bibi guffawed.

"Igor!" Margaret shouted; "let's go! Enough with these heathens!"

Igor put his phone down; "you better watch yourselves," he said to Khalid and Joy.

They turned and stomped away through the onlookers, Margaret yelling, "MOVE, I'M GAY! There's not many of us left here!"

Khalid, Joy, Bibi, Fred, and Gucci watched as they disappeared into the crowd.

Chapter 21: A Flutter

21a: The Sinker

The greeting from Margaret Fork and Igor Off didn't affect Khalid in his first round. He won, overcoming nerves and the flock of players coming specifically to watch "the straight guy from Canada with the big manly grunt who was accosted by the angry lesbian and mad laughing Russian."

The rest of the Canadians got through their first rounds as well. Stefan was relieved to not only win his first match, but also to get a nod of approval from Father Porsche, who had been intently watching.

Ernest was still giving the cold shoulder to his mother and Khalid. During his third round match a couple of days later, he found himself in a torturous battle with Rumi Meierhofer, a powerful yet crafty player from Switzerland. In the first set, his opponent mixed flat pace, slice, and short angles off his backhand to narrowly take the first set, 7-5.

Exhausted, discouraged, and down 2-4 in the second set, Ernest heard a familiar voice yell, "Come on boss! You got this!" A reminiscent whiff of … Axe body spray.

He looked around to see Khalid smiling at him, shaking his hands with both thumbs up. "You got this, boss!"

An old feeling resurfaced. Ernest suddenly felt his heart flutter; he began to half smile back, until he noticed that beside Khalid sat his mother, encouraging him as well. He looked away.

The flutter, which he had not felt in months—the sweet sensation of feeling like he mattered to someone—was enough to energize Ernest's play. Hitting with more power and depth, he came back and won the second set from Rumi, 6-4. After converting set point, he pumped a fist and turned to Khalid, who stood up and cheered. Khalid smiled; it was the first acknowledgement from Ernest in a long time.

He started the third set super tiebreak confidently, first serving an ace—a rarity—and then hitting a hard flat return in the corner. Up 2-0, and only eight points away from victory, Ernest glanced Khalid's way again, looking for more support.

However, he didn't see Khalid watching and cheering him. Rather, he saw Khalid in a lip lock with his mother. Ernest's heart—desperately seeking another lift—sank, rather sadly. So did his play. It all felt like slow motion; the blurred voice of the umpire announcing the score, the balls suspended in the air during long laboured rallies, his opponent's score increasing. His torture seemed prolonged, and all he could do was glance to the stands and watch the boy he loved, love someone else.

When it was over five minutes later—Ernest losing the super tiebreak 2-10, and thus, the match—he quickly packed his tennis bag and ran off the court before Khalid or Joy could come console him.

21b: Rafa

Two hours later, Ernest watched Abby and Scooter also get eliminated on courts beside each other. Scooter tried unsuccessfully to call close balls out to his advantage; the bounce marks on the clay proved he was a cheater. His opponent, as well as the crowd, didn't take to his strategy. Meanwhile, Abby's craftiness served no damage to her opponent from Rome; all European players knew how to deal with variety.

Ernest was relieved; he wasn't the only loser that day.

"Fuck this shit, bruh. Let's go to a bathhouse tonight. I've had enough of Deutschland!" Scooter declared, chugging his beer, as he, Ernest, and Abby sat in the hotel restaurant.

"Screw it, I'm having the croquettes and gelato," Ernest told the waitress.

"Bruh, I thought you were vegan."

"Oh, fuck off!" Ernest and Abby replied in unison.

Scooter continued. "So what do you say? I heard there's a good bathhouse called Rosa not too far from here." He turned to Abby, "Sorry, Abby, I'd invite you but I don't know if that was your thing. Actually, what is your deal? Are you a lez-bot or what?"

"Rude," Ernest snapped. "The term lez-bot is offensive."

Abby didn't seem bothered. "No. I hate labels ... but if I had to choose, I'd say I'm pansexual."

"What is that again? I get them all mixed up," Scooter said.

"I'm attracted to whomever I'm attracted to—boy, girl, and all that's in between."

"I respect that. I don't get it, but I respect it," Scooter nodded, chewing his pretzel with his mouth wide open, making no effort to lower the volume of his smacking.

"Thank you, Scooter. I wish more people would be open-minded like that." Abby smiled warmly.

Scooter turned back to Ernest; "so I guess it's you and me, bruh."

"I don't know. People here don't seem to be into me."

Scooter scoffed; "No way! There's bound to be someone who likes the little guys. Most importantly, you got the Black hipster thing going! That'll score some points!"

Ernest rolled his eyes.

***

Like any city hosting an Olympic Games, Bonn designated a pocket of the city for the athletes. Pride Village, as it was called, was literally sparkling and shiny. Ernest and Scooter walked the streets, delighted to see the multicoloured lights, red carpets rolled out in front of bar and club entrances, and cobblestone roads sectioned off as restaurant patios lit with glittering disco balls.

"Can we just do that?" Ernest asked Scooter, pointing to what looked like a tourist welcoming committee giving athletes backrubs in their chairs as they ate dinner. "I could totally use one of those."

In truth, Ernest just wanted a man to put his hands on him—to feel any human touch.

"Nah, I need dick, bruh. Let's just go to the bathhouse," Scooter replied.

"Fine."

Rosa bathhouse was easy to find, unlike the hidden entrance of the Apollo Spa in Toronto. "Jesus, what is this, a mini Disney castle?" Ernest asked, as they stood in front of the ornate mansion.

"Well, Mickey better be hung!" Scooter laughed.

The interior of Rosa was dark, yet warm and inviting. After exiting the change rooms, Scooter and Ernest entered the hall dimly lit with red light. The doors to the individual rooms were dark wood, the grains clearly visible. "So much more inviting than our cold and sterile Apollo, eh bruh?" Scooter asked.

"I've only been to the Apollo once," Ernest replied. "I don't remember what it looked like."

"Once, that's it?"

"Yeah. I've always been too shy to go to places like this."

"Well, have fun my friend! Just close your eyes and swipe right like no one is watching!"

"Ha."

"See you at the hotel later?"

"You're leaving me?" Ernest asked, worried.

"Well, yeah! I can't be holding your hand. I'd rather be holding something else."

"Right," Ernest nodded. "Have fun."

Scooter vanished into a hallway.

Unlike the long narrow alleyways and linear whirlpools of slate and ice blue of the Apollo, there were multiple rounded passages and a grand swirling staircase, the steps made of stone. Television screens playing porn lit the dark red walls; some areas of the hall completely dark and others with a more intense red light. Ernest climbed the stairs, still fearing he wouldn't find anyone to hook-up with. But the ambiance of the place made him feel better; if nothing else, this could be a fabulous tour of some interesting European architecture.

But four hours later at 3am, Ernest had walked circles, unable to make any connections. There was a chance something could have happened in the sauna when he was chatted up by a Portuguese guy who was competing in the Games for rowing; "you're adorable," the guy said to Ernest, who wasn't sure if that was code for *"I'd like to be plowing you in a few minutes."* Unfortunately, that wasn't what it meant. Another man—tall, muscular, and blonde—smiled at Ernest's prospect, and suddenly Ernest was sitting in the sauna alone again. *Is there anyone here who isn't hot?*

He was tired, sad, and worst of all, feeling sorry for himself. He had lost his match earlier. He felt bloated from eating meat and dairy. Feeling undesired and out of place, he decided he would leave and go back to the hotel to watch another telenovela.

While walking through the halls back to the locker room, Ernest felt a hand slightly brush his forearm. He stopped and raised his head; a tall man was staring down at him, his face faded in the dark.

"Hola," the man said.

"Hi."

"Were you leaving?"

Ernest detected an accent, but not sure which. "Yeah, I was."

"That's too bad."

The man came closer, Ernest getting a clearer view. Below his thinning hair, he was definitely handsome, with his slightly squinty eyes bookended by crow's feet, a pronounced nose, and—to Ernest's worry— noticeably large lips in a giant smile, slightly gummy, and a dimple on each side.

Ernest's self-consciousness naturally led to pessimism: *This man's mouth is too big for my dick. It'll be like sucking a stir stick for him.*

"You're adorable," the man said.

That phrase didn't end well for Ernest the last time he heard it. "Thanks."

"Would you like to talk for a little before you go?"

The politeness of the man's voice was comforting.

"Yeah, sure."

They walked slowly down the hall together, speaking quietly. Ernest learned the man was originally from Spain, but living in Bonn for work.

"What's your name?"

"Rafael."

"Rafael … like Rafa?" Ernest's voice perked up.

He laughed. "I'm a doctor, and I'm 42. And I don't play tennis. But you can call me Rafa if you like. Some of my friends do."

Ernest grinned.

"Are you here for the games? You enjoying them so far?" Rafael asked.

"Uh… yeah. I guess."

"Are you sure?"

"Yeah, I am. Bonn is beautiful. I'm just a little sad … I lost my match this afternoon."

"I'm sorry to hear. But now, you can enjoy the rest of the vacation."

"Thanks. You're right."

Rafael put his hand on Ernest's shoulder. "Listen, Ernest, no pressure, but if you are interested, we can go find a room. We don't have to do anything."

There was no hesitation in his reply. "Okay."

Rafael smiled and took Ernest by hand, then leading him back up the stairs to a room on the second level. "Is it okay if I close the door?"

he asked.

"Sure."

Rafael sat on the edge of the plastic mattress on the bed, gesturing to Ernest to come to him. He smiled, big white teeth emerging from his wide mouth. "You're adorable."

There's that word again. Adorable. But does "adorable" mean "fuckable?" "Thank you. You're very sexy."

"Actually, you're beautiful, Ernest."

Ernest had never been called that before.

Rafael put his hand on the side of Ernest's face and leaned in, eventually their lips touching. Ernest immediately noticed the difference in the sizes of their mouths and found it funny; *this man is going to swallow me whole.* But as it turned into a passionate kiss, the humour faded. Ernest felt something in him.

A flutter.

Rafael firmly embraced him, his hand creeping down and removing his own towel. Ernest felt nervous.

Rafael then reached to Ernest's waist and as he was about to loosen the towel, he stopped, moving his head back.

"Ernest, are you alright?"

"Yeah, why?"

"I could feel your neck tense up just now."

"I'm just a little nervous. That's all. But go ahead."

"You sure?"

"You have my consent!" Ernest blurted firmly.

Rafael moved his face closer to Ernest's again.

"We don't have to do anything you don't want."

"I know. Thank you. I appreciate that."

Ernest exhaled.

"You're relieved. I can see that," Rafael said, then picking up his towel and wrapping it back around his waist. Opening his arms, he said, "Aqui."

Ernest fell into his embrace.

"What do you wanna do?" Rafael whispered.

Ernest looked up at him. "I don't know ... can we just lie down?"

"Yes."

He lay down first, then pulled Ernest to lie down on his chest. As Rafael rubbed his shoulders, Ernest felt his body go limp, and he and closed his eyes. Turning his head slightly aside to rest on his ear, he could hear Rafael's heartbeat. "This is the best part of my trip," Ernest said.

"It's beating for you, beautiful."

Ernest giggled slightly. *That was cheesy as fuck, but I'll take it.*

A few hours later, Ernest felt a nudge on his arm.

"Ernest, it's 10:30 in the morning. We fell asleep," Rafael said.

***

Ernest's blissful feeling was abruptly snapped when returning to his hotel room. Abby, Scooter, Joy, and Khalid were all there, looking panicked.

"Where were you?" Joy asked.

Ernest: "Out."

Scooter smiled; "bruh, you scored last night! See, I knew the Europeans liked the chocolate, don't be such a pessimist!"

"You could've texted me back, you know," Joy said.

"I was busy."

"A short reply, like, 'yes, I'm alive' would've been nice," she replied, further agitated.

"Oh gawd, Mother. Relax."

"What? I was worried! You were gone all night! It's not like we're in Torpedo, okay?"

"Don't worry about me. Just go enjoy yourself as you were!" Ernest said, his voice increasing in intensity.

"What the hell's that supposed to mean?" Joy asked, taken aback.

"Yeah, well you've been pretty busy. And you got a new kid now, don't act like you care about the old one," Ernest said, looking at Khalid.

Scooter and Abby sensed they shouldn't be hearing this. "We'll be downstairs in the restaurant," Abby said as they left the room.

"That's low, Ernest," Joy replied, shaking her head. "I'm still your mother."

Ernest moved his gaze from Khalid back to Joy, raising his voice: "he was *MY* friend, Mother. I'm sure you knew how I felt about h— ... How could you not even tell me? You overshare everything, but then you kept this to yourself?!"

"I know, I'm sorry, okay? It just ... it just felt so nice to have something for myself. For once. But I didn't want to hurt you! I just needed more time!"

"Well too late." Ernest looked down at Joy's stomach. "I guess I'll be third in line now."

Joy, trying to hide the hurt in her voice, said, "I'm sorry, Ernest. I don't know what else to say except that I'm sorry I upset you." She walked past Khalid and out the door.

Khalid spoke cautiously; "boss, she was just worried. We all were."

Chapter 22: The Tale of the Racquet Stuck in the Tree 2.0

Ernest didn't sleep much after returning from the bathhouse. His emotions oscillated between glee, thinking about Rafael, and anger toward his mother.

Rolling out of bed, he picked up his phone; it was 3pm now, and Abby wasn't there.

Out doing touristy stuff, didn't want to wake you up. See you later, read her text. Wanting to avoid any further interaction with his mother or Khalid, he thought about what to do with himself. Then he remembered: Stefan was playing today.

As he entered the viewing area of the court, Ernest saw a hand wave at him. It was Father Porsche, who signaled to take the seat beside him.

As he made his way through the benches, Stefan put his hand up to his opponent to pause play. He was not going to play any points while being distracted by someone walking in his line of sight. Ernest sat down, noticing Stefan glaring at him until he was settled. He then signaled to his opponent to start again.

"Hello, Mr. Porsche."

"I heard you lost yesterday. What happened?"

Irritated, Ernest replied, "well nice to see you too. Yes, I lost. Thank you for the kind reminder."

"Because you don't eat meat. You're weak. You should—"

Ernest didn't want to have this conversation, interrupting, "how's Stefan doing?"

"He's getting through it. But still not playing his best. He should be killing this guy."

Ernest looked at the scoreboard. Stefan won the first set, 6-0 and was up 4-1 in the second.

Five minutes later, after Stefan won the next eight points in a row to finish the win, Father Porsche immediately got up to leave. "Oh well, at least he won. Have a good night."

Ernest walked down to the court level. Stefan was pleasantly surprised to see someone had come to see him play. "Thanks for watching. That's nice of you."

"Of course. You were playing well," Ernest said.

"So where you off to now? You gonna go hang with mommy and your new daddy?" Stefan said, thinking his joke was hilarious.

Ernest shook his head. "Not funny. No, nothing planned. Maybe just take in some sights around the city."

"Okay. Wanna take a short walk? There's a nice forest right beside the stadium."

"Sure."

Stefan led the way toward the trees. It was just past 6:30pm, a short time before sunset. Ernest looked up and took in the sights of the spruces, pines, beeches, and oaks in their various shades of green.

"So, you weren't kidding about your dad," Ernest said.

"How do you mean?"

"That he's a little nuts about you winning."

"Yup. That's Vater."

Ernest grinned.

Stefan sighed. "Sometimes, he's nice though. Whenever I did win as a kid, it was pretty awesome. I remember when I got my first trophy—I think I was five years old or something—he picked me up and hoisted me on his shoulders, like *I* was a trophy. It was like the fuckin' heavens opened up and I was the Prince of Bonn whenever he was proud," Stefan beamed. "That's all I wanted. Just make him proud ... You know, I'll never forget what he said when I told him I was gay."

"What was that?"

Stefan tried his best impression of his father, his German accent becoming thicker: "He said, 'all this time, I tried to make you something you were not. All this time, I knew something was wrong with you. Now I know. You shouldn't mention this to your mother.' It was big disappointment for him. So he pushed and pushed me to win at tennis, as if that would make up for it."

Ernest didn't know what to say. He tried to be upbeat: "But I'm sure he's proud of you now."

"I don't know about that," Stefan said dismissively. "Maybe if I were straight and the perfect manly tennis champ who destroyed everyone on court ... like Khalid ... then, he'd be proud. He always wanted *that* kind of son."

Ernest noticed Stefan's mood had turned melancholy. "Stef, you okay?"

Stefan's face softened and he smirked a bit. "I remember one huge match I had in juniors. I was seven, I lost to a little blonde six-year-old with pigtails. Peggy Bock. I must have been half a foot taller than her. Vater never let me forget that."

"She was six? She must have been good."

"Skill wise, she was decent. But nowhere near me at the time."

"So, how'd she beat you?"

"Moonballs ... death by a thousand moonballs."

Ernest laughed. "Isn't that the death of all of us?"

"It's funny isn't it?" Stefan remarked. "The moonball is the most pussy shot. Yet it humbles everyone so easily, because you don't expect it to. And it thrives on you doubting yourself, and then you just ... beat yourself. Worst way to lose, period."

"I'd agree."

Stefan looked up and stopped walking. He started to chuckle. "I was so distraught when I lost that match. It was at this venue, you know? Vater was embarrassed. I ran out to this very forest and threw my racquet into a tree, and it got stuck."

Ernest laughed too. "You threw a racquet into a tree? How'd you get it down?"

"I didn't." Stefan pointed up to the branches of the giant tree in front of them.

Ernest raised his head to see a vintage grey aluminum Dunlop racquet, weathered and dirty.

Ernest's mouth was wide open. "That's your racquet? It's been there all this time?"

"Ja! That's it!" Stefan howled. "Still fuckin' there! 33 years and no one could get it down! Not one damn person in Germany!" Stefan said, now laughing so hard that he squatted, resting his face on his knees. "My moment of shame, on display, forever!"

Ernest laughed with him; it was rare to see Stefan like this: bright with a big smile; hearty laugh. Stefan almost never let himself be loose. It looked nice on him, Ernest thought.

They stood, admiring the racquet, while continuing to giggle, and then started their way back to the tennis centre.

"Have I told you about my friend from before? Gabe Lamb? He was part of the league years ago."

"Yeah, I've heard his name a few times."

"He was notorious for moonballing. Junking too. Drove me nuts."

"You must have hated that."

Stefan's tone turned sombre again. "He was my best friend. We'd do everything together."

"I heard you guys were close."

"We were." Stefan stopped to look at the sunset. "I actually loved him."

"You did?"

"I even stupidly told him. It was after a practice match one day in Toronto. We'd always go to this little market in Summerhill and get ice cream after. It was like 7pm, you know that time of the day when the sun is setting, and you get that cotton candy orange-pink sky? It was the perfect moment ... golden. I looked into his hazel eyes, the last rays of the sun reflecting in them, and then said it. 'Gabe, I love you. I want to be more than a friend. I think we would be good together.'"

"And?"

Stefan stopped walking again and turned to Ernest, locking eyes. "I leaned in to kiss him."

"And?"

"He held the sides of my face, gently. Like he caressed it. Then he lowered my head and kissed me on the forehead, saying, 'I love you too Stef, but not the same way. I'm sorry.'"

Stefan's sad blue eyes coincidentally reflected the last rays of the setting sun at that moment.

"Then what?" Ernest asked, feeling pity for him.

"I couldn't handle it. I distanced myself after. Basically threw away our friendship."

"Where is he now?"

"I don't know. He just took off. Ghosted everyone. That was almost a decade ago," Stefan sighed. "But I think about him sometimes. A lot, actually."

A few seconds of silence, until a bunch of cuckoo birds chirped and flew out of the branches in formation toward the setting sun.

Their eyes followed the birds.

Stefan continued, "so that day, I dropped him off, went home and called my mom and just bawled like a little girl. I said I was sad because I had lost some big match that day. She listened. I felt like she knew what had happened, even though I didn't say it. I miss her."

One last bird leaped off its branch and soared in the same direction as the group before.

Stefan seemed to be in a trance; "I don't know which day was sadder: the day I lost that match to that little girl, or the day I came out to Vater, or the day Gabe said that to me. Or the day that Vater called me to tell me mom died. There's too may of those days to choose from."

Ernest reached over and put his hand on Stefan's shoulder, patting it softly like the night they were on the side of the road in Torpedo. They looked at each other, without saying a word, feeling more connected than before.

Suddenly, Stefan heard his phone alert and grabbed it from his pocket. Snapping out of his trance, his eyes widened and panicked. "Fuck!"

"What?" Ernest asked.

"It's Bibi. He's in the hospital—again!"

Chapter 23: Executive Meeting 3 — *An Ode to The Sparrow*

Rushing through the Bonn Hospital hallway, Stefan was greeted by Gucci's loud barking. "Sorry, but someone needs to kill that bitch," he muttered to Ernest.

"Terrible," Ernest commented.

They entered Bibi's room to find him asleep, hooked up to an IV; Fred stood over him.

"How is he?" Stefan asked.

"Stable."

"Is he going to be alright?" Ernest asked.

"I hope so. No, I know so," Fred replied, his voice cracking. "He'll be fine," he said, trying to convince the room, most of all, himself.

"What happened?"

"He said he was feeling a little weak early this afternoon. I told him to go lie down, so he did. But then I couldn't wake him up for lunch. His pulse was slow and faint, and he was freezing, so I asked the hotel to get us to an emergency room. I don't know what happened, he's been eating better the last couple weeks since the first round of treatment ended."

"Did the doctor say what it was?"

"Just that he was severely dehydrated and low on potassium."

"That's all they said?"

"Well yeah. But it could be—" Fred's eyes teared, and he covered his hand with his mouth.

"What?" Stefan asked. "Could be what?"

"Shit. I'm not supposed to tell you."

"Fred, just tell us. It's fine."

Fred took a moment to wipe his eyes.

"Fred! Eye contact!" Stefan snapped.

"Stefan! Calm down!" Ernest said.

Stefan lowered his voice. "Sorry. He's my best friend. Please."

Fred took a deep breath, and then nodded. "Right before we left for this trip, he had another scan."

"Yeah?"

"The tumour's spread. They found two spots on his liver," Fred said, barely holding it together.

"No," Stefan whispered, feeling his body cave in. His eyes moved to Bibi, looking smaller than ever, sleeping peacefully on his bed.

How can something this bad happen to someone so good?

"Fuck!" Stefan shouted, then left the room.

Ernest walked to the hospital bed, placing his hand on Bibi's arm. It was cold to the touch, and his skin felt paper thin. On the small table beside him was Bibi's purple writing journal.

"You brought his writing book?" Ernest asked.

"Yes," Fred responded. "He's been writing a lot … says he's been feeling inspired since he got sick."

***

Two hours went by; Fred left to walk Gucci around the hospital grounds. Ernest paced back and forth, while Stefan sat and watched Bibi closely, determined to see any signs of improvement.

"Do you want me to get you something to eat from downstairs, Stef?" Ernest asked.

"No, I'm good."

"You haven't eaten since before your match today. You need to start carbing up for your match tomorrow."

"I'm not hungry."

"What are you gonna do? Just sit there and stare at him for another two hours?"

"If I have to, Ernest, yes, I will. I want to be here when he wakes up. What if he wakes up and I'm not here?"

"Ok, fine. I'm going to get something for *us* in case you want it," Ernest said, heading toward the door.

Bibi suddenly moved his head, seemingly trying to adjust his pillow. Ernest rushed back to the bed.

"B!" Stefan said desperately. "You're awake!"

Stefan turned to Ernest, "See I told you. You just have to have some faith." He turned back to Bibi. "Are you comfortable? You want a new pillow?"

Bibi wearily opened his eyes. Focusing on Stefan's face, he smirked. "Stef, you look like shit," his voice thin and raspy.

Stefan cracked a smile.

"And Miss Woke is here too?" Bibi said, looking at Ernest.

"Are you feeling better?" Ernest asked.

"A bit. I must be a mess. How do I look?"

Stefan grabbed his phone, turned the camera on to selfie mode, and put it in front of Bibi.

"Oh lawd," Bibi said.

"You look good," Ernest said with encouragement.

Bibi's voice perked up. "Sweetie, I look amazing! I bet the nurse is wondering how could I be dying when I look so good?" Bibi cackled.

They laughed.

Bibi's eyes circled the room. "Where's Fred?"

"He took Gucci for a walk. He'll be back."

"Oh, okay. Well then now's a good time for me to tell you."

"What?" Ernest asked. "Does Fred make you feel inferior because he's the white man? I knew it!"

Stefan rolled his eyes.

"Ha! No," Bibi answered ... "Fred always thinks I'm crazy when I talk about it."

"What?"

Bibi looked out the window, "Is he here?"

"No, I just said Fred took the dog for a walk."

"No, not him. The sparrow?"

"What sparrow?"

Bibi leaned in, as if to tell them a secret. "Stef, you know there's this little bird. It's called a song sparrow. It's brown and white. Kinda stripe-y with some spots. Sings a lot."

"Okay?"

"When I was getting my chemo back in Torpedo, this sparrow would always sit on the same branch and stare at me through the window. I know it was the same one every time! I'd open the window sometimes and we'd chit-chat."

Puzzled, Stefan and Ernest looked at each other, then looked back, keeping face.

Bibi continued; "well, just yesterday I saw the same bird near in a tree near our hotel window. I think it followed me here, you know? There's none of those sparrows in Europe."

"Huh?" Stefan uttered, sounding as if Bibi had lost his mind. "Um, okay, B. I think you need to rest a bit more."

Ernest nodded.

Bibi pointed to the journal; "so I wrote a poem about him. Stef, can you get my writing book?"

"Sure."

"Turn to the last page. There's a pen clipped onto it."

Stefan did so.

"The poem's unfinished. I couldn't think of the last part," Bibi said. "But now I think I got it. Do you wanna hear it?"

"Yeah," Stefan replied.

"I'd love to," Ernest said.

Bibi turned to Stefan. "Stef, can you read what I have so far?"

"Out loud?"

"Yeah."

Stefan suddenly felt self-conscious. "*An Ode to The Sparrow*," he read, then looking up. "That's a nice title."

"Thanks."
Stefan read it slowly, mindful not to trip on his words:

"The wings of the sparrow open to the sky,
and soar toward the stars, never reaching too high;
they hold on to clouds, to defy their end,
but soon comes the storm, and the sparrow must bend.

The songs of the sparrow, so sombre, forlorn,
Sing tales of past promise, of which they are borne;
they hum, whistle, and sing a new song,
but fall short of reaching the beauty they long.

The heart of the sparrow—"

Stefan looked up. "That's all you wrote, B. It's pretty great so far. Amazing, actually."

"I have the ending in my head now. Stef, can you write the words down as I say them?"

"Sure." Stefan pulled the cap off the pen.

Bibi cleared his throat, his voice thin and breathy:

"The heart of the sparrow remembers its youth,
amidst broken branches and earth and truth;
it searches and gathers and sows what it gleans,
while it weeps, weeps, weeps for its star-crossed dreams."

A few seconds passed as Stefan finished writing the last few words.

"Bibi," Ernest said, awestruck. "That was … just beautiful."

"Thank you, hun. Yes, another poem down!" Bibi exhaled.

Stefan scanned the page quickly again, pensive. "It is beautiful …

but it's fucking depressing! You gotta stop reading dead old white man poetry!" he said, agitated.

Bibi laughed. "It's so weird guys, I used to get such bad writer's block. But lately the words have just been flowing out of me, ever since I've been thinking about dying. Ha!"

Stefan: "Nope. Not funny."

Bibi: "Oh please! Life is just one big joke. You just don't get it!"

Stefan became serious again. "Why didn't you tell us?"

Bibi: "Tell you what?"

"Fred told us," Ernest said. "About it spreading to your liver."

"Oh, he worries too much. And I knew you would too. I'll be fine."

Stefan and Ernest looked unconvinced.

Bibi smirked again. "Plus, if I die, Ernest, you can have my tennis trophies. They make great table centerpieces."

Ernest chuckled, "oh Miss Butterball."

Bibi then looked at Stefan. "And Miz Prez … I bequeath thee, my porn."

Stefan was aghast. "Your porn? *I* want your trophies! Give your jizz flicks to Ernest!"

Bibi, theatrically: "Ungrateful bastard! How dare you! My porn is categorized! How can you turn that down? Hashtag priorities!" Bibi turned the other way and dramatically plopped back into his pillow, closing his eyes.

Ernest grabbed Bibi's arm; they both started giggling.

Stefan shook his head. "Unbelievable."

Chapter 24: "Make Tennis Gay Again!"

24a. A Precedent

The quarterfinal rounds had extra pressure: winners would advance to the semifinals—the stage where the gold, silver, and bronze medals were decided.

The previous evening with Bibi appeared to have released tension in Stefan. He quickly dismissed his opponent; his powerful forehand and backhand hitting every corner. At the end of the match, Father Porsche stood up and applauded with pride, cheering "Ja!" so loud that everyone else in the stands turned around and looked. Beside him sat Ernest, whom he pulled by the arm to do the same.

"What's wrong with you? Cheer for Stefan!"

"I'm happy he won," Ernest said, "but do we really need to cheer so loud when he won 6-0, 6-1? Plus, do we want to make his opponent feel bad?"

"I don't know about you, Ernest. You don't eat meat, you talk all this nonsense. You're a funny boy."

"It's not nonsense, it's just being respectful. You know, nice."

"I don't agree with you."

"Okay."

"And that's not because you're Black."

"Huh?" *This again?*

"I'm not racist, okay? I'm the same with everyone—Black, White, purple, I don't care."

Ernest chuckled, deciding to leave it as is. "Yes, okay. I understand, Mr. Porsche."

Back at court level, Stefan packed his tennis bag, satisfied with his win. Then, he heard footsteps approach behind him.

"The audacity!" a voice said.

Stefan saw Margaret and Igor standing in front of him, their arms crossed. Though they had never spoken, he knew who they were. It was common for players to watch other players' matches and assess their competition.

And in this case it proved useful; they too were in the semifinals scheduled for the next day; Igor was to play Stefan, and Margaret to play Khalid.

"What?" Stefan said.

"How could you?" Igor said in an accusatory tone.

"How could I what?"

"We messaged you on Facebook, Stefan. You never replied," Margaret said.

He remembered. He didn't want to deal with those messages, so he ignored them.

Margaret: "What kind of leader are you? How could you let them invade your league? Despicable!"

Stefan: "Them?"

"Don't act like you don't know who we're talking about. The breeders. The straight people."

This was the moment Stefan dreaded: having to defend *not* kicking Khalid out of the league to other gay leagues. "It's just one guy."

"And soon other leagues will be expected to do the same! Do you see what you've done? You've set a precedent!"

Stefan huffed. "Listen, I don't like it either, but what am I supposed to do? Ban him?"

"Straight-bash that fucker!" Igor responded.

"Yeah," Margaret said. "We need to make tennis gay again!"

"He just wants to play, then let him." Stefan leaned in, lowering his voice. "One of us will just have to beat him."

Margaret and Igor glared back at Stefan in disapproval.

Stefan zipped his tennis bag and strapped it on his back. "Whatever. You just worry about your own leagues. See you tomorrow," he said, then walking away.

Just before exiting the gate, he felt something hit the back of his head. He turned around and looked to the ground to see a banana peel. He then reached up to feel the smashed banana goo in his hair and on his shoulders.

"How do you like that now?" Margaret yelled, then starting to laugh.

"What the fuck? Screw you!" Stefan said as he pulled gate shut.

24b. "You Need to Check Yourself, Ernest!"

Before departing the tennis centre, Father Porsche invited Stefan for dinner later that evening. "Hotel food is too much sodium. It's slowing you down, Stefan. I could see it in your match. Your split step isn't fast enough. You should come to the house for dinner tonight. I'll make you cabbage rolls. You'll see in your match tomorrow—you'll be faster than Novak!"

"It's okay, Vater," Stefan said. "I like the food at the hotel. And I don't want to tire you out."

"Come on!" Father Porsche insisted.

"How about if I win the gold? Then we can celebrate with a big dinner."

"*If* you win the gold? *When* you win the gold!"

"Yes, yes. We'll see," Stefan said, brushing him off.

"Okay." Father Porsche turned to Ernest. "And what about you? Want to come over for dinner? You're so thin and pale, my God! I know you're Black, but I can still tell you're pale. And that's not racist. I'm concerned."

Ernest looked at Stefan, as if to ask for help.

Stefan shook his head. "That's enough, Vater. Just do me a favour, if you have anything to say about Ernest being Black, just don't say it, okay? Now go home and relax!"

Father Porsche stared at his son. "Okay. Sleep early, you hear me, son?" Father Porsche turned and walked toward the parking lot.

Ernest smiled. "I thought that was really nice of him to invite you for dinner. He really seems to be making an effort."

Stefan raised his eyebrows. "Remember what I told you: it's like the heavens open up when I win, and I'm the Prince of Bonn. But if I lose, that'll be it for him."

"I think it's genuine though. He just wants you to do well."

"People don't change, Ernest. How many times do I have to tell you?"

"Of course they do. Look at my mother and Khalid. I thought Khalid was my friend. And my mother—I just can't believe she's doing this to me."

Stefan thought for a second. "Your mom raised you alone, right? Your dad wasn't around?"

"No. I've never met him."

"And she never had a man all this time?"

"Nope. Just her and I."

"Well, maybe just take it easy on her. Let her have this thing for herself for once," Stefan said.

Ernest stopped. "Have you been talking to her?"

"No!" Stefan chuckled slightly. "Look I'm not taking sides, but, she's done a lot for you. Maybe this is just what makes her happy … You only have one mother. Don't take it for granted. Trust me, I know."

Ernest looked around at the trees. *Point taken.*

Stefan apologized. "Sorry, I didn't mean to tell you what to do."

Ernest diverted the conversation, smirking. "Well, speaking of changing, I did too. I took your advice and put myself out there. Guess who went to a bathhouse the other night?"

Stefan was taken aback. "What? You?"

"Yeah, why not? I'm out of the tournament anyway. Only way I was gonna get laid on this trip."

"Well, that was your choice. I offered—"

"Let's not talk about that okay?"

Pause.

"So," Stefan sneered, "how was it? You meet anyone?"

"Si si! A sexy Spanish man, named Rafa!"

"Well, then." Stefan's shoulders lowered, and he crossed his arms. "Good for you. Did you do it?"

"I'm not saying. A lady never kisses and tells."

"Excuse me."

Ernest was hoping Stefan would be more excited for him.

Suddenly a Grindr alert sounded from Ernest's pocket.

Stefan: "What was that? Gawd, are you in heat now?"

Ernest pulled out his phone. "Oh. I got a message! I'll check it later."

"No, check it now. I wanna see," Stefan said, trying to restrain his curiosity.

"No, why?"

"Come on."

Ernest exhaled, looking at the message on his phone. *Hey cutie. Wanna hook up?* the message read. He looked at the picture; "oh, I don't know about that," he said.

"Let me see his pic," Stefan asked.

"No, never mind, not my type."

Stefan grabbed the phone from Ernest and looked at the profile. "What's wrong with him?"

"He's 6'3"."

"And?"

"And … he's Black."

"And?"

"He'll be …" Ernest didn't want to say it. "He'll be huge! It'll be painful!"

"What? That's racist! Against your *own* race! That's so messed up!" Stefan laughed.

"Oh, come on. You know what they say. *And* he's tall! He'll rip me right in half."

Stefan began to howl. "You're nuts! You're being totally ridiculous right now!"

"Shut up!"

"Just read his profile at least."

Ernest swiped to read it; his face quickly showing disappointment. "No, I don't think that it'll work"

"Why? Did he list his dick size? You scared?" Stefan laughed.

Ernest's face remained serious. "No."

"Well, then what is it?" Stefan snatched the phone out of Ernest's hand and read the screen. Under *HIV status*, it read, *Positive Undetectable.*

"Is it because—?"

"Well … yeah," Ernest shrugged his shoulders, sounding guilty.

"He's undetectable. He can't transmit anything to you."

"Well, still …. Do we know that for sure?"

Stefan moved his head back slightly, concerned. His face creased up. "What? You sound … ignorant."

Ernest became defensive. "You're judging me? The guy who is heterophobic?"

"What you said is ignorant. You think I'm a bigot and *I* even know that."

"Would you sleep with someone with that status?"

"I …" Stefan was flustered. "I'd have to think about it first … but yeah, I would."

"See … you're not sure! How can I believe you?" Ernest said angrily, pointing his finger.

Stefan shook his head. "Don't point your finger at me, okay? You rag on me all the time for being offensive and politically incorrect, and you act like you're all perfect and righteous!"

"I do not!"

"Yeah, you do! And I don't pretend to be this social justice warrior like you."

"You're just mad because being politically correct means you can't act like an asshole anymore!"

"You think you're better than everyone … but you're the same way! You have the same issues and same prejudices as the rest of us! You need to check yourself, Ernest!"

"You know what, fuck you!"

"Fuck you!"

They stood frozen, staring at each other, more disconnected than ever.

"I gotta go rest for my match," Stefan said, turning and leaving Ernest alone in the shade of the oak trees.

Chapter 25: Semifinals — Fuck the High Road!

"You're a disgrace for a president," Igor Off muttered in his heavy Russian accent.

That was one of many comments said to Stefan during their semifinal match. Stefan tried to be the bigger person. To be empathetic. He understood that being the defending Pride Games gold medalist, Igor could have felt threatened by Khalid. Or afraid of difference or change.

But Stefan's patience was wearing thin. Any time the linesmen accurately called one of Igor's shots out, Igor questioned it. On three occasions, he walked on to Stefan's side of the court to inspect the marks—a definite sign of disrespect and cause for default in some professional tournaments. Arguing that the wrong marks were called, he finally yelled at the linesman, "you cannot be serious! … Goddammit! Are you blind or are you straight?" and then urged the umpire to throw the linesman out.

Father Porsche—sitting with Ernest, Abby, and Scooter—was confused. "Why isn't Stefan talking back to this asshole? He needs to tell him off already!"

"That's right, man! Take the Russian commie down, Stef!" Scooter yelled.

Ernest and Abby swapped glares, hoping others in the stands wouldn't look at them.

Stefan remained focused, and after impressively winning the first set 6-3 and breaking Igor's serve and then holding serve in the second to go up 5-2, he looked up to see his father with his hands pressed together, praying to the sky.

He took a deep breath and played the last game with renewed energy, smacking three forehand winners, and arriving at triple match point, 0-40.

Igor served, and Stefan ran around his backhand and clobbered the forehand return inside out past Igor's backhand. He'd won. The Canadian contingent cheered louder; Father Porsche, almost in tears, was now praising the sky.

Disappointed, Igor walked to the net to shake Stefan's hand. Having taken all the insults over the last hour and a half and staying quiet, Stefan could only think one thing: *Fuck the high road!* As they were about to touch, Stefan pulled his hand away. "You're an asshole!" he said coldly to Igor, then walking to his chair.

"That's my boy!" Father Porsche said. "Tell him off!"

An elated Stefan exited the court a few minutes later; Father Porsche stood there, his arms open. "You made it to the gold medal match, son! You're going to win it all! I'm so proud of you!" he exclaimed, pulling his son in for a hug. Stefan closed his eyes, trying to savour the feeling. *"I'm so proud of you."*

***

Like the first semifinal, the next one between Margaret and Khalid was noted not for the tennis, but for the drama. Apart from a venomous stare every few points, Margaret started the match relatively quiet.

Khalid ignored her; barely looking up in between points and playing as usual. It worked; he won the first set 6-2, and then walked to his chair for the changeover.

BUMP.

He looked up; Margaret had intentionally shoved her shoulder into his side, a smirk on her face. "What the fuck?" she sneered. He didn't reply and sat down.

"Did you see that?" she screamed at the umpire. "This guy's a lunatic! He bumped me on purpose! Throw him out! He's abusive!"

"I didn't see that," the chairman said.

Joy yelled from the stands, "Bitch, you're crazy!"

Unfortunately, the bump did rattle Khalid, and nerves crept into his game. His shots fell into the short court, and Margaret capitalized by coming into the net and volleying points away, confirming her nickname as "The Iron Fist." She won the second set, 7-5.

Before they began the third set super tiebreak, the umpire called Khalid over. "I'm sorry but you're going to have to try and lower the volume of your grunt, or not grunt at all," the umpire said.

"What?"

"She claims she's distracted and can't hear the ball being hit."

"I've been grunting this whole time, nobody said anything before." Khalid then looked at Margaret, who yelled, "What? What's your problem?"

Rattled and trying to suppress any noise, Khalid served a double fault, and then missed the next two service returns. The anxiety he felt months ago in the CGO final against Scooter had returned. Netting another easy shot, he knew it: he was having the yips.

Taking a huge breath in and exhaling it out, Khalid repeated in his head, *just hit the ball into the court, and run. Just hit the ball into the court, and run.*

Two long rallies followed, and Margaret showed signs of buckling, mis-hitting a volley and then an overhead. As they changed sides, she led 4-2.

Khalid then saw a familiar face peeking in from the seating entrance. Ernest was watching. Khalid nodded; Ernest reciprocated.

Suddenly perking up, Khalid returned to the baseline, taking small hops before the point started. *Just hit the ball into the court, and run.* His shots landed deeper, and he spun his forehand up as hard and as high as he could, successfully hitting the shots at Margaret's feet or over her head. She threw her racquet on the ground, only giving Khalid more confidence. On match point, he passed her with a cross-court backhand, winning 10-5.

She refused to shake Khalid's hand at the net after. As he cautiously walked past her to exit the court, she grabbed a ball and stepped in his way: "I'm going to shove this ball down your fuckin' throat!" He walked around her and off the court, but Margaret wasn't done. "That'll make you gay, asshole!"

Passing the gate, Khalid picked Joy up and swung her around; "holy shit!" she said giddily, "you're in the finals, babe! You're in it for the gold!"

He put her down and took a deep breath. "Yeah ... against Stefan."

With a warm and comforting smile, Joy put her hand on his arm and gave it a squeeze. "You got this."

"Where's Ernest?" he asked, looking around. "I saw him watching at the end of the match."

"He was? I didn't even know he came."

Chapter 26: Finals — Gold, Bloody Gold

Now was the time to practice superstitions.

Stefan did his usual pre-final selfie social media post, but with some modification: instead of emoting the brooding blue steel expression, he smiled, mouth slightly open. The regular hashtag of #championshipmatchglory was replaced by #grateful2Bhere. It was accurate; he was playing his best tennis, with a chance to win the biggest title in his accomplished tennis life. Most of all, he felt he somewhat gained his father's approval; he just hoped that would still be the case regardless of what colour medal he ended up with.

As Stefan unpacked his massive tennis bag on the bench, he noticed there weren't any changes to Khalid's rituals. On the ground in front of Khalid's chair lay his water bottles in a perfect line, one filled with orange liquid, and the other two presumably water.

"Alright gentlemen, come on up to the net for a photo," said the representative from Lufthansa, the Pride Games sponsor. The finalists approached while not making eye contact and stood beside each other at the net. A couple of snaps were taken, then a "thanks guys. Have a good match," uttered. The sponsor exited.

"Good luck," Khalid said quietly.

Stefan hesitated, and looked up. "Yeah, you too."

They walked to the baseline and began their warm up.

Father Porsche and the Toronto contingent sat in the third row.

"I don't know about Stefan," Father Porsche said. "He's got this look in his eye. Like fear or something."

"I'm sure he's just nervous," Ernest said, feeling some uneasiness himself, looking two rows ahead of him where Joy was sitting.

He caught his mother and Khalid staring at each other, she in her seat and him on court. She gave him a thumbs up and big smile, to which Khalid smiled and responded with a wink; he then placed his hands on his heart and extended them to her. Joy beamed.

Ernest looked away; the love connection between them still stung. But he looked back at his mother again—a big wide smile, hands clapping to encourage Khalid—Joy was joyful. He found himself grinning slightly. He hadn't seen her happy like that in a long time.

She suddenly turned around and saw Ernest staring at her, smiling cautiously and slightly lifting her hand to wave. He looked away.

"I think Khalid's forehand is way too strong for Stefan," a man behind Ernest said. They turned around. "I caught a few of their earlier matches," the man continued. "The straight guy's going to be tough."

This was not something Father Porsche wanted to hear. "Who are you?"

"Holy shit. Francesco!" Scooter said, walking down the aisle to sit beside Abby.

"Scooter, good to see you! It's been a while," Francesco said.

"Good to see you too, bruh!" Scooter gave an introduction, "Guys, this is Francesco, he used to be the president of the old league in Toronto."

"You're Francesco Zappone?" Ernest asked.

"Yeah."

"You played in the tournament?" Father Porsche asked.

"No, I'm recovering from an injury right now, so just watching for these Games. But I used to play with Stefan when I lived in Canada."

"I'm Ernest. I've heard about you."

"Oh yeah? Stefan and I used to be pretty competitive back then. We actually have some unfinished business."

That was a diplomatic way to say it, Ernest thought. He had heard that Stefan and Francesco were rivals on court, and frenemies off it.

"I'm Otto. Stefan is my son."

"Hello. Good luck," Francesco said. His eyes stopped on Abby, peculiarly.

"Have we met?" he asked.

"Maybe ... I don't remember," she replied.

They turned their attention back to the court; the warm up was over.

***

Unlike their one-sided semifinal in Toronto, this match was closer. Both players camped in the corners of the court, protecting their backhand and eager to clobber forehands as much as possible. Stefan got most of his first serves in, starting the point on the offensive. He dictated points with his trusty forehand and won the first set 6-3, to which his father raised his fist in encouragement.

"Get him!" Margaret shouted from the stands, cackling with Igor. Neither player acknowledged them.

Khalid was more aggressive in the second set, spinning his forehands even higher to Stefan's backhand. Now hitting from his weaker side above his shoulders, Stefan struggled to maintain the same depth as in the first set. Khalid moved in on shorter shots, either smacking them to the other corner, or feathering them for a drop shot.

Then Stefan's serve began to fail him. Down 3-4, he double faulted twice to lose his serve. Khalid quickly closed the second set with two big service winners.

The Pride Games finals differed from the rest of the finals of the league; the third and deciding set was not a super tiebreak to ten points. Rather, Stefan and Khalid had to play out the set in full to six games.

Back in the stands, Ernest had been thinking of the question he wanted to ask for the last hour and a half. He got up and moved to the row behind, sitting beside Francesco, who was joined by two friends.

"Hi, Francesco," Ernest said.

"Hey Ernest. These are my friends, Kevin and Geff. They're from the UK."

They nodded and smiled. "Hi, nice to meet you Ernest," Geff said.

"Hello," Ernest replied.

"So, where are you from?"

"Torpedo Valley, Canada."

"Lovely. So how have you been liking Bonn so far?" Kevin said.

Ernest didn't want to waste time on pleasantries; he ignored them, and leaned into Francesco. "So, can I ask you a question?"

"Uh, okay sure," Francesco replied.

Geff raised his eyebrows and pursed his lips, mumbling to Kevin, "Well excuse me, I thought Canadians were supposed to be polite."

Kevin nodded in agreement. "That bitch."

Ernest continued. "Francesco, I've been wanting to find something out. Can you tell me why the Torches' league ended? Nobody seems to want to talk about it."

Francesco's smile quickly disappeared. "Oh, that's a long story."

"Okay?"

"I don't really want to get into it right now."

Ernest was disappointed.

"All I can say is, I've never been so ashamed."

Ernest was intrigued. "Really?"

"Yeah ... Ernest, is Stefan your friend?"

"Well, yeah."

"With all due respect, Stefan knows the answer to your question, and he needs to make it right. Hopefully, when the chance presents itself, and he's ready."

"Huh? Can't you just tell me right now?"

Francesco then looked back down at the court. "They're starting the third set. You better get back to your seat."

"Right."

On court, Stefan rummaged through his bag, finding his trusty book of notes. He read the various strategies listed: *Go to the net; hit down the centre of the court; visualize yourself as your favourite player*

... Stefan continued to scan the list, then stopping on number 7: *Win ugly*. The changeover time was up; he put his book down.

Then, catching his eye as he walked to the baseline were Khalid's three water bottles; perfectly lined up. Stefan stepped closer to them, slightly lifting his foot to kick them over.

But then something stopped him.

He shifted to his right, leaving the bottles as they were. He looked up at his father and Ernest, who were clapping and cheering for him.

The quality of the match rose in the third set; rallies got longer, balls deeper, and Stefan and Khalid were grunting louder than ever.

At four games all, the fifth deuce, Stefan hoped the nerves—the yips—that sometimes invaded Khalid's game would make an appearance. He suspected they were creeping up; in the past five minutes, Khalid's balls were falling shorter in the court, and he seemed flat-footed. Stefan approached the net and Khalid slid on the clay, tossing up a lob. It sailed high past Stefan's head, then caught an opposing gust of wind that blew it back toward baseline, bouncing just inside. Stefan tossed his racquet to the ground in horror. Break point for Khalid.

Stefan then went for a big serve in the corner; Khalid mis-hit his forehand. They both watched as the ball floated back, hit the tape of the net, and after appearing to sit on top of it forever, bounced on Stefan's side. Joy and Father Porsche screamed at the same time, but for different reasons. Khalid was now leading 5-4, and would serve for the gold medal win after the break.

Khalid sat, toweled off his face, and repeated in his head; *Don't let the nerves get to you. Just hit the ball into the court, and run.* He tipped his head back and closed his eyes, trying to find some calmness.

Meanwhile, Stefan had plopped himself on his chair, stunned at his bad luck. His anger only grew.

He then remembered something and looked into his tennis bag. Ernest's wooden racquet. He pulled it out and raised it for Ernest to see. Although they had not spoken to each other since arguing the day before, Ernest nodded. Stefan then bashed it on the ground, the sound of it snapping and breaking in half causing everyone to stare. He felt better, having released some anger and not wasting in on an actual racquet.

"I'm sorry Stefan, but I'm still going to have to give you a warning for racquet abuse, even though that wasn't your racquet," the umpire said.

"That's fine. Just needed to get that out."

Stefan picked up his racquet and began to walk to the baseline as Khalid sat, still closing his eyes.

THEN, SUDDENLY—

In the left corner of his vision, Stefan saw a figure in the stands in all black with a ski mask running on to the court towards Khalid. He was holding a knife, its blade below his clenched fist, about 15 feet away from Khalid's back.

Without thinking, Stefan ran toward the man and body-checked him. Then a piercing scream from Joy was heard.

Khalid turned around to see that Stefan and the man had fallen to the ground, red clay flying. As the man got up, Stefan jolted up and forward, punching the man in the face. He fell to the ground again, and was restrained by a couple of spectators who ran on court.

"What's happening?" Father Porsche screamed, as he, Ernest, Scooter, and Abby ran down the stands.

Meanwhile, Stefan found himself being held up by Khalid, who shouted in his face, "Boss, just breathe, just breathe! Oh my God, your shoulder!" Stefan looked down to his right to see blood gushing to the side of his collar bone.

It all became hazy, and Stefan felt his legs become jelly underneath him as the sharp pain near his shoulder increased. A court official grabbed him from behind while Khalid continued to hold him up from the front; but any strength he had drained like the oozing blood, and Stefan's knees buckled.

"We have a stabbing on the grand court, I repeat, a stabbing on the grand court," a security officer yelled into his radio.

"Stefan! Son!"

Stefan, now on a stretcher, watched as his father followed and continued to call for him, tears running down his face: "Stefan! I'll be right there, son! I'll be right there!" Amidst the chaos, Stefan realized this may have been the first time he saw his father cry.

As the paramedics lifted him into the back of the ambulance, Stefan looked up one last time to see Ernest's and Abby's faces staring back at him in fear. Their faces comforted him, and he closed his eyes. The doors shut and the sirens began to blare.

Chapter 27: "I'm Not a Hero" and Other Revelations

"You've tarnished our league forever! We're over because of you, Stefan!"

Stefan woke up from his nightmare to find himself in the hospital. His father, Ernest, Abby, Scooter, Khalid, Joy, Bibi, and Fred stood over him. On the back of his left hand, he felt a soft licking and looked over; it was Gucci, showing the first sign of affection for him.

"Stefan," Ernest said softly. "How are you feeling?"

"Ok, I guess," Stefan drowsily replied. He looked down to see his chest and entire arm had been heavily wrapped.

"Oh my God, son! I was so worried about you!" his father said.

"Are you in any pain? You are, I can see it in your face," Ernest said. "Someone get the nurse, he needs more drugs."

"No, no," Bibi said. "The more painkillers, the more constipated he'll be." He then turned to Stefan. "Trust me, sweetie, or you'll be trying to push rocks out of your ass."

Khalid stepped forward, looking solemn. "Boss, I can't believe you did that. You're a hero."

Joy nodded in agreement, her head leaning on Khalid's arm. "He's right. You are."

"Amazing," Abby remarked.

Stefan had never been called that before. "Well, I don't know about that."

"You took a knife for a straighty! You rewrote the Monica story! You stopped Günter! Definitely heroic!" Bibi said.

They laughed.

"Who was that crazy guy? Why was he trying to stab you?" Stefan asked.

"We don't know. The cops arrived and took him away."

"It doesn't matter," Ernest said. "You put yourself in front of injustice. I don't know what to say," Ernest said, grabbing Stefan's hand.

Stefan grinned reluctantly; "you all would have done the same."

Father Porsche shook his head. "Oh I'm not sure about that ... You were so close to gold! Now the gold medalist of the gay people ... is straight?"

Everyone tried to ignore that comment.

Stefan looked at the smiling faces staring at him, admiring him, still uneasy. His eyes scanned from them to the back of the room, to the sun shining through the window, then landing on Khalid.

Then a mirage of images flooded his mind: pulling the power on Khalid during karaoke night; the glitter bomb exploding at the Canadian Gay Open; the Apollo Spa, the Costco membership form on Khalid's windshield telling him to *STAY IN YOUR LANE*.

"No, I'm not," Stefan mumbled.

"Stop being so humble. It's not cute." Bibi said.

"I'm not kidding. I'm no hero, guys," Stefan insisted.

"I think you're just exhausted," Father Porsche said.

"Yeah, you need some rest," said Abby.

"Do you want me to get the nurse to give you a sleeping pill?" Ernest asked. "Or maybe just a sedative to relax you?"

"Ernest, stop," Stefan pleaded.

Ernest spoke faster. "Of course, you're probably overwhelmed with all of us crowding you. Guys, let's just give him some space."

"Ernest?"

"Come on guys, let's go."

"I planted the glitter bomb!" Stefan shouted.

"Huh?" Ernest spat out.

"I planted it. And I pulled the power when you sang karaoke that night, and I sent you to the Apollo Spa!" Stefan confessed looking at Khalid, and then down.

The room was silent.

"So I'm no hero. I'm sorry, Khalid ... I don't know why I did those things. Everything just seemed so easy for you," he said with shame. He looked at Ernest. "I'm sorry."

Ernest noticed that in his confession, Stefan's German lilt seemed to be more prominent. Stunned, he restrained his anger. "Why are you apologizing to *me*?" he said coldly.

A pause.

Ernest then rushed out of the room past Khalid and Joy, still shocked. Walking down the hallway as his eyes began to well, he turned the corner in hopes of finding a moment alone.

"Ernest? Is that you?"

He stopped; Rafael, the man from the bathhouse was standing there in a white lab coat. Beside him was another man dressed in street clothes.

"Rafael? You work at this hospital?"

"Yeah. What a coincidence. What are you doing here?"

"My friend—actually, no, he's not my friend—got hurt today."

"I'm sorry. Is he okay?

"I think so."

Rafael then turned to the other man. "Amor, I'll see you at home later," to which the man smiled at Ernest and walked away.

Ernest's shoulders sank. *Amor*. "That's your—?"

"My partner."

"Oh."

"Yeah. Maybe we can have you over for some dinner before you leave?"

Ernest wasn't sure if that was code for a threesome, but he didn't care. "I'm leaving tomorrow and have some stuff planned, so I don't think so."

"Okay then."

They stared at each other awkwardly.

"Well, I hope your friend—or not your friend—is okay. You take care of yourself Ernest," Rafael said, giving him a hug.

"You too."

***

Ernest walked further down the hallway and sat on a bench. Placing his face in his hands, he felt the sting of tears rushing his eyes and looked at the ground. Seconds later, a pair of shoes were beside his, and then he heard Khalid's voice: "I'm probably the last person you feel like talking to right now, but I just want you to know, I'm here." He sat down.

Ernest rolled his eyes. *First Stefan, then Rafael, and now the straight guy. Not more drama, please.* "Sorry, I don't feel like talking to you."

"That's fine."

Ernest then began sobbing, burying his head in his hands again.

"But I'm not leaving your side until you tell me to, boss," Khalid said.

Ernest blew his nose. "I thought Stefan might be behind everything. But I didn't want to believe it. I'm such an idiot."

"No, you're not. You just want to believe there's something good in everyone. It's a good thing."

"No, it's naive. Dumb."

It seemed to be a confessional day, Ernest thought. Everything—the events of the day, the resentment toward his mother and Khalid, the horror of Stefan's actions—all weighed too much on him.

Whatever. Just let it go. Just let it go.

He took a deep breath. "I'm sorry I've been an asshole. You see Khalid, I have a problem liking people who don't like me back."

Khalid responded as gently as he could. "Listen, It's not that I don't like you. Cause I do. I'm so sorry I didn't tell you about me and your mom."

Ernest braced himself.

Khalid continued, "but boss, I'm not your type, and you're not mine.

You're my friend ... no ... you're like a brother to me."

Ernest knew Khalid was going to say that. "Jeez. Those words are a stabbing on their own," he smiled slightly.

Khalid, noticing Ernest's grin, returned the favour.

"Well, if you think of me like a brother," Ernest said, "that means you're dating our mother, you fucking pervert."

Khalid chuckled, "whatever you might think, I really do care. I've been saving money like crazy and have been interviewing for legit jobs. I'm a reformed fuckboy!" His tone then turned serious. "I'm gonna take care of her. Of us. I love her."

"I know you do," Ernest mumbled.

Khalid put his arm on Ernest's shoulder.

They sat for a few minutes. Ernest's heart was torn in two; one half feeling lighter for letting go of his anger; and the other broken, for the sensation—the fluttering feeling—that Khalid's hand on his shoulder would be in, and always be in, the spirit of brotherly friendship, and nothing more.

Joy walked down the hall toward them reluctantly. Khalid smiled and nodded at her, signaling all was good. Her face lit up and she looked at Ernest, who stood up slowly and embraced her. "I'm sorry, Mother. I've been so selfish. You've done so much for me. I'm sorry I forgot that you deserve to be happy too."

"No, I was selfish," Joy said. "I'm sorry, darling. I shouldn't have kept that from you. I should have been honest. But Ernest, *you are* my happy."

Khalid joined them, hugging Joy from behind.

She rubbed her belly. "It's been a crazy day and this baby's tired me out. We should probably get back to the hotel."

"Sounds good."

They turned and walked to the elevator.

Joy turned to Ernest, giddily; "you know the other night, Khalid and I did it up the butt, and I totally thought about you."

Ernest was appalled. "Mother!"

"Joy!" Khalid shook his head.

They burst into giggles. Joy gazed at her son, her heart elated that this was the first time in months he didn't despise her. Ernest sighed, eager to put the day behind him.

But that was not to be.

Ernest looked down, noticing a few dark maroon spots on the stark white hallway floor. He walked slower and looked closer, eventually turning back behind them to see the trail coming from the direction of Stefan's room. Ernest's eyes then went back forward, finding the drops were coming from his mother; her beige flowing shirt was stained in dark red blotches at the back.

"Mom, you're bleeding!"

"What?" Joy said, then looking down and screaming, "oh my God!"

"Ernest!" Khalid panicked, putting his arms around Joy. "Call the nurse now!"

PART FIVE

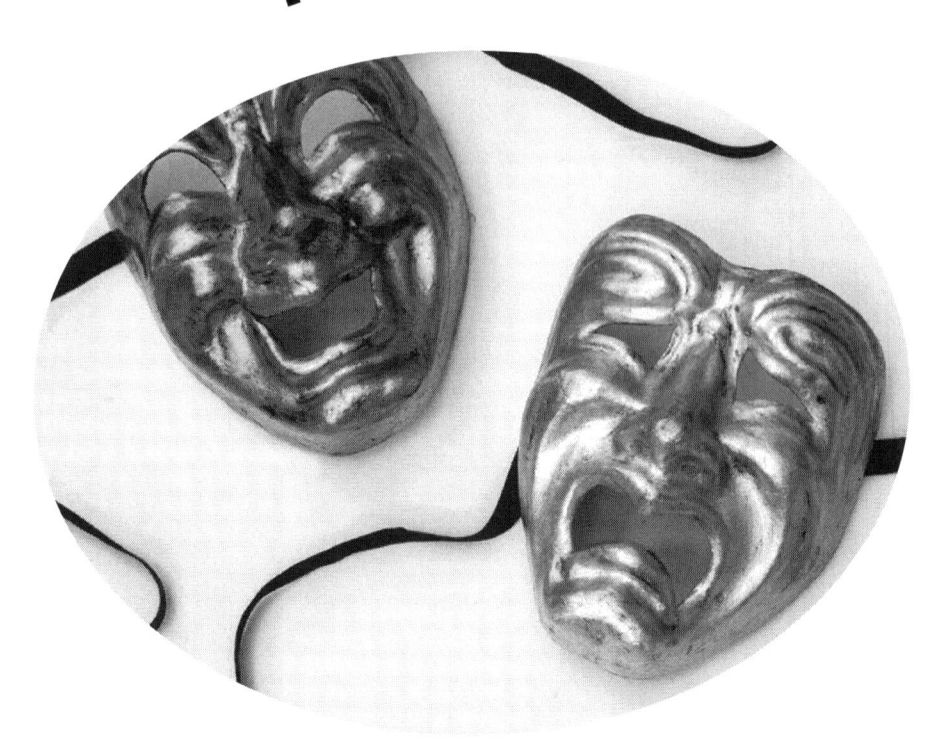

Chapter 28: Red
Torpedo Valley, Ontario, Canada
September 2020

She thought it may be too soon to go out for a party, or do anything that might be "fun." But Joy needed to get out of the house. Since returning home from Bonn a month ago, she had avoided all social interactions. She subbed out her yoga classes and had Ernest or Khalid run her errands.

She thought a dark dress would be appropriate. Not a black one—this wasn't a funeral—but the league's year-end tennis banquet. Grey then. Any colour that would not remind her of the streaks of maroon and ruby and fire engine red—hers and her baby's blood—splattered all over her skirt, hospital gown, and the doctors' and nurses' gloves back in Bonn that day. Funny, she thought; red—once her favourite colour that she had associated with vibrancy, life, and love, now meant loss, absence … of life. Her nails had grown out but there were still small chips of her bright red nail polish that she couldn't bother to clean off.

It wasn't funny as in humour, obviously. Rather, funny as in surprising, unexpected, and foolish to think that her love of red would never change.

Sitting in front of the vanity mirror in her bedroom, she twisted her hair around the curling iron, let it sit for a few seconds, and then released and teased it for loosely tossed curls. Finishing the last few locks, she gazed at her reflection, which seemed to have shrunk within the thick mop of her hair. This was good, she thought; it would hide her face if she spontaneously started crying, a common occurrence recently.

Joy's mood ranged from numb to hysterical and back in the month leading up to this evening. At the moment she felt the former; she put her fingers directly on the hot curling iron just to make sure she could still feel something. "Ouch," she whispered to herself, then quickly pulling her finger away.

I can still feel that. So, I'm not dead after all.

She wore no fake eyelashes, eye shadow, or red lipstick; rather a simple light pink gloss and a bit of concealer for the dark circles around her eyes. It didn't matter what makeup she would put on. Nothing could be done to pretty up the dim expression since she heard the words uttered by the German doctor in that emergency room as he lowered his mask and called the time of death: "I'm sorry, Joy." And just like that, she was frozen in grief ever since.

There was a knock at the door.

"Mother, you almost ready?" Ernest asked.

"Yeah."

Ernest stepped forward reluctantly; he had felt like he was on eggshells around her lately. "Can you tie my tie?"

"Sure."

She turned to face him and began to fold it, like she had done so many times before. "You know how to do this."

"I know. But you always do it perfectly." He noticed her eyes began to tear and her bottom lip quivered.

"You alright? We don't have to go tonight," he said.

"You know, I used to tie your father's tie before you were born," her voice breaking. She then cleared her throat and finished the knot—a perfect Windsor—just in time to wipe the tears before they left her face and hit the floor.

Now didn't seem like the right time to ask the questions Ernest had always wanted to know. Instead, he reached over and hugged her, not saying a word.

"Your father would be very proud of you, Ernest," she whispered in his ear. He held on to her tighter. "You make *me* so proud."

She looked back in the mirror and grabbed a tissue. "Shit! You ruined my makeup." They smiled as Joy reapplied her concealer.

Khalid appeared in the doorway. "I think your cats are in heat. I keep finding Rafa trying to hump Rodge."

"I know."

"Are you guys ready to go?"

"Yeah."

Joy brushed her make up one last time and fiddled with the sleeves of her dress. "Do I look okay?"

Khalid's face lit up. "You look beautiful."

Chapter 29: The Year-End Banquet

29a: A Mask4Masc Spectacular

Every year-end banquet had its theme. The previous Torches' banquets were legendary for being over the top and unforgettable. The 2012 theme was a tribute to Madonna; other than one member getting accidentally stabbed in the eye by another member's acrylic nail during an aggressive vogue-off, the evening was a smash. In 2014, there was the Moulin Rouge theme, which was notable for its orgy at a member's house after the party with more than ten guests testing positive for chlamydia a few days later. The 2015 banquet was the "Dress as your Favourite Diva" theme, highlighted by a scrap between members garbed as Mariah Carey and Whitney Houston snatching each other's wigs off in a hotly contested lip synch battle; it inevitably turned into a fist fight with Whitney sweating profusely, claiming victory over "that dog whistling bitch."

Despite his failing health, Bibi managed to plan the first banquet in Torpedo Valley: "A Mask4Masc Spectacular," he called it. Members were encouraged to wear any mask—fancy, costume, humorous, medical or whatever—of their choosing.

This was good for Stefan. Since being the hero for taking a stabbing for the straight member, then the bigoted asshole for bullying him before that, he wanted to keep a low profile. He sat at a corner table by himself, believing he was inconspicuous with his Barack Obama mask.

"Good mask choice," Bibi said to him.

"Everyone loves Obama! I can't go wrong! Do you think it sends the wrong message? Should I take it off right now?"

"Well, Miss Woke might think you're doing Blackfa—actually no, keep it on! I don't want people to know I'm talking to you. Your approval ratings are at an all-time low."

Stefan looked at Bibi's jeweled mask with peacock feathers on the side. "What are you? Some sort of bird?"

"The most beautiful one, of course. A peacock."

"Pardon me."

"Okay, enough gabbing, gotta start the show."

Meanwhile, at another table, Abby, wearing a butterfly mask, and Fred, in a Chewbacca one, waved for Ernest, Khalid, and Joy to join them.

Dakota walked over and whispered to Abby, "Oh my God, Ernest's mother. God bless her. How'd she lose the baby?"

"That's not really for me to say. Sorry."

"Of course. Well, she looks great." Dakota walked back to her table, to which Angelica said softly, "did you hear she miscarried? She still looks amazing though."

Abby gave Joy a hug. "Are you okay?" she whispered, staring deep into Joy's eyes.

"Yeah. Right now I am. Thanks for asking," Joy said, putting on a smile.

"If you need anything, even just to talk, you let me know."

"Thank you."

Abby turned to Ernest. "Ernest, great mask. Always the revolutionary."

"Why, thank you," he said. "Not everyone knows who Guy Fawkes is."

"Guy Fawkes? Who's that? I thought that was the V for Vendetta mask."

"That's what I said," Khalid said, wearing a Batman mask.

"It's the same thing," Ernest replied.

"It creeps me out," Joy said, putting on her Catwoman mask.

Abby's face lit up. "Catwoman and Batman? Straight people are just the cutest!"

The lights dimmed. Bibi's voice, although frail and thin, filled the speakers. "Hello bitches, and those who do not identify as such! Welcome to tonight's year end banquet, the Mask4Masc spectacular!" The audience cheered, and Bibi appeared on the stage.

Bibi had started a second round of chemoradiation since returning from Germany. Although very weak, he insisted he emcee the banquet, even though Stefan felt it would be too exhausting. But he knew being in front of a crowd energized him, and he joked and improv'd with members, basking in the spotlight.

The banquet always had some less exciting parts, including the review of the league's financial statements led by Dakota; at those times, most members headed to the bar. The only point of interest was the brown furry animal mask she wore.

"Hey Dakota, is that a beaver on your face?" Scooter yelled from his seat. "You just can't get enough of them, eh?" He howled at his joke so much that the leather mask he wore almost jiggled off.

"It's a chipmunk, you dummy. And what kind of mask is that, Scoot? The S&M party is at the Black Eagle!" she quipped.

"I'm Bane. You know from Batman?"

"Oh. Doesn't Bane get it on with Batman at some point?"

"I'm working on it!" Scooter yelled back, then turning to Khalid. "Bruh, my invitation's still open! The bathroom's right over there."

As always, Khalid took it in good spirits while the members laughed.

"God, I just love that straight guy," someone said.

"Yeah, I just love how he's so cool with everything," somebody else chimed.

Stefan rolled his eyes; the fawning over the Khalid never ended.

That exchange also raised eyebrows for another reason: beside Scooter sat his mother; he had brought her as his guest.

29b: Player of the Year and Favourite New Member Awards

It was time for the annual awards. Bibi started off with the "in-jest" awards—a Torches' banquet tradition—these were joke prizes, or funnier, less hurtful way to insult members. Winners were determined by member votes. This year, the categories included:

1. Best On Court Drama Queen—self-explanatory
2. Best Off Court Drama Queen—self-explanatory
3. Best Stevie Wonder Line Calls—recognizing the player who makes the worst line calls
4. Favourite Lesbian—self-explanatory
5. Best Delusional Player—recognizing the lowest ranked player who thinks they should be seeded number 1 or playing on the top court
6. Best Fake Injury when Losing to Hold on to Your Ego—self-explanatory
7. Best Kim Jong-un Award—recognizing the player who launches the hardest missiles at net players without apologizing
8. Best "I'm a Top" Façade—self-explanatory

Some recipients didn't accept their award so graciously. "What do you mean I'm a drama queen, bruh?" Scooter yelled at Bibi, then the audience. "Whatever, give me my damn trophy!" The members awkwardly laughed. Bibi seized the opportunity to talk to Scooter's mother, following him to his table. Sticking the microphone in her face, Bibi asked, "Now Mamma Scoot, do you know what kind of event this is?"

Wearing a red cardigan this time, she leaned forward. "Yes, I do now."

"Oh you do, do you?"

"Yeah," Scooter replied, his mood changing instantly. "I finally came out to her," to which the audience clapped and cheered.

"Well good for you, honey," Bibi replied. He turned back to his mother. "Now was that a surprise for you Mamma?"

She smiled. "No not really. I always knew he liked boys."

Crowd laughter.

"But I just didn't think he was that much of an asshole," she giggled, just as Betty White would, then sat back and sipped her herbal tea. Scooter joined in with the crowd laughing, then kissed her on the cheek.

Bibi walked back to the stage. "Now, our big awards!"

These were the "legit" awards, mainly because they were actual prizes. This year, they were gold tickets to the next Canadian National Bank Open at York University, where the professionals would compete.

"Our Player of the Year Award goes to…" Bibi opened the envelope at the podium, "It's history … Khalid Adam!"

It *was* history. He had already been the first straight person to enter the league. He made the finals of the Canadian Gay Open, won the titles in Detroit and Montreal, and the Gold medal at the Pride Games. And now this.

Stefan sighed, echoing his father's thoughts, *who would have thought the best player in the gay league would be a straight person?* He was amused. This was his worst fear all those months ago when he first met Khalid. He took a deep breath, and exhaled.

Oh well. Just let it go.

He stood up, started to clap, and took his Barack Obama mask off. The members, pleasantly surprised to see his face, cheered louder.

Bibi handed the trophy to Khalid like it was an Oscar. "Girl, it's your Halle Berry moment!" he exclaimed, to which Khalid had no idea what he was referencing.

Khalid looked out into the blinding lights, trying to make out faces. "This is crazy. I just wanted to play tennis. Thank you everyone. This wouldn't be possible without you all. Especially you Bibi, and all those sitting at my table."

He looked at Ernest and Joy.

"Ernest, thank you for making me feel part of the family, boss ... and Joy, I love you!"

Ernest's heart fluttered, only slightly.

"Oh my God, he's so dreamy," someone swooned.

"I love you too, baby!" Joy screamed, hugging her son from behind.

Khalid then noticed Stefan standing in the corner, smiling at him. "And you."

Everyone braced themselves; they had anticipated this since the Pride Games and learning about Stefan's previous antics.

"No matter what anyone says, in the end, you put yourself in harm's way for me," Khalid said. "I'll never forget it. Thank you, Stefan."

Stefan nodded politely.

"I just love these little straight people," Bibi said as Khalid left the stage. "Do we not love them, crowd?" The audience agreed. "Now that's enough of that, I'm about to hit my rag."

The next award was Favourite New Member. "I think we should have Miz President give this one out, don't you?" Bibi said to the audience. Stefan shook his head.

"Oh look, she's shy. Stef, get up here!" Bibi insisted.

Stefan slowly walked up the stage, whispering in Bibi's ear, "I told you I wanted to be low-key, B. I was just going to give a short obligatory 'hello' near the end, like I said."

"No, I'm trying to repair your image, trust me," Bibi hushed back, reassuring him.

Bibi reached over and grabbed Stefan by the shoulder where he had been stabbed the month before, causing Stefan to hurl over in pain.

"Ow! What are you doing? It's still healing!" Stefan whispered.

"Sympathy votes, hun," Bibi muttered back.

"How'z the shoulder doing, Stef?" Bibi said clearly into the microphone.

"It's okay," Stefan replied. "Slowly it's getting better. Thanks."

It worked. Stefan felt the audience look more kindly back at him.

Stefan raised the mic. "On to the next award. Our favorite new member is …"

Bibi opened the envelope and handed it to Stefan. Afraid that another accolade would be given to Khalid, Stefan was happy to see a different name. "Abigail Abby Elle."

Ernest, Joy, Khalid, Scooter and Fred hollered as she walked up to the stage and received the award from Stefan.

"Congratulations, Abby," Stefan said as he reached for a hug.

"Thank you," she whispered.

But instead of hugging him, she gently held the sides of Stefan's head, giving him a soft kiss on the forehead.

A memory stirred in Stefan. *There was something about the way her hands tenderly caressed the sides of his face. About the way her lips felt against his forehead. The way the light reflected in her eyes,* he thought.

"Thank you very much," Abby said. "It's amazing to be part of such a welcoming and accepting family. I have made so many special memories with many of you and cannot wait to make more."

Applause.

Stefan's memory became more clear, and he felt himself in a trance. *The graceful and slow manner in which she spoke. The handsomeness of her features.*

She continued: "But I really don't deserve this award. I'm not really a new member."

A few faces in the audience were puzzled.

"I used to play with the Torches a long time ago. But then I took time away for myself."

The crowd seemed to sit on the edge of their seats, not knowing where this was going. Bibi and Stefan hung on to her every word. She turned to Stefan, removing her butterfly mask.

The way the light reflected in her eyes. Stefan never noticed before. Her eyes. They were hazel. *And the last person to kiss him on the forehead was ...*

Suddenly, it became clear. Stefan recognized who was speaking. "Stefan ... Stef. It's me, Gabe. But now I'm ... well, me," she said.

Abigail Abby Elle. Gabe Lamb. One and the same.

"I'm sorry I didn't tell you sooner."

Stefan's eyes widened, and then welled. "Gabe? It's you! I thought I lost you!" he gasped.

The members were completely stunned, their jaws agape. Some of the former Torches' members—including Scooter—shook their heads, in disbelief that this was the same person, or that they hadn't recognized her. "What the fuck?" someone blurted.

"You're *the* Gabe?" Bibi shouted, "the one that Stef never stopped talking about?"

"I'm so sorry! I thought I drove you away when I told you that I loved—" Stefan's voice cracked.

"No, it was me. I'm sorry I didn't say goodbye. You deserved better than that."

"Gabe ... um, I mean Abby! Sorry!" Stefan stammered. "I don't know what—"

He saw her open arms coming at him, and then wrapping around his shoulders as she buried her head in his chest. "I missed you so much," he whispered.

"Me too."

The crowd clapped harder than before. Still in her embrace, Stefan closed his eyes.

Bibi walked up to the microphone. "Well, that's some high fuckin' drama! I think we all need another dessert after that!" He turned to Khalid. "Sorry Khalid, you ain't the special one of this league anymore!

We got ourselves a new unicorn! Ha!"

Khalid and Joy howled; the audience giggled in relief. The tension in the air had been stifling. "But really, thank you, Abby. Welcome back to the league. That was beautiful," Bibi earnestly said as Stefan and Abby walked off the stage. "Now, I think we just need to take a little breather so I can go air out my pussy," he said, to which the audience howled with laughter, eager to lighten the drama in the room. He placed the mic on the podium and scurried to the washroom.

Ernest, Khalid, and Joy rushed to Abby at the side of the stage, smothering her with hugs and well wishes.

Meanwhile, Stefan gazed at her in awe. "I wish I could have been there for you. You know I would have done anything for you. I loved you … well … I still love you."

"I know. I wanted to tell you before. It took me a while to feel good about myself. But I'm there now."

Stefan shook his head and smiled. "You don't need to explain yourself. I'm so happy for you, Abby."

29c: "Some Fucked Up Telenovela"

"You okay, B?" Stefan asked.

"I'm fine. It's just a lot happening, you know?"

They stood in the banquet washroom, Bibi patting the sweat off his forehead with a paper towel.

"Well, you're doing a fabulous job."

"Thanks. I'm gonna go outside now and get to airing out my—."

"You do that."

Stefan washed his hands and looked into the mirror as Bibi exited. He looked a bit flush himself, considering what had just transpired. *Gabe Lamb. I found him. Well, her. I found my Lamb. Holy shit,* he smiled to himself.

Then, a familiar voice was heard, deep, slow, and menacing.

"Excuse me. Mr. President."

In the mirror, Stefan saw a stall door open behind him, ominously creaking, revealing an ornate mask that one might see at an Italian carnival; royal blue with gold and purple accents that caught and refracted the lights on the washroom ceiling, its brilliant flash temporarily blinding him. The figure walked forward slowly, the sounds of his footsteps echoing off the walls, ringing in Stefan's ear louder and more chilling with each step. Looking directly into the eyes of the mask in the reflection, he knew who it was.

"Francesco Zappone." he said. "What are you doing here?"

Francesco stood behind him. "You know why, Stef." He took his mask off.

Stefan looked around to see if anyone else was in the washroom.

Francesco spoke firm and curt; "I've been sitting at the back of the room this whole time, wearing this mask, waiting to tell everyone that I'm moving back to Canada permanently."

"You're ... moving back here?"

"Yeah."

Stefan forced a nervous smile. "Great."

"And I'm planning to rejoin the league."

"You are?"

"Oh yeah. It's going to be fun."

"Uh, yes." Stefan felt his mouth go dry.

"But there's something that needs to be cleared up first. You see, people still think I'm responsible for the old league crashing."

"Oh."

"Don't act like you don't know."

Stefan looked down at the floor.

Francesco's voice lowered. "You know what you did. You need to come clean, my friend. You have to tell them what happened at that party." He noticed Stefan's eyes darting around, refusing to make contact with his. "Look at me when I'm talking to you, bitch!"

Stefan raised his eyes, locking with Francesco's.

Francesco stepped closer; they stood nose to nose. "You need to make this right. Or else, I will."

He backed away, put his mask back on, and left the washroom.

Stefan turned back to the mirror, splashing his face with cold water. *Fuck. Fuck. Fuck.*

Then, he heard the ominous sound of another stall door open. Someone had been there the whole time.

Ernest stepped out; his face disturbed.

"Stefan … what did you do?"

***

Bibi came back inside and picked up the microphone. "Okay everyone, I'm fresh again. So we are at the last award, but first, a word from our president. Come back up here, girl."

Stefan walked up to the stage, unfolded a piece of paper from his pocket, wearing a pensive smile. "Hi everyone. I hope you're having a nice time tonight."

A couple of hollers, then silence.

He looked down at the paper, but was unable to read his scribbles. "Um. Uh," he stuttered. He took another breath and gazed before him; a sea of curious faces stared back. His eyes stopped on the blue, gold, and purple Italian carnival mask at the back of the room, the figure wearing it with his arms crossed.

"So, now was supposed to be the time that I boast about how fabulous our first year as a league in Torpedo Valley was, and how great the executive and the members were, and all that exciting stuff. All that's true of course, but I think it's important to say that what I'm proud of the most is that our league is founded on openness, honesty, and integrity. I hope you all feel that you can come to this league as your true, authentic self." He cleared his throat. "I want you all to look at the back of the room because we have a very special guest tonight. In the fancy blue mask is Francesco Zappone, who you'll remember was the last president of the Toronto Torches."

The members began swapping puzzled stares, then looked to Francesco as he slowly removed his mask, politely nodding and smiling at everyone.

Stefan continued. "I know there may have been rumours about why the Torches' league ended a few years back, many of them pointing to him. And in the spirit of truth, I just want to clear that up." He paused. Exhaled. "You see, a couple of years ago, the Torches had a Halloween event at the Prestige Tennis Club, as we had all our events there before. But something happened that night that caused them to cancel their contract with us, and we were never allowed back."

"Whoa. Sounds serious." Joy whispered to Khalid.

"After we had cleared out the party room that night, the staff thought the facility was empty. But that wasn't the case. Members were still there. And someone ended up walking in on a couple of people at the back of the locker room …"

"Ah, shit," Scooter mumbled, as he sank lower in his chair.

Anticipating what Stefan would say next, Ernest felt his shoulders tighten. Abby felt her throat clench. Khalid clasped Joy's hand. Bibi felt nauseous, and he knew it wasn't from the chemo.

Gathering his courage, Stefan took a deep breath and then let it come out like a bullet: "That night, a six-year-old child of one of the Prestige club members walked in on two people in costume … doing some rather indecent activities. It was me … I was dressed as Pikachu and the other member was dressed as … Hello Kitty!"

He then looked down, unable to look anyone in the eye and continued as if he was reliving the nightmare: "The little girl started to cry. She screamed 'why are you hurting Hello Kitty? Her back is broken!'"

GAY GASPS.

"Oh my God!"

"Holy shit!"

A piercing scream came out of Bibi's mouth, followed by "Oh sweet Jesus, someone hold me!" Fred ran upstage immediately to help Bibi stand.

Amidst the chaos, Scooter had shrunk almost to the bottom of his chair, his face looking down.

Angelica, noticing him, shouted, "Scoot, weren't you dressed up as Hello Kitty that year?"

"No, no I wasn't," he said, refusing to make eye contact.

"Yes, you were! You were Hello Kitty!" her finger pointing at him like a sword pointed at his head.

"Okay, okay, I was!" Scooter admitted, defensively. "Yes, it was me!" He took a pause and decided it was time for him to come clean too. "This will probably shock everyone, but I'm a bottom, okay! ... Why do you all look down at us in shame?!" he yelled, his eyes watering.

"Oh, for Christ's sake," Scooter's mother said, rolling her eyes.

Stefan tried to regain control of the room. "Anyway, that was why the Prestige Club and all our sponsors cancelled us. They were horrified by what the gays—*what I*—did. And Francesco didn't abandon the league and escape to Italy. He disbanded it because he couldn't bear knowing that something so offensive and obscene had happened under his presidency."

Bibi and Fred came closer to the front of the stage. Still in disbelief, Bibi leaned on the podium and focused on Stefan. "So all this time, I never knew ... you actually *are* a top?"

The buzz in the banquet hall eventually settled after a few seconds; Stefan stood alone in the spotlight. *It was all too much,* Stefan thought. *Just let it go.*

"I'm sorry. I've done a bunch of horrible things, and I'm ashamed of all of it. But it's too late. I'm sorry I disappointed everyone ... I'll be stepping down as president, effective immediately."

He walked off the stage and headed to the exit. Francesco stopped him. "I just wanted my name cleared, I didn't mean for you to step down. But thank you for doing the right thing, Stefan."

Stefan nodded and headed for the door. He looked back and saw Ernest staring back at him with heartbreak and pity.

Despite admitting the horror of his past, he felt a little lighter. *Nothing more to hide.*

AND THEN ...

As Stefan was about to leave, another voice was heard on the microphone. It had an Australian accent.

"You think you're so noble," the voice said.

Everyone looked back at the stage.

"Confessing all that, and expecting everyone to forgive you. But you won't get away with it, Stefan!" the voice continued. The figure then reached for their Iron Man mask and snatched it off, snapping the string in the back.

Stefan stepped back in horror. "Margaret Fork! What are you doing here?"

"After the Pride Games, I went back to Australia to find a bunch of ..." she paused and hurled slightly, as if she was about to vomit, "a bunch of straight people wanting to join our league! I was right! You set a precedent! Look what you did to our sacred queer institution! It's now poisoned with these mouth breathers!"

Stefan shook his head. "You can't fight it anymore, Margaret. We need to include everyone. It's only fair."

"How dare you speak of fairness!" she yelled back. "This was our space!"

"You came all the way here from Australia to spew this same old shit?" Bibi said.

"No, that's not all," Margaret replied, then turning back to Stefan. "You see, we have some unfinished business, don't we … Thtefan?"

THTEFAN?

Stefan's eyes grew wider. "What?"

"I never told you what my maiden name was, did I, Thtefan?"

Stefan shook his head.

"It's Bock," she said firmly, then smirked.

A flood of images rushed into Stefan's mind. *The clay courts in Bonn, 1987. His father looking down at him after losing that match. The pink tutu-ish skirt. The gap in her front teeth. The banana goo smooshed on her face.*

Peggy Bock.

Margaret Fork. Peggy Bock. One and the same.

The crowd was confused.

"Peggy? Little Peggy Bock?" Stefan gasped, feeling his breath shorten and his heart beat louder.

"Yes, it's me!" she said. "My life was hell after I beat you for that trophy when we were kids! Your father tortured me at all the junior tournaments after that day! He'd boo me, heckle me … And not just at that one match! You remember … he even threw bananas at my head!

"Is that why you became a lesbian?" Bibi quipped.

"You shut up!" she said back.

Stefan could not believe what the night had turned into. *Some fucked up telenovela.*

"Peggy—I mean, Margaret, I'm sorry! He … well *we*, we were terrible to you." he said.

"Your father would say to me, 'I said I'd get you back for beating my boy!' I was traumatized! I kept thinking he was going to show up at every one of my tournaments! So my parents moved us to Australia to start anew! I even took on the formal version of my first name just in case."

Stefan was horrified.

"This was all because of you, Stefan! The bullying! The bananas! And now the straights!" Margaret dropped the microphone and jumped off the stage. Grabbing a fork from one of the dinner tables, she held it up high like weapon and charged toward Stefan, screaming.

In a split second, Stefan saw Peggy Bock/Margaret Fork running full speed with a fork in her hand, about to tackle him. Suddenly from the corners of his eyes, he saw Ernest, Khalid, and Abby run into her from different sides; they all collided and rolled on the floor, crashing into Stefan, who landed on top of them.

"Orgy!" Scooter shouted.

Members rushed toward them, restraining Margaret while she continued to yell. "I'll get you Stefan! I'll get you, you hear me?!"

"Security! Security!" Francesco yelled, as he ran out the door for help.

A few minutes later, the crowd in a tizzy, Stefan picked himself up and watched the guards escort Margaret out of the ballroom.

His eyes fell on Ernest again, looking back at him with despair.

"I don't know what to say," Ernest said.

"Neither do I," Stefan responded.

And with that, Stefan Porsche turned around and disappeared into the corridor.

***

After another break to let things quiet, Bibi leaned on the podium, too weak to stand. Fred held the mic for him. "Now my darlings, there can't be any more drama, cause I've got no more shit to lose." He looked to Fred; "honey, can you please announce the last award for the night, my pussy's melted."

"Of course, darling," Fred smiled. Bibi then clung to the podium as Fred opened the envelope.

"The last award is Miss Congeniality. And the winner is … Butterball Bibi Deveraux! Oh my God, babes you won!" The audience cheered, eager to bring back the positive energy from earlier.

Fred put the envelope down to hug Bibi, but he couldn't. Instead, he and the crowd watched Bibi's eyes fade and then shut, his limp hands let go of the podium, and his body fall. There was a sharp thud caused by the back of his head colliding with the ground; his beautiful peacock mask flew off his face, its jewels flying into the air.

Fred dropped to the ground immediately, desperate to wake him up. "Can someone call an ambulance, now?!"

Chapter 30: Executive Meeting 4 —
"I know the ending to my book now"

The next morning, and another panicked rush to the Torpedo Valley hospital, dash through the cold white hallways, and deep breath before entering Bibi's room to see what had become of his dear friend. Another moment of pause to take in what he looked like lying there helplessly, appearing to be smaller and smaller, and the machines attached to him getting larger and larger. It had all become routine.

I'm tired of this shit, Ernest thought.

Bibi was asleep on the bed, and Fred sat on a chair beside him, Gucci crouched at his feet.

There was something different.

"What's on his face?" Ernest asked.

"The mask you mean?" Fred replied.

"Yes. Is he having trouble breathing?"

"Yeah. The doctor might need to intubate if it doesn't improve."

Ernest's shoulders lowered. "Oh."

Bibi had been rushed to the emergency room the prior evening, his body unable to handle the dramatic twists of the banquet. No visitors were permitted; the doctor felt he was too weak, his iron and potassium levels having plummeted. In addition, he had endured getting stitches sewed into the back of his head from his fall. He needed undisturbed rest to stabilize, and was brought into the Intensive Care Unit earlier that morning.

"So … do they know if he's going to get any better, or is that just a stupid question at this point?" Ernest asked.

"The last chemo and radiation treatments took so much out of him, so they decided to stop the treatment last week."

"Yeah, but isn't the tumour just going to keep spreading?"

"I know." Fred whimpered. "He hasn't woken up since we brought him here last night."

Ernest looked around the room, noticing a jacket on one of the chairs.

"That's Stefan's," Fred said.

"He's here?"

"Yeah, he came about 20 minutes ago. He left but said he'd be coming back shortly."

Ernest walked closer to the bed, placing his hand on Bibi's arm. It was cold.

He looked at the table; there lay Bibi's purple journal. "You brought his writing book?"

"Yeah," Fred replied.

Ernest picked it up, and skimmed through the pages.

"He's got around 75 poems in there. But he said he still needs to write one final one, to bring everything together. So we bring the book everywhere we go, in case he has an idea," Fred said.

"That's good," Ernest nodded.

***

After watching Bibi sleep for an hour, Ernest headed to the hospital's cafeteria. Passing rooms and catching glimpses of patients lying in their beds, looking up at the ceiling in a daze, he noticed a sign above a frosted glass door at the end of the hall: *Meditation Room*. He looked through the tiny square of clear glass inside; he saw the top of someone's head.

It was Stefan, sitting alone on a white chair in front of a plant. His eyes were shut and hands clenched together, as he seemed to be mumbling to himself. A prayer of some sort. Ernest walked to the cafeteria.

"Sir?" the cashier said.

Ernest looked in her direction, but was focused on nothing in particular.

"Sir? What did you want to order?"

Ernest rubbed his eyes. "Sorry. Zoned out there. Just a mint tea, thanks."

Fifteen minutes and a few circles around the hallway later, Ernest returned to Bibi's room. Fred was on one knee, sobbing and holding Bibi's left hand, slowly slipping a diamond ring on his fourth finger. He spoke softly as Gucci lay peacefully on the floor.

"Oh my God!" Ernest said. "Fred, I'm sorry to interrupt you. Are you—?"

"I have to do this. Before time runs out. And … I just think if I gave him a reason to wake up, then maybe, I don't know …." His voice trailed off, and he fully broke down into tears. "Sorry—I just need a minute, can you watch Gucci?" he said as he rushed out of the room.

"Yes, of course."

Ernest sat in the chair beside the bed, sipping his tea and rubbing Gucci's head. He looked closer at the ring.

A few minutes later, he heard footsteps at the door behind him. "Fred, it's really beautiful."

"It's not Fred."

Ernest turned around; Stefan was standing there. They locked eyes; the only sounds heard were the pulse monitor beeping.

Stefan pulled the chair and sat beside Ernest in front of Bibi, gently patting Gucci on the back.

"I saw you in the meditation room earlier," Ernest said.

Stefan nodded. "You're probably too young to remember this, but they used to call those prayer rooms."

"I've heard that."

"Of course, then the crazy new age millennials came in and had to change it. Not politically correct."

"Well, meditation room is more inclusive."

Stefan looked back at Bibi, his eyes sad and heavy. "When I was a kid, my mom told me that if I prayed, God would give me anything I wanted. Like it was so easy."

"Did it work?"

"Sometimes, I guess. Sometimes not. A few years ago, my mom had a stroke and was in a coma for a few days. Even though I was far from her in Toronto, I prayed like crazy. She never woke up. So that was a time when it didn't work."

"Oh."

Stefan continued; "but I think she wanted me to have faith or whatever. Or else without it, we would all just die in our sleep. There'd be nothing to wake up for."

A few seconds of silence.

"Look at what Fred gave him," Ernest said, pointing to Bibi's ring.

"Wow. You know that bitch, she'd love any bling."

Ernest chuckled quietly.

Stefan lowered his head to Bibi's ear, whispering, "come on, B, wake up. I believe you can, even if you don't believe it yourself. Wake up. So *I* have something to wake up for." He wiped a tear rolling down his cheek, then leaned back into his chair.

Ernest moved closer. "Stef,"

"Yeah?"

"Can I ask you something?"

"Sure."

"Why did you start the new league?"

Stefan dreaded having to explain, but he knew he would face it eventually. "Yeah ... about last night ... are you going to cancel me now?"

"I don't care about that," Ernest interrupted.

"You don't?"

"No. People change. Contrary to what you think, people change."

Stefan's face eased.

Ernest continued. "Some change for the better. Some for the

worse, like your friend Peggy. Or Margaret. Or whatever her name is."

Stefan chuckled.

"I just want to know why you started this league here in Torpedo."

"Because. Tennis ... this league ... it's everything to me. I thought if I was going to do any good, it would only be through tennis. If I was going to make my dad proud, or erase my mistakes, or become a better person, it would only be through tennis." He sighed, sounding resigned. "I thought I was a better person, but I'm not. I still have so many things I can't get past. So many things I can't shake." He moved a little closer to Ernest, staring deep into his eyes. "But I think, that's maybe why I met you."

"What?"

"You're crazy, Ernest. You look at the world, and you see all the good that's possible. I don't know how you do it."

His mouth slightly ajar, Ernest felt his heart beat. "That's kind of you to say. But we both know, I'm not perfect."

Stefan looked away. "I know. And I'm miles and miles away from it. I'll never get there." His eyes scanned Bibi, then the walls, then landed back on Ernest. "But, maybe I'm just a little closer, because of you. You make me want to get there."

Stefan slowly moved his hand and placed it on Ernest's. Not having noticed their faces had moved closer together, they gazed into each other's eyes for what seemed like forever. Stefan then glanced at Ernest's lips, two small light pink pillows against his caramel skin. He put his hand on the side of Ernest's face, gently pulling him closer. Ernest let himself be swept, closing his eyes. Stefan did the same, moving forward, their lips about to touch.

The pulse monitor made one prominently longer beep. Gucci's head popped up to the bed, her eyes alert.

Then Bibi's voice: "What kind of jungle fever shit is going on in here?"

Stefan and Ernest opened their eyes and jumped up.

"B? Oh my God! You're awake!"

"Well, well … what did I interrupt?" Bibi asked, his naughty smile never wavering.

"Nothing. Nothing at all," Ernest said.

Bibi coughed, then smiled again, looking at Stefan. "Ain't you supposed to be catchin' them all, Pikachu? Or did you get forked by your BFF Margaret?" he cackled.

Stefan smirked, shaking his head. "Unbelievable."

"How are you feeling? Do you need anything?" Ernest asked.

"I'm fine. Maybe a drink of water?"

"Of course." Ernest grabbed a plastic cup from a nearby table and filled it with water from the fountain in the room. "Oh wait, I think I have a metal straw in my bag," he said, reaching into it and shuffling through the contents.

"No! Ernest Law, don't you dare give me a metal straw!" Bibi defiantly said.

"Ok, fine. What is up with you and that? Do you know how bad plastic is for the ocean?"

"Hush up and give me the water!"

Bibi took a sip and noticed the diamond ring on his finger. He promptly choked and spat it out. His eyes opened wider as he held it up to his face, admiring its brilliance. "How long have I been out?!"

Stefan and Ernest laughed. "Fred will be back shortly. He just went out for air."

"Well I'll be damned … it's pretty, isn't it? Well, good thing I'm not dead, I guess." Bibi said. "Wait, am I? Of course, the only time I land a man and get my bling is when I'm dead. Ha."

They chuckled harder. "Thank God, B. Thank God, you're here," Stefan said.

Ernest grabbed the journal. "I hope you don't mind, but I read some of your poems. The publishing house is going to love them; they're gorgeous."

Bibi smiled. "I hope so."

It was silent again. They looked out the window at a tree.

"Where are the birds? Is my little sparrow here?" Bibi asked, then looking sad to see it wasn't there. "I guess not."

"But we're here," Stefan said, grabbing Bibi's hand.

Bibi took Ernest's hand with his other one. "I know. Thank you," his voice weakening, the sparkle of tears in his eyes. "You know that I love you guys, right?"

Bibi took the tissue Ernest handed to him, drying his eyes. Clearing his throat and adjusting his position in the bed, he suddenly sounded chipper: "Enough of that now. I'm happy today." he smiled. "I have an idea for a poem! Stef, do you mind writing down the words as I say them?"

"For sure, B."

"I know the ending of my book now. It's a good day."

Stefan opened the book to the last page.

"This one will be called *Infinity*," Bibi said.

"*Infinity*," Stefan repeated.

Bibi recited it as Stefan scribed, him and Ernest clinging on to every word.

Chapter 31: *Infinity*
April 2021

Fall had turned into Winter which had turned into Spring. It was seven months later.

Today was the opening day of the TVLGBTQ2+TA league's second year. Abigail "Abby" Elle stood behind a beautifully set table—complete with organic fruits, vegan and gluten-free muffins, and free trade coffee—in front of the gates of the Torpedo Valley tennis courts. Just as the year before, a rainbow of balloons hovered overhead. Putting her clipboard down, she raised the volume of the small speaker on the table. Carly Rae Jepsen's *Call Me Maybe* was playing.

"Well hello, Miss President!" Francesco said as he went in for a hug.

"Francesco! Welcome back to the league, officially!"

"Thank you. It's great to be back!"

She handed him a can of tennis balls. "Court one."

"Thanks." Francesco looked down at the clipboard. "How was the membership turnout?"

"Good! We had a bigger response than last year! The current members referred a bunch of people to us. And guess what? They're straight!"

"What?"

"I know!" She picked up the clipboard, scanning the list. "We have a few straight friends of Khalid—Jeremy ... Rick. And some couples! We have a Kim and Kurt. Mateo and Stephanie. How more hetero sounding is that?"

"How fabulous and progressive of us!" Francesco said. "You know, all those years ago when I joined the old league, I never thought I'd see this day."

Abby scanned the group of members on the courts and in the registration area. "I know. Looking at everyone, I can't even tell who's gay or straight or whatever."

"Damn metrosexuals. Messing up our gaydar."

More members arrived, including Dakota Pearl, the returning treasurer and webmaster, and Tommy Trinh, the director of the rebranded Canadian Open.

But key members of the executive were missing.

"Where's our vice president?" Francesco asked. "Is Khalid slacking already? I don't know, you better set him straight! … well, you know what I mean."

"He's coming soon," Abby giggled. "Which reminds me, I need to step away for a bit." She turned to Dakota. "Can you watch the welcome desk? I just have to be somewhere. I'll be back with the rest of the gang shortly."

Dakota smiled. "For sure."

"Thanks."

***

Five kilometers away, amidst the maze of black, grey and white headstones, Stefan stood alone in the Torpedo Valley Golden Meadows Cemetery. He knew this day would come, and he anticipated he would be weeping uncontrollably. To his surprise, he was rather subdued, echoing the serenity around him; the wind breezing lightly through the emerald green grass; the vibrant yellow and pink and purple flowers in bloom; the sun smiling down and warming his skin. He fixed his eyes on the rose-coloured tombstone at his feet, kneeling to brush his hands along its top and over the engraved lettering, which read:

Butterball "Bibi" Deveraux
June 15, 1983—November 25, 2020
~Miss Congeniality~

Standing back up, he looked up to the pastel blue sky with fluffy white clouds, shutting his eyes and stretching his arms out with his palms up. He took a deep breath in.

The moment was interrupted by the sounds of footsteps approaching, and then stopping. Next, a gleeful shriek: "Oh my God!" Joy shouted, walking over and placing her hand on Stefan's arm. "The headstone's so beautiful! He would absolutely love this," her voice choking up.

"I hope so."

Ernest put his hand on Stefan's shoulder, giving a quick kiss on the lips. "How are you holding up? You okay?"

"I'm good, actually. This place is beautiful, isn't it? The trees, the flowers, everything. I just want to take it all in."

"Whoa. You sound like a hippy dippy new age tree hugger. Not sure how I feel about that."

Stefan smiled. "I'm sure there's still a healthy dose of asshole in me."

Fred, Khalid, Abby, and Scooter were there too, standing quietly, admiring the beauty of the polished headstone, randomly spotted with gold specks, and ornate patterns etched along the top and sides.

"You chose well," Abby said to Fred.

"Stefan and I chose it together," he said. "When we saw it, we knew."

"Yeah," Stefan said. "I think Bibi would think the white or grey or black would be too basic for her. And you know she'd come for us for that."

Slight giggles.

They placed roses, hydrangeas, and irises in front of the stone, as Gucci approached and sniffed the grass, eventually laying down.

Fred pulled a silver and white paperback from the inside of his jacket. "Who wants to have the honour? I won't make it through."

They all looked at Stefan. "It's all you," Abby said.

Fred handed the book to Abby, who handed it to Ernest, who handed it to Stefan. Its front cover read *The Iron Iris, Poems by Butterball "Bibi" Deveraux*. Stefan opened it to the last page, and showed it to Ernest. "This one, right?"

"Yeah," Ernest said. "Definitely."

Beneath the collage of sounds—crickets, fluttering wings of birds, rustling of leaves—they could hear a whistling melody of some sort; the sparrows were singing.

"This one's called *Infinity*," Stefan said.

Some in the group lowered their heads, some closed their eyes, others looked at the headstone; all were focused on Stefan as he read to honour his beloved friend, his voice slow and steady, while valiantly trying to hold itself together:

"The lonely moon begins to loom,
but the sun shall rise, and roses bloom;
As I chase time, destined to lose,
Alas, night breaks, I cannot choose.

But morning light will wake and grant,
a life anew; extend thy hand,
to steal my heart, as thou only can!
Bestow such honour—may I stand?

Behind thee, beside thee? And thee to me?
Forever and ever; one never shall see,
or break or tarnish, or steal from me,
My Shining Gold: My Family.

For dear, dear, dear infinity,
For dear, dear, dear infinity!"

The End.

REFERENCE GUIDE: THE GAME OF TENNIS

What is Tennis?

Tennis is a racquet sport that can be played individually against a single opponent (singles) or between two teams of two players each (doubles). Each player uses a tennis racquet to strike a rubber ball covered with felt over or around a net and into the opponent's court. The object of the game is to manoeuvre the ball in such a way that the opponent is not able to play a valid return. The player who is unable to return the ball will not gain a point, while the opposite player will.

Tennis Scoring

A tennis match is composed of points, games, and sets. A set consists of a number of games (a minimum of six), which in turn each consist of points. A set is won by the first side to win 6 games, with a margin of at least 2 games over the other side (e.g. 6–3 or 7–5). If the set is tied at six games each, a tiebreak is usually played to decide the set. A match is won when a player or a doubles team has won the majority of the prescribed number of sets.

Points:

A point in tennis is the smallest subdivision of the match, the completion of which changes the score. It begins with a serve by one side's server to the receiver on the other, and continues until one side fails to make a return to the other, causing the opponent to win the points.

Games:

A game consists of a sequence of points played with the same player serving, and is won by the first side to have won at least four points with a margin of two points or more over their opponent. Normally the server's score is always called first and the receiver's score second. Score calling in tennis is unusual in that (except in tiebreaks) each point has a corresponding call that is different from its point value. The current point score is announced verbally before each point by the umpire, or by the server if there is no umpire.

Number of points won	Corresponding Call/Value
0	"Love"
1	"15"
2	"30"
3	"40"
4	"Game"

For instance, if the server has won three points so far in the game, and the non-server has won one, the score is "40–15".

When both sides have won the same number of points within a given game—i.e., when each side has won one, or two, points—the score is described as "15 all" and "30 all", respectively. However, if each player has won three points, the score is called as "deuce", not "40 all". From that point on in the game, whenever the score is tied, it is described as "deuce" regardless of how many points have been played.

In standard play, scoring beyond a "deuce" score, in which the players have scored three points each, requires that one player must get two points ahead in order to win the game. This type of tennis scoring is known as "advantage scoring" (or "ads"). The side which wins the next point after deuce is said to have the advantage. If they lose the next point, the score is again deuce, since the score is tied. If the side with the advantage wins the next point, that side has won the game, since they have a lead of two points.

Sets:

A set consists of a sequence of games played with alternating service and return roles. It is played until a player or team has won at least six games and that player or team has a two-game lead over their opponent(s).

Tiebreak Sets:

A tiebreak set is played with the same rules as the advantage set, except that when the score is tied at 6–6, a tiebreak game (or tiebreaker) is played. Typically, the tiebreak game continues until one side has won seven points with a margin of two or more points.

Super Tiebreak Sets:

A super tiebreak set, sometimes used in matches prior to final rounds, is a tiebreak game (or tiebreaker) that is played when each player has won an equal amount of sets. The tiebreak game continues until one side has won ten points with a margin of two or more points; the winner of the tiebreak game, or super tiebreak set, wins the match.

Matches:

A match consists of a sequence of sets. The outcome is determined through a best of three or five sets system. The first player to win two sets in a best-of-three, or three sets in a best-of-five, wins the match

Tennis Terms/References/Professional Players (in alpha order):

Ace: A serve that is unreturned, either due to its speed, placement, or both.

Ad Side of the Court: The left side of the court of each player, so called because the ad (advantage) point immediately following a deuce is always served to this side of the court.

Backhand: For right-handed players, the backhand is a stroke that begins on the left side of their body, continues across their body as contact is made with the ball, and ends on the right side of their body. It can be executed with either one hand or with both and is generally considered more difficult to master than the forehand.

Backswing: The wind up of the racquet behind/beside the players body before the racquet swings forward to make contact with the ball.

"Bagel": Tennis slang for the score of zero games won within a tennis set.

Baseline: The line at the back of the court; if a player hits a ball that lands past the baseline, it is considered out and that player loses the point.

Bjorn Borg: Retired Swedish tennis player, born 1956. Winner of 11 Grand Slam singles titles.

Boris Becker: Retired German tennis player, born 1967. Winner of six Grand Slam singles titles.

Break/Service Break: The game a receiver has won from the server that marks a lead within the set.

Break Point: A point which, if won by the receiver, would result in a break of service; arises when the score is 30–40 or 40–ad. A double break point or two break points arises at 15–40; a triple break point or three break points arises at 0–40.

Changeover: The brief break—usually 90 seconds—in which the players change sides of the court in between games; players usually sit, drink, or towel themselves during the changeover.

Cross-court: Shots hit diagonally across the court.

Deuce: Score of 40–40 in a game. A player must win two consecutive points from deuce to win the game; a player who has won one point after deuce is said to have the advantage.

Deuce Side of the Court: Right side of the court of each player, so called because it is the area into which the ball is served when the score is deuce.

Double Fault: For each point, the server gets two chances to serve, called "first serve" and "second serve". If the server hits both serves either out of the service box or into the net, they have served a double fault, and have lost the point.

Drop Shot: A shot that is softly hit or tapped just over the net so that the opponent is unable to run in fast enough to retrieve it.

Flat-footed: Tennis jargon for a player who is not energetic and not playing on the balls of their feet. Flat-footed players appear to be slow to react to the ball and do not move to the ball fast enough to hit an effective shot.

Forehand: For a right-handed player, the forehand is a stroke that begins on the right side of the body, continues across the body as contact is made with the ball, and ends on the left side of the body.

Groundstrokes: A general term for forehands or backhands that bounce within the baseline of the opponent's court during a point.

Günter Parche: German tennis spectator, born 1954. Known for stabbing the number 1 female tennis player Monica Seles on court during a tournament match in Hamburg, Germany on April 30, 1993. He later admitted that the attack was motivated by his desire for Seles' rival Steffi Graf to return as the most dominant player in women's tennis at the time.

Junk/Junker: A junker player is one who uses junk—a variety of unconventional spins and/or balls of slow speed—to disrupt their opponent's timing and cause frustration in order to win the match.

Lob: From a poor defensive position on the baseline, the lob can be used as either an offensive or defensive weapon, hitting the ball high and deep into the opponent's court to either enable the lobber to get into better defensive position or to win the point outright by hitting it over the opponent's head.

Manolo Santana: Retired Spanish tennis player, born 1938. Winner of Four Grand Slam singles titles.

Maria Sharapova: Retired Russian tennis player, born in 1987. Winner of Five Grand Slam singles titles.

Match Point: The last point needed to win the match.

Match Retirement: The player concedes a match due to injury or unforeseen circumstances in which that player cannot complete the match.

Michael Chang: Retired American tennis player, born 1972. Winner of One Grand Slam title.

Moonballs/Moonballer: A moonballer is a player who consistently hits moonballs/lobs—shots hit very high and of slow speed—to disrupt the timing and cause frustration to their opponent. Moonballs are typically a beginner level shot.

Monica Seles: Retired American (born in Yugoslavia) tennis player, born 1973. Winner of Nine Grand Slam singles titles. While being ranked the number 1 women's tennis player, was stabbed in the back with a knife on court during a tournament match by spectator Günter Parche in Hamburg, Germany on April 30, 1993. Parche claimed the attack was motivated by his desire for Seles' rival Steffi Graf to return as the most dominant player in women's tennis at the time.

Novak Djokovic: Active Serbian tennis player, born 1987. Winner of 20 Grand Slam singles titles.

Overhead Smash: a hard, serve-like shot, to try to end the point, usually hit at the net.

Pace: The speed of a shot.

Pat Cash: Retired Australian tennis player, born 1965. Winner of One Grand Slam title.

Pusher: A player who stays on the defensive and "pushes" the ball back with very little speed without deliberately hitting a winner. Pushers will often win points by eliciting errors from their opponent or tiring their opponent out.

Rafael "Rafa" Nadal: Active Spanish tennis player, born 1986. Winner of 21 Grand Slam singles titles.

Rally: Following the service of a tennis ball, a series of return hits of the ball that ends when one or other player fails to return the ball within the court boundary or fails to return a ball that falls within the play area.

Roger Federer: Active Swiss tennis player, born 1981. Winner of 20 Grand Slam singles titles.

Seeding: A player's position/ranking in a tournament that has been arranged based on their ranking so as not to meet other ranked players in the early rounds of play; typically the higher a player's seeding is, the more favourable draw/path they are given in the tournament.

Serve: The shot to start a point. The serve is initiated by tossing the ball into the air and hitting it overhead into the diagonally opposite service box without touching the net. Players can also serve underhand (below their hips) as a surprise tactic to throw off their opponents.

Serve-and-volley: Method of play to serve and immediately move forward to the net to make a volley with the intent to hit a winner and end the point.

Service Box: The boxes in the court delineated by the net, sideline and, service line that the server must hit the serve diagonally into to start a point.

Service Line: The line that is parallel to the net and is located between the baseline and the net. It marks the end of the service boxes; serves that are hit outside the service line (and sidelines) are considered out and the player must hit a second serve (if that was a first serve) or has hit a double fault (if it was a second serve) and therefore lost the point.

Sideline: The lines at the side of the court; if a player hits a ball that lands outside of the sidelines, it is considered out and that player loses the point.

Slice/backspin/underspin/"chips": Shots with slice/backspin/underspin, or "chips", are shots that spin/rotate backwards as it is moving. Slice/backspin/underspin on a ball, or chips, propelled through the air imparts an upward force, and will often bounce lower and less forward.

Steffi Graf: Retired German tennis player, born 1969. Winner of 22 Grand Slam singles titles including the "Golden Slam" in which she won all four Grand Slam Titles and the Olympic Gold Medal in 1988.

Topspin: Shots hit with topspin are shots that spin/rotate forwards as it is moving. Topspin on a ball propelled through the air imparts a downward force, and will often jump high quickly after it bounces.

Volley: A shot returned to the opponent in mid-air before the ball bounces, generally hit near the net, and is usually made with a stiff-wristed punching motion to hit the ball into an open area of the opponent's court.

Winner: In regards to tennis shots, a winner is a shot that is hit so well that the opponent does not touch it with their racquet, often due to the its very high speed, force and/or placement.

Yips: A sudden and unexplained loss of ability to execute certain skills in experienced athletes. Symptoms of the yips are losing fine motor skills and psychological issues that impact on the muscle memory and decision-making of athletes, leaving them unable to perform basic skills of their sport.

ACKNOWLEDGMENTS

My most sincere gratitude to the following people/groups/organizations for your wonderful contributions; whether you have inspired me, encouraged me, played tennis with me, contributed to this story, and/or allowed me to literally put you in this story, I thank you:

Lee Moore & Jeff Orr, Aldwin Era & Jason Patterson, Edsel Colaco, Vong Sundara, Ian Salmon, Hau Truong, Tommy Trinh & Perry Ryno, Richard Chong & Michael Waterson, Luke Ng, Phil Hutchins, Andre Lafantaisie, Ocean Phi Long Le, Dave McLaren, Ray Kwa & Robbie Manuel, Cameron McGill, Artour Kassimov, Artemisa Raudel Villaroja, Jeremy Abergel, Bart Kraczkowski & JP Gloria, Ernest Wong, Jeff Morgeson, Jonathan Scott, Ketan Marballi, Chris Ng & Darryl Stewart, Kevin Tang & Geff Parsons, Tom Dando, Roman Pavlicek, Christian Drongowski, Luciano Burgos, Stephanie Beals & Mateo "Brah" Cano Serna, Felien Torres-Lyn, Jaime Padua, Jeannette Padua, Neil Gagasan, Lori MacInytre, Sabrina Marino, Joey Cheng, Pamela Mauro, Erika Torres-Lyn & Sean Lyn, Deena Huertazuela, Sandra Degli Angeli, Beverly Bambury, Professor Michael Cobb, Professor Anna Wilson, CIBC (My GPP & PMO families), Jodi & Prada Rose, Joel Rodrigues, The Glad Day Bookshop, The Merchant of Tennis, The Ontario Tennis Association (OTA), The Bramalea Tennis Club, The Castlemore Country Club, The East York Tennis Club (EYTC), The Toronto Lesbian and Gay Tennis Association (TLGTA), The Gay and Lesbian Tennis Alliance (GLTA), and my very first tennis teacher, Isabelle McDougall.

Thank you Ali Dean, Bobby Nijjar, Melissa Paladines, and Nathan Tarrant for guiding me with your genius, humour, sensitivity, and countless hours of therapy.

Thank you Liz Parker for being the daffodils in winter and reminding me to follow my bliss.

Thank you Sohee Yoo for painting this story with vibrancy and joy.

To the straight people—you courageous souls—who bravely joined our league and made it a better (and less dramatic) place, I salute you; In particular, Kurt Magney and Kim Huynh, the latter who happens to be The Queen of F*cking Everythaang ("F*cking" as in the adjective, not the verb).

This book is a tribute to the wonderful friendships that tennis has given me, the following Queens in particular: Queen Monica—Rumi Meierhofer, The Queen Bee—Bobby Nijjar, Gong Li & Amélie—Ricky Shi & Alex Onave, respectively, and THE one and only Queen of Sheba—Frank Zappone.

Thank you to my parents who taught me how to play tennis by hitting against a school wall in Brampton, and later for telling me that if I had any more tantrums on court, they would immediately take me home.

Thank you to my family—my ironwoman sister, Arnelle Adigue, my nephew, Isaac "Bruh" Martins, and the ray of sunshine that is my niece, Gabby Tiqui.

And you will probably never read this, but to Rafael Nadal (Si, si, I will marry you!) and my number 1 of all time, Monica Seles—thank you for making me love this sport.

***

Quote from Tom Boehner reprinted under terms of fair use.

Medical information courtesy of The American Cancer Society. www.cancer.org

Information in the Reference Guide: The Game of Tennis courtesy of Wikipedia. en.wikipedia.org/wiki/Tennis

ABOUT THE AUTHOR

Jeffrey Sotto's first novel, *Cloud Cover*, won an Independent Publisher Book Award (IPPY), a Best Indie Book Award (BIBA), and a Literary Titan Book Award. *The Moonballers: A Novel about The Invasion of a LGBTQ2+ Tennis League … by Straight People (GAY GASP!)* is his second book. He lives in Toronto, Ontario, Canada, and can be found on Facebook, Instagram at jeffreyasotto, and his website at jeffreyasotto.com. He will gladly accept all friend/follower requests if it means advertising/book sales/fame/fortune/etc.

Dubbed the "mini-Michael Chang" as a junior tennis player in Brampton, Ontario, Jeffrey's dreams of sports glory were dashed when, at age 11, he—devastatingly—stopped growing at five-feet and a quarter of an inch (GAY GASP!). He has been a member of the Ontario Tennis Association (OTA) since 1992, and the Toronto Lesbian and Gay Tennis Association (TLGTA) and international Gay and Lesbian Tennis Alliance (GLTA) since 2003. He also competed in the 2010 Gay Games in Cologne, Germany, where he lost in the first rounds of singles, doubles, consolation singles, and consolation doubles (yes, losing every match and set possible—and managing to down some fat German bagels along the way).

Without a doubt, his best shot is his moonball.

Printed in Great Britain
by Amazon